Praise for the Night Stalkers Series

"Top-notch military romance with to-root-for characters and a phenomenal attention to technical details... It has everything readers could want... This is a not-to-be-missed read."
—*RT Book Reviews*, 4.5 Stars, for *Bring On the Dusk*

"Buchman's writing is full of visceral, adrenaline-packed scenes and authentic military details, while his characters enjoy simmering chemistry, with love scenes bordering on the poetic."
—*Publishers Weekly* for *Light Up the Night*

"The perfect blend of riveting, high-octane military action interspersed with tender, heartfelt moments."
—*RT Book Reviews* for *Light Up the Night*, 2014 RT Reviewers' Choice Award Nominee for Romantic Suspense

"Quite simply a great read. Once again Buchman takes the military romance to a new standard of excellence."
—*Booklist* Starred Review for *Take Over at Midnight*

"A thrilling, passionate story in which love sparks in the midst of helicopter warfare."
—*Barnes and Noble Review* for *Take Over at Midnight*, a Barnes and Noble Best Romance of 2013

"Exquisitely written, sensory loaded, and soul satisfying."
—*Long and Short Reviews* for *Wait Until Dark*

Also by M. L. Buchman

The Night Stalkers

The Night Is Mine
I Own the Dawn
Wait Until Dark
Take Over at Midnight
Light Up the Night
Bring On the Dusk
NSDQ, a Night Stalkers novella in
the *Way of the Warrior* anthology

The Firehawks

Pure Heat
Full Blaze
Hot Point

Delta Force

Target Engaged

By BREAK OF Day

THE NIGHT STALKERS

M.L. BUCHMAN

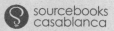

sourcebooks
casablanca

Published by Sourcebooks Casablanca, an imprint of Sourcebooks, Inc.
P.O. Box 4410, Naperville, Illinois 60567-4410
(630) 961-3900
Fax: (630) 961-2168
www.sourcebooks.com

Printed and bound in Canada
MBP 10 9 8 7 6 5 4 3 2 1

Chapter 1

U.S. Army Captain Kara Moretti sat in her coffin and flew. She had the best damn job in this woman's Army. The boys from back in the neighborhood would crap their pants if they could get a load of her right now. Her "coffin"—technically a GCS, ground control station—was a secure, air-conditioned cargo container.

Outside, it was a steel box, tucked away on the hangar deck in the belly of the helicopter carrier USS *Peleliu* currently stationed off the coast of Turkey.

Inside was a whole other world, one bristling with technology. It was her kingdom and she loved it. One side wall inside had a rack supporting a pair of long, white transit containers that actually did look like coffins, big ones. One was empty, but inside the other eight-meter-long white box rested a disassembled General Atomics MQ-1C Gray Eagle worth a cool thirty million.

As remotely piloted aircraft went, it was about the hottest RPA flying anywhere in the world. The one normally in the empty box—she'd named it *Tosca* after a not very bright but very loyal opera heroine—was even now climbing up into her sweet spot just shy of the stratosphere. Twenty-nine thousand feet up and looking down, that's what she was good at—among so many other things. *Tosca* was a talented lady and Kara was the girl to fly her. She was the brains behind the RPA...

or maybe the opera conductor…or… She'd think about that later.

At six miles up, the RPA would appear to be the same width as a single human hair held out at arm's length. And not a big thick hair like one of Kara's own long brunette ones, but rather like a fine blond one that belonged to Justin Roberts—not that she'd notice such things, especially not on him—presently flying his helicopter at the other end of this exercise's battlespace domain.

The orders for this training scenario had been simple: "Show them what we can do, but not how we do it."

U.S. Special Operations Forces held cooperative international training to serve one of two functions.

Usually it was to enhance an ally's skill while scaring the pee out of a nearby enemy. Under those conditions, the SOF worked patiently to transfer knowledge and skills. They'd recently run a major exercise with the Polish JW Grom counterterrorism unit. The three-day simulated fast-response invasion had been staged close to the Ukrainian border to put Russia on notice that U.S. and Polish forces were nearby and watching closely.

Other times—like this one—the goal was to humble the ally when they weren't trying hard enough. Sharing borders with Syria, Iraq, and Iran, the Turkish forces should not be playing favorites. Despite that, their attitude was, "We may hate the people doing the genocide and destabilizing the entire region, but we hate the people that they're killing even more. So we don't see a thing."

It was worse than the neighborhood rivalries that used to sweep through Kara's part of Brooklyn. Sometimes it was just gangs, but sometimes it was way worse. Just because she wasn't in one of the Five Families didn't mean she was stupid or something. The garbage cartel. The cheese cartel. Liquor cartel. Restaurants. The list went on, and that didn't even include the drugs, gambling, and prostitution. It was quieter now—the New York Mafia had mostly turned to the business of doing business—but that didn't mean the past was forgotten or that flare-ups didn't occur.

There were times when Kara wondered why she was out here fighting other people's wars rather than being a Brooklyn cop like two of her brothers and Papa.

'Cause then you wouldn't have the coolest job in the Army, that's why.

She and her assistant, Sergeant Santiago "Tago" Marquez, sat side by side in the coffin at the GCS stations. Two big, comfortable armchairs faced the flight and sensor controls of the MQ-1C. Ahead and to either side they each had three large screens that fed all of the visual and remote sensing data from the Gray Eagle. Below it was flight tracking and a full array of flight instruments and controls. A third chair, presently empty, sat close behind her when there was too much happening and they had to pull in a third operator.

She and Tago each held dual joysticks. Her controls included flight and weapons. He was the grand master of the sensor arrays, constantly twisting and tuning them to give her the information she needed before she knew she needed it.

"Hell of a team!"

She held up a hand for a moment and received a high five just as they did before every mission.

Tago didn't speak, of course. In a full year he'd

probably spoken a dozen words during an actual operation, and two dozen out of one. But he didn't need to; he was that far inside her head. Sometimes it worried her a little, like what kinda muck was he gonna find in there that even she didn't know about? Never worried her for long though; he was too much fun to fly with.

The other great thing about Tago was that he was almost a foot taller and much wider than she was. The run-of-the-mill assholes would take one look at him, hovering close beside her like a big brother, and scoot for the hills.

There were a whole lot of suckers back at Cannon Air Force Base sittin' on their ever-widening butts with their McDonald's coffee and McGut Bomb breakfast. All doing their time in some godforsaken Clovis, New Mexico, suburbia-hell so they could fly a Predator RPA over Afghanistan or Yemen from Cannon AFB's deep bunkers. It was good work if you could get it and didn't mind cooking your ass in the Southwest desert.

Two years ago, she'd been one of a kajillion other flyboys and gals working the command consoles.

Then the Night Stalkers' recruiter had showed up and her life had changed.

"We fly for the U.S. Army's 160th Special Operations Aviation Regiment," the Captain had said. "We have been over-reliant on U.S. Air Force and NSA satellite intelligence assets."

A pretty ballsy statement in the middle of a USAF base. She liked that plenty for starters.

"We're going to be integrating a dozen Gray Eagle RPAs directly into our operations."

They had her right there.

First, SOAR was so seriously cool that they called themselves the Night Stalkers, which rocked. One of the best nicknames in the forces.

Second, they hadn't said "drone" or "UAV—unmanned aerial vehicle." She wasn't some lame-assed *drone* pilot. And her craft wasn't *unmanned*, or it wouldn't need a pilot. The pilot simply wasn't aboard the aircraft. The Gray Eagle was a remotely piloted aircraft, and, by God—

Third—she was the woman to fly them.

"We're seeking specialists for transfer from remote pilotage here in New Mexico to being embedded directly with our helicopter units. Would all those interested please—"

There'd been advantages to being five-foot-five and having three older brothers. You learned to be quick. She headed the sign-up queue before the guy even finished the briefing. Tago had been her shadow.

True to the captain's word, after two additional years of training, she was sitting on a warship in the Mediterranean and kicking baddie-guy ass—usually. That she was using her skills to spook an ally tonight was one of those changeups that kept life interesting.

Interesting, hell. Super sweet!

"This is *May*. Ready for my run."

"Roger, *May*," Kara answered Trisha in her MH-6M Little Bird helicopter. Short for *Mayhem*, the name of the tiny, heavily armed attack helo was a perfect match for its petite female pilot. They were both hyperactive and both lethal.

The entire company was on hold five minutes to target awaiting Kara's "Go" signal.

It was weird that it was hers to give, but then a lot of things were in the 5th Battalion, D Company of SOAR. Everywhere else, an RPA pilot was just another pilot — and one often looked down on. The 5D was trying out having the RPA flier also be the AMC.

Archie Stevenson, the former Air Mission Commander, had just departed for the States with his wife and kid. Something about them all working at the White House, which had a coolness factor of its own. Turnover had been as odd as everything else in the 5D.

Rather than pulling someone else off the birds into the AMC role, they were dumping it on their new eye-in-the-sky person as a trial.

For seven days without break she'd sat at tactical displays as she and Archie tore apart every single mission he'd commanded — at least the ones she was authorized to see. With an unusual candor for an airjock, he'd spent the entire time showing her every single thing he'd done wrong.

"The things you do right will come from your instincts. Hopefully you can learn from my mistakes." He'd had crews shot down, good friends shot down — some recovered intact, others crucified by hostiles.

"Good luck," and he'd been gone.

Well, Kara sure liked the sound of being AMC. And she had no intention of letting such an opportunity slip out of her grasp now that it had fallen into it.

The other choppers reported in.

Merchant and *Maven II* flew with *May*.

Vengeance, the lethal DAP flown by Lola Maloney, hovered close behind. Where a Little Bird attacked, a DAP Black Hawk helicopter weapons platform demolished.

"Ah'm ready as can be, little lady." And that would be the big hammer for this operation, the massive twin-rotor MH-47G Chinook *Calamity Jane*. No need for Justin Roberts to identify himself—his Texan dripped off him like...

Like you're not going to be thinking about in the middle of your first solo mission as AMC, girl!

But she'd caught him working out in the weight room on the lower decks a few times, sweat sheening his face and arms, drenching his T-shirt until it clung to his muscled chest. Damn, but he was a handsome one.

Focus!

Kara had each of the helos located clearly on her screen. Not because they were visible, but rather because of their encrypted locator beacons. Except for the Chinook, they were stealth-modified helicopters so they didn't show up on her radar or, except for scattered moments, on her infrared imaging. Normal vision showed nothing at all either, since it was three in the morning in the Turkish wilderness and the helos were all painted black and running without lights.

The Turkish Special Forces, the OKK, on the other hand, showed up brilliantly to the advanced sensors aboard the RPA. Tago had them zeroed in both on infra-red and through their radio transmissions as backup.

Kara didn't speak Turkish, which didn't really matter because their radios were encrypted. But they didn't have the American ability to distort a signal's transmission so that it looked like it was coming from somewhere else. *Tosca* wasn't smart, but she had Electronic Intelligence down.

The Turkish Special Forces would think they were

well hidden—*not!*—and knew where the attack was coming from—wrong again!

Now to kick their heinies good and hard with a lesson in true stealth.

She leaned forward and whispered into the headset mic, not that it mattered how loud she spoke in the coffin. "Go!"

And like magic, two hundred kilometers away, the tiny indicators that were the Night Stalkers' 5th Battalion, D Company went.

—◦◦◦—

Captain Justin Roberts gave the collective control between his knees a little nudge forward. Fifteen tons of helicopter carrying a platoon of U.S. Rangers and their gear eased forward as smooth as a baby's behind.

Every single time he flew his big MH-47G "Golf" Chinook helicopter, it was a surprise—a surprise of how much fun it was. Like they were meant for each other since long before they met.

SOAR only flew three primary types of helos, all deeply modified to the 160th's specification. The Little Bird, the Black Hawk, and the Chinook Golf. His girl was the monster of the outfit. *Calamity Jane* was definitely a Texas-sized lady: big, powerful, and dangerous.

"I feel the need for a song."

"Oh God, spare us." Danny Corvo spoke up from the copilot seat. From there he was Justin's second set of eyes and the master of the helo's general health and well-being.

"*Oh, give me a home*," Carmen cut in from her position at the starboard gun close behind Justin's seat.

Carmen Parker was hot shit with an M134 minigun that could unload four thousand rounds-a-minute of hell on anyone who messed with her. She was also king, er, queen of the bird—the absolute last word on maintenance and loading.

"*Where the Chinook helos roam*." Talbot George was always off-key at the side gun behind Danny's copilot position, but he sang with heart, even if with a distinctly British accent.

"*And the flights are at night every day*," the three of them sang together in splendidly awful harmony.

Danny groaned as if in the throes of death-by-torture agony.

As usual, Raymond Hines kept his own counsel at the rear ramp gunner's post. The Chinook was the size of a school bus inside. Tonight, in the cargo area between the cockpit and Ray's rear post, thirty U.S. Rangers and their three ATVs were counting on SOAR to sling them into position. On the outside, the *Jane* was half again as wide due to the long auxiliary fuel tanks hung low along the fuselage. They gave her a massive operational range, completely aside from the refueling probe that Justin could extend beyond the edge of the rotors for a midair tank up if needed.

The big rotors fore and aft let her lift her own weight in cargo; even in high-hot conditions the Chinook outperformed most everything around.

By the third chorus their harmonies were better, so Justin hit the transmit switch for the last of it. It got the answering transmission he was hoping for.

"Justin, honey?"

"Here for you, sweetheart." Kara Moretti just slayed

him. From the first briefing where she'd moseyed in all dark and Italian and perfect, his head had been turned hard enough that he kept checking his neck for whiplash. Then when she opened her mouth and poured out thick Brooklyn... Two months later and he still didn't know what to do with that, not a bit of it. It was all... wrong, yet it was *so* right. Her voice should be some sweet *bella signora*, like the one he'd spent a week with while stationed at Camp Darby outside of Pisa on the Italian coast a couple years back.

Instead Kara was—

"You do that to me again and you're gonna be singing soprano the rest of your life. We clear, Cowboy?"

—a hundred percent, New York. "Y'all wouldn't do that to me now, would ya?" He laid it on thick.

"Castrate the bull calf? In a heartbeat. And I ain't your sweetheart."

"I'll hold him down while you trim 'em," Lola Maloney called in from the DAP Hawk.

He was about to say something about how it made the meat taste more luscious and tender—which was why they castrated most bull calves—but he couldn't figure out how to phrase it without it sounding crude and perhaps tempting her to start looking for some neutering shears when Trisha cut in.

"Roger that! We'll pin him, you chop and cauterize. Use a really hot iron."

Claudia Jean Gibson at the controls of the *Maven II* didn't speak much, but he could feel her out there agreeing with them.

Justin winced in imagined pain, as he was sure every man on the comm circuit did. He figured maybe it would be better if he kept his mouth shut. Once the women of the 5D got on a roll, wasn't no man on God's green earth who was safe.

At a dozen kilometers to target, the whole flight of five helos dropped from ten meters above the ground to three. No time to sing now.

The overlap imaging inside his helmet took serious concentration when flying true nap-of-earth. The NOE software suite fed him programmed satellite terrain models that let him see the big stuff up ahead. Live infrared from the nose camera told him when he was about to eat a tree or the side of a house. And Kara's feed from the Gray Eagle provided the tactical landscape to overlay on the other two. All of it projected on the inside of his helmet's visor along with key engine and flight indicators—most of which he left up to Danny to manage as copilot.

They were doing what no other helicopter pilots anywhere could. Two hundred and fifty kilometers per hour and no higher off the dirt than a horse. They hugged mountainsides and deep valley bottoms like they were birds of prey on the hunt.

He loved slinging his helo over the low terrain.

Now they were getting down to it.

―――

Kara was briefly mesmerized by watching the helos fly across her display. The 5D pilots were the best, and everyone knew that, but, damn, they were fun to watch. She could pick out each pilot simply by how they flew across the terrain.

Trisha was the slick knife, straight slices from point

A to point Z, skipping the twenty-four places in between as if they didn't exist. Claudia so smooth that she blended into the landscape, and Lola Maloney practically bebopped ten tons of gun platform across the sky. Dennis flew his *Merchant of Death* almost as aggressively as Trisha.

And then there was the cowboy.

In his massive Chinook, he should have lumbered; instead he soared. *He SOARed. Hyuk! Hyuk!* She could practically hear Justin and that deep laugh of his—the man was absolutely convinced he was the funniest thing around.

He flew as if he were settled back in his saddle loping over the prairie, not dodging through the rough and arid wasteland of central Turkey. That's assuming he was a real cowboy and didn't just have the hat and the drawl. Probably tried line dancing once at some Dallas cowboy bar and bought a hat in the gift shop.

Tago flashed the close-up tactical feed showing the Turkish OKK's positions onto Kara's side screen. She forced her attention away from watching the perfect harmony of Justin's lope over the wilderness.

The OKK still squatted right where they'd been all along, hunkered down in a valley like sitting ducks. She'd thought they were better than that.

They were better than that!

They were…

Right where they knew they'd be seen!

The SOAR flight was sixty seconds out.

Come on, girl. Think! Think! It's gotta be a trap.

Assume that it was. Then what did that tell her? It was…

Like the time the idiot boys had clambered out onto the roof of Keating Hall and decided to flour-bomb some random college girls as they trooped up the front steps. But they'd made a crucial tactical error. For their initial target, they'd bombed the female cadre of the Fordham University Army ROTC program—Cadet Captain Kara Moretti in the lead.

The flour bombers had left two boys at ground level to engage and flag likely targets, slowing them down. The initial rooftop attack had worked all too well, leaving Kara and her cadre enveloped in a cloud of hot-pink-stained flour and raucous laughter. But not for long.

Kara had signaled Cadet Master Sergeant Merry to deal with the two lookouts on the ground. When it was Sergeant Merry, one girl versus two civilian boys was plenty.

Kara had led the rest of her team straight into the hall at a fast trot, leaving a long line of hot-pink dust up the marble stairways. Three hand signals and they'd split up and cut off all angles of escape. Ten minutes later, her entire cadre had headed for the showers, smiling.

The disorganized attackers were left dangling upside down—wearing very secure impromptu harnesses fabricated from handy fire hoses—off the edge of the roof four stories in the air.

They'd been rescued soon enough, though it had been hours before they'd thought to track down their two spotters on the ground. Those two were eventually unearthed in the bushes outside Keating Hall trussed with their own shoelaces and gagged with each other's dirty underwear. Kara had always liked the way Cadet Master Sergeant Merry thought things through.

That's what the group of OKK clustered in the Turkish valley was doing; they were the distraction. Slowing SOAR down and drawing their focus. They needed to be spanked, but the real threat would be ranged and ready somewhere nearby. The question was: How close?

Forty-five seconds out.

Once she thought it through, it was obvious.

"Little Birds, split and circle the hills." She rattled off helicopter names and target coordinates. "They have shooters placed high at these locations. Land on their heads."

"*Vengeance*," she called to Lola's gunship. "Climb to three thousand feet. Your primary targets will be…" She listed off more coordinates. "Make some noise and light once you're up there." It was against the unspoken rules to ask a stealth helicopter to make noise, but Lola didn't argue.

Chief Warrant Lola Maloney might command the 5D when they were on the ground; experience counted more than rank here—another thing to appreciate about the Night Stalkers. But during an operation the Air Mission Commander called the shots.

Kara could really get into this AMC role. She spoke, and the tactical map reflecting the team's actions shifted and morphed into seriously bad news for the OKK.

Not that she was power-trippin' or any such thing. But she could see it, like one big gestalt, right where the Turkish Special Forces had to have parked their butts if they were good without being truly great like the U.S. Special Ops Forces.

Key hideout positions would be tromped by the Little Birds coming up over the backs of ridges.

The DAP Hawk, well able to defend itself, would perch high to attract attention and draw simulated fire.

Now for the hammer blow.

"Texas," she called to Justin. "Come in fast and low. Fast-rope six Rangers down on top of the small hillock at the southwest corner to draw their attention." She circled the target hill on her screen so that it would transmit to the tactical display shining on the inside of his helmet's visor.

"Then fly and land here." She drew a line that circled behind a low ridge—cutting an arc around the OKK team sitting as bait—where she'd found him a small dip in the landscape that would provide cover while unloading the rest of the Rangers.

The OKK would be trying to follow his circling, which would draw the ground troops' attention away from the first Ranger team, who could then start taking potshots at the bad guys' backs to distract them from the main force.

"Let the rest of your Rangers loose here. Then climb to a thousand feet directly below the DAP Hawk to offer your gunners prime shooting."

Nobody responded.

They didn't need to. This was SOAR. All of the training in what could be reliably assumed had been taken care of during the two years of training in the 160th, which was after having a minimum of five years flight experience elsewhere in the armed forces.

She'd thought herself a real hotshot pilot of her RPA, until the first day of SOAR training. It had been a very humbling moment. She'd kicked ass ever since to make sure it didn't happened again. The SOAR instructors weren't just good; they were Night Stalker pilots themselves and knew shit that she'd never even dreamed of back in the 27th Special Operations Wing.

The SOAR fliers simply reacted to her commands. Once in the inner ring of the engagement, they only used radios for emergency communications like this last-moment change. Otherwise the Night Stalkers flew missions in absolute silence. Though she'd have to find a way to curb Mr. Texas during transit times. She'd just ignore the fact that his song had made her laugh so hard that Tago had offered to thump her back.

Kara had nosed the RPA over into a dive while handing out instructions. *Tosca* fell from six miles down to three in that thirty seconds of full-powered dive.

Fifteen seconds to first contact.

Tago had picked up on what she was doing and marked two areas of hillside. "Clean!" he said over the intercom just to emphasize that they were unoccupied sites. They wanted to spook the OKK, not kill them.

Kara targeted two of the simulated Hellfire missiles mounted on the Gray Eagle and let them loose. They went supersonic in seconds. Nine seconds and three miles later, the Hellfires slammed into either side of the valley wall high above the OKK encampment and blew up with a light-show blast from two hundred grams of R321 tracer powder that had replaced the usual warheads.

There would be a nice bright flash and a resounding *Bang!* that would echo through the valley.

At five seconds until the helos' arrivals, every OKK trooper was now looking at the two flashes and wondering what was going on up on the vacant hillsides.

More crucially, the blast was going to dazzle their night-vision gear and force them to blink at the wrong moment.

Kara pulled *Tosca* back into level flight and circled above Lola's DAP Hawk to watch the Turks' downfall.

Just like Alexander the Great twenty-five hundred years earlier, the 160th SOAR and the U.S. Rangers swept across the land of the Turks with the ease of a Brooklyn gelato vendor selling cones on a scorching July day.

—∿—

Justin called over the intercom to Lieutenant Clint Barstowe, the leader of the U.S. Rangers, about the change in plans.

Raymond would be dropping the rear gate and rigging the two thick FRIES fast ropes to dangle off the stern. The forty-millimeter-diameter rope would allow the Rangers to slide down to the ground and deploy in seconds without having to land the helo. Because they'd be passing behind a low hill, the OKK might not even realize the helicopter had paused to let down troops.

To emphasize that, Justin floated up into the Turks' view for a moment, moving slow. Then he ducked down fast behind the hill, pausing only long enough to deliver the Rangers, and then raced to the far side and slowed again as he let himself float once more into brief view. It would look as if he'd simply done a slow cruise the whole way.

Now the trick was to stay completely out of sight.

Kara had found him a deep notch of dry arroyo just like back home in Amarillo where he'd learned to fly.

He'd been dating a cattle rancher's daughter at the time, Francine of the long legs and not a single brain cell between her cheerleader ears.

One day her daddy had taken him up in his little R22 helicopter to search for some stray cattle and, more likely, to scare the crap out of Justin. Instead, Justin had earned his rotorcraft license as fast as he could and flown three seasons for Hank Freeman while Francine continued to work her way through the entire football squad.

Justin had the ball now, and like the All-State tailback he'd been, he was gonna stay fast and low.

He slid the body of the Chinook right down between the banks of the arroyo. From down here only the sixty-foot sweep of each of his front and rear twin rotors stuck out beyond the edges. He kept a close eye for any growth higher than the stubbly brush or any particularly tall boulders that might be wanting to clip off his rotor blades.

Danny also rode the controls. There was too much for one person to concentrate on. Per prior training, Justin watched the arroyo and the right-hand bank. Danny kept an eye on the arroyo, but mostly watched the left-hand bank. And they both watched the threat detector like hawks, just in case there were a couple bad buys stationed down in the arroyo.

Should have been; there weren't. *Missed opportunity, guys!*

They kept the Chinook moving along sharply, which meant the Rangers had better be hanging on as he bobbed and weaved twenty tons of helo like it weighed twenty kilos.

There was Kara's hill.

A good choice. *Nice job, sweetheart!* If it were up to

him, he'd confirm her as the new permanent Air Mission Commander on this basis alone. She'd known exactly what he needed and made sure he'd received it.

He slewed the Chinook sideways as he bled speed.

"Unload in ten, nine…" He didn't have to continue his countdown over the intercom; everyone would have the count now.

At five he saw by the indicator light that the rear ramp was once again open and lowered.

At two he came to a stop.

Raymond began calling distance-to-contact as Justin lowered them into position. He was still in hover, none of his wheels on the ground. Justin's pilot seat was a dozen meters in the air over the dry arroyo. The middle of his helicopter was above the steep side of the carved riverbed. The Chinook's only point of contact with the earth was the trailing edge of the rear ramp twenty meters behind him, against a small flat spot he'd picked out as they slewed into place.

In ten seconds, the remaining twenty-five Rangers and their three heavily armed ATVs were out.

"Ramp clear," Raymond called.

Justin nosed down the face of the slope to gain some speed, rode the ground effect for a moment as momentum built, and then hammered skyward toward the firing position that Kara had identified.

Lola's DAP Hawk would have been invisible, except every ten seconds or so the crew was kicking out a decoy flare. It was a perfect solution to Kara's instruction to be visible. The flare was designed to burn bright and hot as it shot to the side so that any incoming missile would target the flare instead of the helo.

Rather than firing a large cluster in every direction as would normally be done, Lola Maloney was firing one here and one there. No way to pin down the exact location of the black-painted helo itself.

He slid in below her—tight, quiet, and dark.

Then he called to his crew.

"Remember, simulated rounds only. We don't want to be hurtin' their behinds any more than we already are. Weapons free."

It was strange not to hear the jarring buzz saw of the miniguns that usually penetrated the roar of the twin turbines mounted at the rear rotor. There was also no stench of cordite that often wound through the cabin when firing from a stable hover.

For this exercise, their weapons were firing light beams, not lead.

But that didn't mean the Turkish Special Forces stood a chance, not with SOAR on the scene.

—◦◦◦—

Kara checked her mission clock. It was all over in ninety-seven seconds.

Five helos and thirty U.S. Rangers had just taken down a hundred OKK spread across eight locations without breaking a sweat.

Kara knew that a report to that effect was going to go public, unless the Turkish military got its act together about actually helping in Syria and Iraq. Turkish pride was on the line; Kara didn't doubt that they'd cooperate.

"Bring them dogies on home, boys and girls."

"Yee-haw!" Justin called out over the radio and whirled down to gather his Rangers back aboard. The

DAP Hawk remained on guard station above him even though they were in "friendly" territory.

Kara jolted at the sound of the cowboy's call and reviewed her own words. What in the world had she been thinking? *Bring them dogies on home?*

Captain Justin Roberts was six-two, built like, well, a cowboy, and had hair the color of wheat. He was also arrogant, as impressed with himself as a fresh-inducted benchwarmer parked in the Mets dugout, and from Texas—which all on its own was like eighteen strikes against the guy. That was two full innings worth of outs, just for one guy.

"Want some flight time, Tago?" Dumb question.

At his eager nod, she waved for him to take over flying the Gray Eagle *Tosca* back to the U.S. side of Incirlik Air Base a hundred kilometers south of the exercise area. A ground team awaited her there for a rearm and refuel. She needed twice the length of the warship for a runway, so a ground team made sure that her *Tosca* was always ready with whatever mission package Kara needed. It was nicer this way, not having the ground team always underfoot.

She climbed out of the deep armchair to stretch her legs and paced up and down the length of the coffin. She kept an eye on Tago. He had about half the flight hours he'd need before he'd have a chance at his own bird, but he was good and didn't need much of an eye. Once he was close enough, the software would take over for an automated landing.

"Don't just float along, Sergeant. You'll never get any better that way. Shake her out a bit."

He answered with a snap roll and a climb into a full

loop that he didn't quite manage. She considered showing him the trick, but she remembered learning more
from her failures than her successes, so she'd let him be
for a couple more attempts.

The rest of her attention? She'd better be using that
on herself.

Bring them dogies on home?

Damn.

No way was she going to be getting weak in the head
for a handsome hunk of Texas meat.

Back home, Carlo was much more her style, though
she wasn't stupid enough to fall for his constant plead-
ing. He too was typically arrogant and male. At least he
was Italian, from the neighborhood, and had a to-die-for
tenor voice that was leading him to opera houses around
the world. He'd been trying to get into her pants since
they were both twelve, with no success.

But better him than Captain Justin Roberts.

Chapter 2

JUSTIN BROUGHT THE *CALAMITY JANE* BACK TO THE stern of their ship, the USS *Peleliu*. The aging Landing Helicopter Assault ship had been taken over from the Marine Corps when they'd tried to retire her.

It was a crazy mash-up of a ship. The Navy's next-sized class down from the big aircraft carriers, she could carry twenty-five hundred personnel, thirty helos, a half-dozen Harrier jump jets, and a bellyful of amphibious assault craft and vehicles including trucks and tanks. The latter loaded and unloaded through a rear gate in the stern that opened into a massive well deck awash at sea level and reaching deep inside the ship. She was designed to deliver an entire Marine Expeditionary Unit to the beach, any beach in the world, fast.

SOAR's 5D had taken her over as a mobile platform to prowl the troubled oceans of the world. Now—including all of the 5D, the fifty U.S. Rangers, a handful of Delta Force operators, and the Navy people to run her—she boasted barely six hundred personnel and under a dozen helos. She was a dozen stories from keel to superstructure, so they practically rattled about inside the eight-hundred-foot ship. Her flattop deck stretched over two football fields long and most of one wide.

The air boss signaled Justin to stand off the stern while the other helos came in from tonight's training exercise.

He and the *Jane* had only been aboard for a few

months, and he'd already flown in dozens of live ops in addition to these training exercises. The 5D maintained a blistering op schedule even by the standards of the 10th Mountain Division where he'd been stationed before applying to SOAR. The heavy flight demands were fine with him; he liked the challenges.

But there'd been one mission which he could only infer had actually happened. They'd all gone on leave for one week, one lousy week, and he'd missed something big. That still stuck in his craw. They'd lost the Little Bird helicopter named *Maven*. And then her pilot and the head Delta Force operator had gone missing for two weeks afterward.

Next thing you knew, a brand-new helicopter had been delivered to take the lost gunship's place. Then Captain Claudia Jean Casperson and Delta Colonel Michael Gibson were married and back on the ship—serving together no less.

Marriages were another of the things he couldn't get over about the 5D. Families normally didn't happen in the same unit of the military. Hell, sex wasn't supposed to happen in the military at all—as if that made one lick of sense. *Come on, people, corral a clue. Why would a career guy want anything less than a soldier babe?*

But the 5D was a horse of a whole different color.

Chief Warrant Lola Maloney, pilot of the *Vengeance*, was married to Tim, who'd recently made the jump from backseater to copilot. Her crew chief Connie was married to Big John who handled the other side gun on the DAP Hawk. Trisha, the Little Bird pilot, and another D-boy…

It was just weird.

Made a man wonder just how extreme these folks were that they could get away with such things.

And that thought, as almost every other one over the last two months, led him back to Captain Kara Moretti. The babe was hot, no arguing with that. Just about blew his hat off when she'd strolled into the *Peleliu* briefing room that first time. They had joined the 5D the same day.

But it was way more than that. Carmen, his starboard-side gunner, was hot in a San Francisco redhead sort of way. Funny, a great shot, a joy to look at, but that was all. Kara was short, feisty, pain-in-the-ass New York... and his brain switched off and his body switched on every single time she walked by. Or he heard her voice over the radio. Or he thought of her...

The only celebration of their joining the same day had been a massive hostage rescue in the heart of Somalia twenty-four hours later. SOAR was never dull, that was for dang sure.

The landing officer finally called Justin's chopper forward and he settled down onto the stern of the *Peleliu*.

Thoughts of Kara were so distracting, he almost landed with the rear unloading ramp of his Chinook hanging out over the sea. Man, the Rangers would have loved that. First they get to humiliate the OKK—which the boys had done a damn fine job of—and then their pilot exits them into the night ocean in full gear, probably killing the lot of them.

He shuffled forward to where the landing officer indicated before letting the *Jane* settle onto the ship. He tried to make it look as if he'd just been settling slow, but the LO wasn't buying that fifty-thousand-pound mosey for a second. Neither was Danny. Justin could feel the eye roll even worse than when he was singing.

Once down on the right spot, the first thing he did was pull his helmet and scrub at his hair so that his head could breathe. Second thing he did was reach behind the seat and grab his cowboy hat. There were so many Yankees and West Coasters in SOAR that a man had to take a stance about something. He only ever wore a white straw Cooper Stetson in the heat, because there was nothing like a classic. In winter he wore a black felt High Point, but there wasn't a whole lot of winter around the Horn of Africa or in the Mediterranean, so that one had stayed in his cabin so far.

After unloading and cleaning up behind the Rangers, who never left anything quite the way it should be, his crew tackled the postflight lists together. Not his duty, but get it done and get them to their supper had always worked for him. Ma and Dad had always helped clean the stalls, as had every camper at their ranch.

It was almost sunrise. The *Peleliu* and the 5D worked at night and slept during the day, so suppertime was fast approaching. SOAR's motto wasn't "Death Waits in the Dark" just for the sake of saying it. That's when they flew and how they lived.

As they worked over the postflight checklists and switched back to live ammunition, the sun gave a warm glow to the Mediterranean horizon. Nothing much to see here—a hundred kilometers offshore left Turkey below the horizon. Cyprus was a smudge to the west and Syria and Lebanon were low hints to the east. Most everything about was water, empty water.

Unlike the big aircraft carriers, the *Peleliu* and her

helicopter company wandered the seas alone. No destroyers, frigates, oilers, or other craft were about. The Landing Helicopter Assault carrier was always on the move. Since she wasn't attached to a war, she was ignored by most and well able to defend herself.

It was a matter of thirty minutes to get the *Calamity Jane* back to shipshape.

Thanking the crew, something he made a point of after every flight, he headed up along the deck as they each dropped down into the bowels of the ship to await mess call.

The Little Birds and DAP Hawks were already serviced and shrouded with nylon covers along the flattop deck of the *Peleliu* like so many cowpats. Shrouded so that no one would see them clearly by daylight. The grapes—purple-vested fuel handlers—were already pumping Jet A gas into the *Calamity Jane*. The reds were double-checking the ammunition, even though the SOAR crews hadn't fired a single live round.

As soon as they were done, the deck crews would shroud her, the biggest cowpat of all, at least three times the size of any of the other choppers. Though she wasn't stealth, it made for a consistent presentation to unwelcome surveillance.

The nature of the company's aircraft was just one more weird thing about the 5D. Courtesy of the raid on bin Laden's compound, Justin had discovered along with the rest of the world that there were stealth helicopters. That most didn't know they were part of SOAR was just the way the Night Stalkers would want it.

And if one crashed in Abbottabad, Pakistan, that meant there were at least two on the raid.

And if there were two... He just hadn't expected ever to see one during his career, much less fly with a whole company of them. But here they were, carefully hidden from seeking eyes, their covers softly lit by the oncoming dawn that now was turning the sky gold and knocking the last of the stars out of the heavens. As one of the 5D's pilots, he was left to wonder what he'd done right with his life to end up here.

His sister, Bessie, had gone Air Force and flew an AC-130 Spooky gunship for them. Dad had done a tour with the Navy on a destroyer. That only left the Army for Justin, because a Roberts didn't follow in anyone's footsteps. Not even if they were kin.

The ranch was his big brother's job. Rafe had joined their parents in the horse ranch business. A place Justin had thought he'd end up himself, until shortly before the end of his first tour.

He now flew the heavily modified Boeing MH-47G Special Operations version designed for and flown only by SOAR—the Percheron of the heavy-lifters. He truly appreciated the beautiful and noble craft.

During that first tour he'd come to love the simpler CH-47 Chinook that he'd flown for the 10th Mountain Division. She wasn't just any old helicopter, but rather served as the workhorse of the Army helifleet.

Still, he'd thought to do his tour and head home... right until his world had been blown apart, literally.

He did his best to shunt the memories aside, because they sure weren't good ones. Often they kicked him into a tailspin of epic proportions.

"Hey, Captain Roberts."

He must be losing his tracking skills to let Kara come

up on him without him noticing. "Howdy yourself, Captain Moretti." He should have expected it. She was always doing that to him, sliding in under his radar even when he was watching out for her rather than momentarily lost at sea.

And this time it was predictable. All the commanders and lead pilots were headed toward the same room for debriefing. The Navy Lieutenant Commander of the *Peleliu* had established an office in the base of the communications superstructure that towered a half-dozen stories above the vast deck. Four tiers of flight ready rooms, command-control spaces, and flight control tower topped by great towers adorned like overladen Christmas trees with antennas, radomes, and other sensing equipment.

"'Howdy'?" She looked up at him sidelong from most of a foot down—though no man would be fool enough to call her petite, unless he was *looking* for a black eye.

He could never tell when she was teasing or getting all…New York. Well, he had his pride and responded with a "Yep!"

"Do people actually speak like that where you come from?"

"A' course! In Amarillo we speak like Americans, not Yankees."

"Gimme a frickin' break, Cowboy. If all Americans sounded like you, the rest of the world would need translators so that the translators could understand them."

He reached for the heavy, soundproof door that led into the communications structure, like Pa had raised him, but she beat him to it as if it was some sort of a competition.

The movement placed them so close that his nose was practically buried in the back of her hair. Closest together they'd been in two months aboard.

SOAR's customers, especially the edgy ones like Delta and SEAL, grew longer hair or beards to blend in with crowds. Only in the 5D did command allow quite so much imitation of their customers. His short hair was the exception rather than the rule.

And Kara Moretti's was a downright sin in the other direction. Most of the women let their hair grow down to their shoulders, which was nice to look at. He'd always had a weak spot for longer hair.

But because Kara flew in a box and didn't have to worry about harness restraints and other hair catchers, she'd let her dark brown hair, with just a hint of gold, flow down to the middle of her back. On a military woman it was stunning, evocative, and made him want to dive his hands into it.

She smelled of...not New York. And for certain not hot helmets and battle sweat. Kara Moretti's hair smelled of—she'd hate the allusion—his favorite mare's mane after a long run on a cool fall day. All the promises of a filly now full grown and just filled with life.

As he'd noted earlier, the woman was just killing him.

They filed into Lieutenant Commander Boyd Ramis's office. He'd taken over a flight-ready pilots' waiting room and outfitted it with comfortable chairs and couches, a small conference table, and a desk that was less ostentatious than it might have been.

Most merely waved at Ramis or nodded. Justin always made a point of saluting. Some might think he was sucking up, but after he saw how much the man appreciated it in his quiet way, Justin never missed. Ramis returned the salute sharply.

Ramis might believe he was a forward-thinking, up-and-coming commander, but it was clear he had found his highest post and wouldn't be progressing upward any further. He was the kind of commander who'd have your back but wasn't the strongest leader.

The four other women of SOAR had gathered around the coffee urn. A glance out the LCDR's window revealed the sun just cracking the horizon over the flat line of the shining blue Mediterranean, so the coffee would be decaf. The Night Stalkers would all be asleep in a few hours.

Justin knew from experience that even if it was decaf, the urn would still be filled with Navy mud that could corrode stainless steel faster than salt water. He'd thought he had an iron gut until his first time aboard a Navy ship. On that day he'd meant to take an orange juice from the small fridge, but then he got to thinking about the proper color for coffee being about the shade of Moretti's hair and somehow ended up with a cup of the lethal sludge instead. He'd never made that mistake again.

Lieutenant Barstowe, the commander of the Rangers, came over and thumped him on the back. "Nice job, Roberts."

"Thanks." He wouldn't mention that he'd almost unloaded the entire platoon into the ocean.

"Next time I want to go for a swim, I'll be sure to give you a call."

"Aw, shucks, Lieutenant. Just wanted to make sure y'all were on your toes."

Barstowe laughed and thumped him on the back again before taking a seat.

Justin almost tripped over the senior Delta operator who had come up silently beside him. Colonel Michael Gibson was spooky that way. The man was so stealthy that you never knew where or when he'd be.

Unless his wife was around.

It was like he became more in focus when he sidled up beside the astonishing blond. It wasn't that Claudia Jean Gibson was so beautiful, which she was, but it was the quietness that seemed to flow around her. The woman flew her tiny attack Little Bird helicopter that way: smooth, clean, quiet—with the precision of a scalpel and the effect of a tactical nuke. The woman was beyond lethal, which, Justin supposed, made her a good match for the D-boy colonel.

He watched them move off and sit together on a bench below the window looking out over the shining ocean. Close, like they belonged together. Without them touching, speaking, or even looking at one another, you could feel that they were a unit.

It was easy to imagine sitting like that with Kara, except not so much with the quiet part. She wasn't a wild spark of a thing like the Boston redhead Trisha O'Malley, but the woman had no problem speaking her mind.

Sitting like a unit with Kara Moretti...

That thought sent a jolt up his body and not just through his groin.

During the exercise, the woman had slipped inside his head. She'd given him exactly the route he needed, even taking into account the *Jane*'s much larger airframe. And he knew that the change in plan had been completely last second, but she'd had the insight that turned pitched battle to easy victory without one single hesitation.

Justin had flown with a lot of Air Mission Commanders who couldn't communicate an order half as clear, never mind strategize it to begin with. And the number who would have seen the trap and successfully reallocated resources on the fly he could count on a single hand—one with most of its fingers left in a fist.

Women didn't make Justin Roberts feel like a yokel, nor men either. But Kara Moretti most certainly did. No way he'd have seen what to do with five aircraft in the fifteen seconds she'd had to retarget the attack.

Even feeling the fool, he wanted to get closer to her. Being near her was more important than… His mind was already lost. Either he should sit close by her, or he should step off the ship's stern to soak his head in the ocean a while.

To see if there was a spot near her, he turned slowly so that it wouldn't show quite where his attention was focused.

Don't mind me. Just casually scanning the debriefing room and sipping my coffee—Crap!—black because I forgot to put in cream and two sugars.

—⁓—

Kara watched Justin turn to face her with all the subtlety of a juggernaut, his white cowboy hat rotating with the rest of him like the top beam of a scanning radar. She wasn't sure why, but she knew he was tracking in on her.

LCDR Ramis's office was fairly crowded with the five pilots, six including her, plus Connie, the best mechanic in all SOAR; Barstowe from the Rangers; Gibson and Trisha's husband, Bill Bruce, from Delta; and Sly Stowell, the Navy's hovercraft pilot. Even though he hadn't been part of this exercise, Kara had learned that Sly's advice was always good. A couple of Navy officers and Ramis rounded out the crowd, yet Kara still knew she was Justin's search target.

She ducked her head to pay attention to Lola and Trisha, who had taken seats to either side of her on the couch.

"It was awesome. I popped over that ridge crest you pointed me at." Trisha had hands in motion imitating angles of attack.

Kara wondered how soon she'd be wearing the cranberry juice from the open bottle that Trisha was waving about like a baton.

"…easing way back on the collective. I was almost dead silent as I rode the ground effect down the cliff face. When I got to just one rotor from their hidey-hole, I spun to face them and hit them with the floods. Billy was riding copilot and grabbed the PA. 'Bang, you're dead!' he told 'em. Just that. That man is such a crack-up. You totally rocked it, Kara. You nailed their butts."

She glanced at Bill. If the D-boy ever put more than two words together, she hadn't heard it. So not like Justin who always had a joke or a wry comment waiting. Bill was totally the strong, silent type. Also undeniably brave as he had not only married but also rode with Trisha.

One rotor diameter. Kara still wasn't used to how the

helicopter pilots measured distance. If you were "one rotor" out, you wouldn't be scraping yourself off a cliff wall. On the Little Bird it meant that Trish had hovered a half ton of weaponry a dozen meters from the bad guys with no warning. She'd bet that had really bruised some egos.

Kara would have commented on it being such a wild maneuver, but had long since learned that in addition to being a certifiable lunatic and flying like a wild woman, Trisha might well be the most skilled pilot here. Even Lola Maloney, the chief pilot of the DAP Hawk *Vengeance* and leader of the 5D, gave Trisha respect.

And friendship.

Kara was only starting to learn just how tight-knit a group the women of SOAR constituted. The 160th regiment had five battalions of four companies each, and every single woman flying for the Night Stalkers was in the 5D. The first woman in, a Major Emily Beale, had retired when she had a child. And Kee Stevenson was on temporary assignment to do some training with the HRT. Apparently, being one of the nation's top snipers, she was the one training the FBI's elite Hostage Rescue Team, not the other way around.

All of the women in the entire 160th were in this room. And here she was, one Kara Moretti, late of the 3rd Special Operations Squadron of the USAF 27th Special Operations Wing at Cannon Air Force Base in bumfuck New Mexico.

No pressure, girl.

She'd been here two months and she still didn't have her feet down. She'd been eye-in-the-sky on a hostage rescue on her second day in, and the same on a black-in-black op invading Azerbaijan a month later. A mission that no one had or ever would know about, except for the four others who had flown it.

"How did it feel doing your first sortie as our AMC?" Lola asked her in the suddenly silent room.

Kara startled.

Somehow the debriefing had begun and she'd missed it. Everyone looked at her intently, even LCDR Ramis. Except Justin who was staring at her as if she was a total screwup…or maybe a lost circus clown who'd wandered away from Barnum and Bailey at Madison Square Garden and onto a Navy ship in the middle of operations.

"Maybe you should tell me?" It wasn't like her to be cautious, however it was the only way to mask her sudden nerves. She was mostly sure that the op had gone well, but only mostly.

"We've all heard Trisha's assessment." Lola offered a bit of a laugh. When Trisha was excited, her voice tended to expand to fill any space she was in. "Claudia Jean?"

"Captain Moretti offered clear instructions in a timely and accurate manner under difficult circumstances. It was neatly done."

Lola nodded. "Captain Roberts?"

Justin was still staring down at Kara from where he stood across the room—concentrating fiercely on something.

The silence stretched long enough to be awkward.

"Yo, Roberts!" Kara snapped at him when she couldn't take it any longer.

"Uh." He looked around quickly. "What?"

Trisha snorted, but her expression was unreadable when Kara turned to look at her.

"Chief Maloney asked for your opinion on Kara's first op as Air Mission Commander," Clint Barstowe offered helpfully from where he stood close beside Justin.

Justin shook himself, almost losing his hat.

Why a man who stood six-foot-two needed another six inches of hat was beyond her. It looked like a big, white, "shoot me here" target. Right in that thick head of his.

"Beautiful." Then Justin snapped to, his deep-blue eyes raking over Kara once more before he looked over at Lola.

Trisha sent an elbow into Kara's ribs hard enough to hurt for reasons she didn't understand. Trisha widened her eyes as if that was supposed to communicate something.

By the time Kara turned back, Justin had finally shifted his attention to Lola.

"The timing and clarity of her direction really was as purty—"

He actually said it *purty*!

"—as could be. I was flying along, just breaking into final eyes on the target and she drew me a new map. Imaging showed up right on my visor, so as I didn't even have to look aside. Simply told Clint, shifted my track, and it worked, slicker'n bat guano. Afterward, when I had a moment to inspect the area, I saw that she'd chosen the absolute optimal points for troop deployment. Now that's what I call beautiful."

He almost convinced her that he was talking about her job as AMC, but his eyes slid sideways just enough to once more catch her gaze.

Kara finally understood Trisha's elbow. Mr. Too-Tall,

Too-Handsome Texan had just called her "beautiful" in front of the entire top echelon of the USS *Peleliu*.

Death was too good for what she was going to do to him.

Chapter 3

JUSTIN TRIED TO BEAT A HASTY RETREAT FROM THE debriefing room.

Escape was definitely his best option.

He'd simply never look at Kara Moretti again. Maybe he'd wear blinders around the ship like the ones he put on his brother's horse team when he was hitching them up for the Tri-State Fair. Rafe was the only Roberts not to serve, because a horse had kicked his knee hard enough when he was a boy that it had given him a lifetime limp. At the moment, Justin sort of wished he was the one the horse had kicked.

But Justin made the mistake of breaking his newfound law by glancing at Kara as he was tossing out his untouched, pitch black, and now dead cold coffee.

She very subtly pointed behind her back out toward the sunlit flight deck. Everyone else was heading down the internal ship's ladders to the mess on the 02 Deck in time for their meal. The vast open slab of the ship's flight deck would be about as private as you could get.

He considered ignoring her signal, but she'd just been approved as the 5D's AMC by group consensus. If he made her angry enough, she just might fly him into a dead-end canyon at full speed.

This time when he beat her to the door and held it for her, she simply scowled and walked through. In silence, she led him around the base of the communications superstructure and onto the narrow service walkway, all that perched between the superstructure and the thin rail that protected them from a five-story fall into the sea.

He rounded the corner out of sight of the flight line, and she turned to face him like a cornered mountain lion. Actually, more like one on the attack.

"What the hell, Roberts?"

He considered many lines of response…and retreated into the truth.

"Y'all make a man think of many things that are completely inappropriate, ma'am."

"Like what?"

Like the way I can smell you on the breeze right now slipping off the warming day. "Some things are probably best kept between me and my horse."

"You two that close?" She rested her fists on her hips. But instead of scowling up at him, Kara had a cocky grin like she knew the answer to everything. Her humor was sharp, biting, but always made him laugh. And the smile she put back of it always held a surprising warmth. Even as ticked as she was with him at the moment, he could see that deep kindness shining through. He wondered if she knew that about herself—he suspected not, or she might be likely to beat it into submission.

"You might say. I can tell her secrets and she promises not to tell anyone but another horse. Way I see it, that's a safe enough bargain."

"And just what exactly are you keeping between you and your horse? What's so goddamn inappropriate that I—"

Justin wasn't quite sure what came over him. Kara Moretti frustrated him worse than his brother, Rafe, which was sayin' a handful. She knew precisely which buttons to push to make him twitch.

Justin took off his hat, because that's what you did before you kissed a lady.

He caught her mid-word, which turned into a muffled "Mrgrf!" of surprise. He fully expected a slap—another good reason to take off his hat and protect it from being knocked into the sea—and he'd absolutely earned it.

But it didn't come.

She tasted even better than she smelled. Her lips were warm and soft. He'd half expected them to be made of as much steel as her spine and attitude. Instead they gave and molded to return his kiss.

"Mrgrmmmph!" It seemed like a happier sound; he was fairly sure it was.

When the blow came, it didn't connect with his jaw.

Instead, her fist hit the center of his chest and only just hard enough to knock them apart.

"Shit, Roberts!" Kara cursed. "You can't be doing something like that."

"Sorry, ma'am. Warned you it was inappropriate."

"You kiss me and you call me ma'am? Crap! You really are from Texas."

"Born and bred."

"Like your horse who keeps secrets so well."

He nodded. "Much like. Except she's a she and I'm not. There's also the matter of a different number of legs, though I do hope that I kiss better than she does. She tends to slobber a bit." Also, this conversation was not the least like any he'd ever had with a woman he'd just kissed. Whose lips still hovered close enough that he could feel the warmth of her words on his cheek.

Kara took a step back and bumped against the rail.

Justin forced himself to lean back against the gray steel of the superstructure still cool with the night. It brought some tiny bit of rationality back to him.

He rubbed at his jaw. "Odd, I don't feel a slap."

"You were expecting one?"

"Must admit I was."

"And still you kissed me."

He slid his hat back on. "Seemed worth the risk. You taste sweet, Kara Moretti."

"Do *not* be saying shit like that."

"Give me a reason not to."

She narrowed her eyes at him for a long moment before tipping her head toward the rail she was leaning on. Her hair swung like a wave softer than those rolling by behind her.

"You want a reason? Fine. I'll give you two words. Hat. Ocean."

The woman did know how to make her point.

Still, he didn't have a palm print in red on the side of his face. Made it downright difficult to not be grinning as he looked down at her.

Men had stolen kisses from Kara before.

When they were both six, her nearest cousin had claimed first rights...and his nose had bled all over his cannoli.

Carlo di Stefano, now turned opera singer, had won her first real one at thirteen. Hadn't earned the slap until he'd grabbed onto her breasts that had only recently put in an appearance.

There'd been others, some welcomed, many rebuffed.

And she had fully expected to be rebuffing Justin Roberts.

Instead she'd barely resisted melting against him at the *Peleliu*'s port rail.

"That will never do."

"What won't?" He still leaned back against the communication structure's gray steel, looking ever so much like he was a cowboy leaning up against a fence post in the middle of some Texas prairie rather than wearing a sand-colored T-shirt, Universal Camo ACU trousers, and tan Army boots.

"You kissing me and me not..." She trailed off because it sounded stupid to say it after not doing it.

"...slapping me so hard that I see stars for a week."

"Yeah, that." She couldn't help but smile. He read her far too easily.

"Don't be doing that!" Justin's voice was suddenly sharp.

"What, slapping you?"

"Well, I appreciate you not giving me what I deserved. But stop that smiling thing you're doing. It's what has gone and got me in trouble in the first place."

Kara bit her lower lip and tried to look somewhere else to hide her smile. Behind her lay nothing but the calm Mediterranean; Turkey was out of sight over the horizon. A small cluster of fishermen worked the water out near the horizon with a net and a couple cranes. Even though she traveled alone, not many were foolish enough to approach a ship the size of the *Peleliu* uninvited.

Fore and aft offered no view, just the narrow service

walkway. Upward ranged several stories of communications structure, then a couple stories more of radio masts
and radar.

Straight ahead.

Justin Roberts.

He was far too handsome for his own good, or
for hers.

And he was proving himself eight kinds of a gentleman. Except for the kissing part, and even that, he'd
warned her.

In high school it would be, "Yo, Moretti. Get your
cute tush over here, so's I can check it out. 'Cause
there ain't no way it feels as good as it looks." Army
wasn't always that different from high school. Though
switching to SOAR had been a huge improvement. In
two years of additional training and two more months
of mission-qualified service, a couple of men had tried
to befriend her, clearly hoping for more, but Justin had
been the first to cross the line in any way.

And he had apologized beforehand, which was about
the most backward thing on the planet.

She studied those sky-blue eyes. Masked from the
morning light by his hat brim, they watched her closely.

"You're still doing it, Moretti," he warned her in a
deep voice.

"Smiling at you?"

"Yep! Not fair to do that to a man who's just hopin'
to live through the next few minutes."

"You know, my papa always said I've got a naturally
sunny disposition."

At that Justin laughed in her face. "You've got a
naturally *dangerous* disposition."

"Then why did you kiss me?"

At that his face quieted. After a long moment, his lips shifted into a lazy, self-contented smile. It looked damn good on him.

"Must say, I did it because I wanted to. Have for some time."

If Kara was being honest, she'd have to admit that while she hadn't felt that way, the chance to kiss him again registered pretty high on her to-do list.

Kara didn't like lists much; tended to attack them until everything was crossed off so she could throw the damn thing out rather than having it sitting on the corner of her desk scowling at her all the time.

She pushed off the rail and took a slow step toward him across the narrow steel walkway.

"You're still smiling," he noted.

"I seem to be." Without touching him, just the slightest breath of air separating their chests, she tipped her head back to look up at him.

Still he didn't lean down to kiss her, his eyebrows pulled together in fierce concentration as he looked at her.

Sometimes men were so dense. She slid a single finger up along his jaw, could feel the roughness that said he hadn't shaved since waking, and hooked him down to her with the slightest of pressures.

His second kiss was as gentle as the first one. Slow, testing, luscious. Justin might look like some macho, gorgeous Army jerk, but his kiss was a caress that teased her into leaning closer, wanting more, until she'd have tumbled into his arms if his hands weren't braced on her shoulders.

When she moved to deepen the kiss, he eased her back.

She could feel a heat soaring to her cheeks that she was glad her darker complexion would mostly hide. He wanted to kiss her, but he was stopping, which meant that she was just as awkward as—

"Whoa, girl." Justin let out a breath. "Just whoa. You could kill a man with a kiss like that."

"Really?"

"Don't sound so darned pleased with the idea. Especially not when I'm the man."

Kara grinned up at him. Maybe it wouldn't be too awful to spend some time with a Texas cowboy. At least long enough to take him out for a test drive.

Chapter 4

"So?"

Trisha asked before Kara even had a chance to put down her dinner tray. Kara scanned the officers' mess to see if it was too late to sit somewhere else, but the other women of SOAR had already shifted to make room for her.

Her choice of seating was kinda all over the place. Most people had a spot and hung with their own. Kara moved around some and had only landed at the room's center table with the SOAR women once or twice over the last two months.

The 75th Rangers always took a cluster of tables on the side closest to the chow line; the ability to get speedy seconds and thirds was an essential element of their existence. She'd only sat with them a few times. It was odd to sit with a combat unit when you didn't carry a gun for a living—it broke some invisible bond of theirs whenever she joined them. It also made them uncomfortable that her jokes were often raunchier than theirs. She'd grown up in Brooklyn. What did they expect?

The Navy officers ranged across the front and the other side of the mess area. She spent most of her meals with them. Had more connection to them than the women of SOAR. She was never off ship for a mission, just like most of the Navy personnel. The ship was more intimately their home than anyone else's. You could feel the stability of them. Also, one in six sailors were women. Sitting with them was more comfortable than with the Rangers, but she was still an outsider. Still Army.

And no way was she sitting with the tiny cluster of Delta operators in their quiet back corner. Nobody even sat *near* them. Only Trisha and Claudia Jean, who had both married into Delta for God alone knew what reason, ever crossed over.

She sighed and settled across from Trisha and next to Lola, hoping this wasn't about what she thought it was about. They were such a tight group; another reason she hadn't sat with them much.

As a group they unnerved her, and they also filled a table. Until the recent departure of Kee Stevenson and her teenage daughter, Dilya, there hadn't really been room to join them. Kee was also one of those force-of-nature types that Kara both admired and found a little scary. With her gone, the group looked a little less unnerving. A little.

Connie Davis and Claudia Jean Gibson rarely spoke—scuttlebutt had them as the best mechanic and best Little Bird pilot in all SOAR—which only added to the risk factor of joining them. It was a gathering practically designed to terrify men and humble mere human females.

As Kara was finally settling onto her seat, Justin wandered in beneath that tall, white hat that almost reached to the overhead gray-painted pipes and cable runs. He did a casual scan of the room.

She looked down before she could be caught staring at him. Half alien from another planet and half man she really wanted to kiss again. Which made him even more alien. Sex was fun, a take-it-or-leave-it scenario for Kara. But that kiss, that stupidly simple kiss, had been incredible.

Tray. Focus on your tray. There's food there.

The chief steward and her crew had served up beef stew and fresh-baked sourdough bread that smelled amazing.

"C'mon!" Trisha urged her, then took a large spoonful of stew and hissed against the heat. Unable to speak, she waved her spoon at Kara to speak.

Kara went for a subject change and turned to Lola. "Is she always this nosy?"

"You have no idea," Lola commented drily: "Why, what does she have to be nosy about this time, or is it just her normal pushiness?"

Kara did her best to shrug it off, realizing her tactic was on the verge of backfiring on her.

"Cowboy," Trisha managed to gasp out. Then she took a breath. "Wow! The stew is hot, but really good. So, how was the cowboy? Hot but good? He *shore* is *purty*, ain't he?" Her fake Texas sounded ridiculous in a Boston Irish accent. Kara recalled an elbow in her ribs; no question Trisha had caught the meaning of Justin's misstep in the debrief.

"You're married."

Trisha sighed happily. "I am. Doesn't mean I'm blind though."

"Why should I answer you?"

"Because"—Connie spoke up in that soft voice— "Trisha has over a ninety-seven percent success rate of getting answers with her pestering. Most choose to spare themselves the pain and simply provide requested information."

Kara eyed the woman. Connie might look like the girl next door with her light-brown hair feather cut to her jaw, but Kara knew there was also a genius lurking behind those eyes. A genius with a photographic memory who just might have actually tallied Trisha's success rate.

Kara held out her hand toward Trisha, who stared at it in puzzlement for a long moment before she reached out to take it. Kara offered one short handshake.

"Hi. My name is Captain Kara Moretti, and I'm one of the three percent."

Trisha made a raspberry sound at her as Connie smiled and Lola burst out laughing. Claudia Jean nodded her quiet approval and turned back to her stew.

—◊◊◊—

Justin sat with Lieutenant Barstowe and some of his Rangers. It was like old home week, just sitting with some guys and shooting the breeze. It was one of his favorite parts of being home.

Most of Roberts Quarter Horse Ranch, the RQR, was a premier American quarter horse breeding and training center. But Ma had a soft spot for training up the young ones in roping and racing for rodeo.

One of the treats for the resident campers had always been a campfire dinner. In summers, the campfire was used far more nights than the stove in the big farmhouse kitchen. The family always joined in for the meal; it was one of the things he missed most when serving overseas. The Texas stars, steaks sizzling on the cast-iron grate, an ice chest of cold Coke, and comfortably sore legs from a day in the saddle.

Sitting with the Rangers gave him some of that same

feeling despite the steel-gray room and the bolted-down tables with raised edges to prevent losing a tray in a storm. He'd arrived in the middle of the retelling of the "Taking of the Turks."

By the time they were done, Justin had reached a couple of conclusions. First off was that a U.S. Ranger was as full of himself as your average Texas rodeo rider. Second that they were actually pretty well justified to feel that way.

Sure, he'd faced his share of rocket-propelled grenades, shoulder-to-air missiles, and other such nasties during his time in the Afghanistan War. But that was far different than crawling through a muddy ditch to find an hombre with an AK-47 and a passel of anger to unload. The Rangers got down on the ground and faced it foot by foot.

"Got a theory," he told them when the Turks had once more been browbeaten in story as well as song.

"Hit us." Barstowe grinned across at him.

"Well, you guys are the working horses of Special Ops. All y'all get out there and beat down that track day in and day out."

There were nods of approval and a few hooahs.

He eased back and dunked some of the good crusty bread into the stew. "Now my job and that of my fellow SOAR fliers is leading you ground-pounders where you need to go. I figure us as the purebreds of the crowd."

As they razzed him, he shouted them back down, though it was seven to one at his table.

"Seriously, guys. You're gonna put a pair of Army boots and some little ATVs up against a lady as beautiful as my *Calamity Jane*? Just not in the same league, pardners."

That bought him some nods and some crap about gettin' down and gettin' dirty if he wanted to find out what it was really all about.

"Now them boys," Justin cut them off and nodded over toward the Delta operators in the corner. Delta often did joint ops with the U.S. Rangers and drew most of its candidates from them. These guys were probably all hoping to make it one day. "They're like the good old boys. They're the ones who take home so many of the rodeo's prizes that the competition for everyone else is who all can come in second. Like they're so good that they aren't playing fair."

"Damn straight." Barstowe slapped one of his men on the shoulder. "You could take on Gibson with one hand behind your back. Right, Johnson?"

"Hooah, Lieutenant!" Not there was a way he could give any other answer and retain Ranger pride. Though his worried look got another round of laughter going.

"And what does that make the Navy?" Chief Petty Officer Sly Stowell dropped his tray beside Justin's.

"W'all"—Justin shot a grin over to the Rangers—"all your best rodeo boys need someone to do the driving between the events."

There was a round of laughter among the Army guys.

Sly nodded calmly until they quieted. "I can see how you might make that mistake."

"What mistake?" Johnson leaned forward, wanting to make up for no way he could beat Colonel Gibson.

"Thinking that all of you would have a place to ride if it weren't for the Navy carting your sorry selves every which way and keeping you safe for the other twenty-three hours and fifty-eight minutes of the day.

Did you really take the Turks' asses down in ninety-five seconds?"

That got him razzes and cheers and more stories of the night's operation. The Rangers jawed tales back and forth right through a dessert of honeyed fruit that really balanced off the richness of the stew.

"Excuse me, Cowboy. Can you direct me to Captain Moretti?"

Justin turned to look up at the man standing close behind him. His accent was Yankee, though Justin couldn't pin it down. He was a lean guy, with black hair and skin almost as dark as Kara's.

He gave a nod toward the table where all of the SOAR women sat together. "The pretty one."

Justin wasn't quite sure why he said it just that way. The women of SOAR were not only amazing examples of soldier fitness, but also collectively women who were a true joy to look at.

But Justin didn't like the guy. Didn't want to be helping him for some reason.

"A woman. Well, they didn't tell me that. Excellent! Thanks, pard." The guy clapped him on the shoulder as if they were old buddies and moved off.

Justin definitely didn't like the guy.

He also didn't like that he walked unerringly to Kara despite the insufficient description.

Nor the fact that ten seconds later Kara rose and headed out of the officers' mess with the man.

It wasn't jealousy.

Except that Justin could feel an urge deep in his hands to disassemble the stranger into tiny pieces, break him up like kindling, and toss him on the campfire.

Chapter 5

"Captain Moretti?"

"I think we already established that, didn't we?" Kara tried to keep the snide out of her voice, but didn't succeed very well. It was clear from his accent that he was City and Upper West Side. Yeah, Brooklyn was rising in profile and trendiness—God help them all—and the Upper West Side of Manhattan was no longer the bedrock of old money, but it still felt that way. Though this guy looked more low-lifer, like the Upper West Side was phony and he should sound Morningside Heights. Besides, coming from where he did, he'd be a fan of the Yankees rather than the best baseball team in New York, the Mets.

"We need a secure place to speak. Where is your GCS installed?"

"You need to identify your ass better than *Major Wilson* before we go a step further." She dug in her heels along the two-man-wide corridor outside the officers' mess. Her ground control station coffin was close— walk about fifty meters down this corridor, descend a ship's ladder, and step onto the hangar deck—but she wasn't about to tell him that. "Gotta know you way better before I take you into a secure location."

"Hello, Willard," Colonel Michael Gibson's voice sounded softly from behind her. "Saw you walk through. Do we have a problem here?"

"Your parents named you Willard?" Kara continued to razz him to buy herself a moment to analyze the unexpected interruption. "Willard Wilson? I'm guessing they didn't like you at first sight. Not even a little if they named you that. What are we supposed to call you, Willy Willy? Square Willy? Nah, that's what they must have called you in school. Maybe we'll call you Willy Nilly."

Mr. Delta Force Colonel, Mr. Number One Soldier in the U.S. Military, knew the man by name. She could feel her hackles going down. Recommendations didn't come much higher.

"Got a mouth on ya, don't cha, Brooklyn?"

"Special for you, West Side." His fake Brooklyn accent was totally lame. He was one of those guys who was so convinced that he was charming that even the dumbest broad could see through it. And Kara was far from that stupid.

The man looked pleadingly at Michael.

"Don't be looking at him when you're asking to get around me. Can't even fight your own battles?"

"I wasn't expecting a goddamn—"

"You'll want to listen to him," Michael cut the man off.

To the best of her knowledge the ever-so-silent D-boy never cut off anyone. And it wasn't her that he was cutting off, but rather this Major Dickhead. And in the process telling her that the guy wasn't as much of a dickhead as she was thinking. Like eight layers of communication in six words. No wonder they'd made him a Delta boy.

"Can we get the hell outta here, lady? We're drawing

a crowd." The ill-named Willard Wilson was looking over her shoulder.

She glanced back and spotted Justin standing there, stopped two steps outside the mess. His pure white hat and golden hair only emphasized the age of the yellow-painted *Peleliu* corridor. There were even spots of rust showing through on the steel walls. Though that made Justin look just that much newer and shinier.

His face showed he was wondering if he should move in fast or what. Kara appreciated the backup, not that she needed it with Michael Gibson standing beside her, but it was thoughtful of him. Then she had an idea and flashed a subtle hand signal for Justin to hold fast. She saw him shift his stance slightly in answer before she turned back to the Major.

"You're going to be talking air assets?"

He glared down at her and then nodded reluctantly.

"You show up on the *Peleliu* and you single me out of the crowd, that tells me one piece you need. What else do you need with the 5D, big or small?"

He shifted from scowl to consideration.

"'Cause if you need big, that"—she nodded to Justin—"the tall drink of water in the cowboy hat, is probably the best Chinook pilot there is."

"And who are you to be saying that?"

There were moments in a soldier's life that were just sweet. You ground through daily crap. You made Captain. All the bad stuff with the good. But every once in a while the universe just lined up her little lines of fate, and you got to really rub a superior rank's nose in it.

"Because, Major Willy Nilly—still can't believe your mama named you that—you are talking to the

5D's Air Mission Commander." That she'd been the AMC barely an hour was information he didn't need. "It's my job to know my people and the 5D only takes the very best."

Which actually was a fact she hadn't taken in about herself yet either. If Justin was in the 5D, he hadn't been just a good pilot of the MH-47, he was one of the best on the planet. And if she was here—

Watch it, girl! Ego will spin your head.

"A drone jock who's an AMC?" Wilson asked Michael with a *Who is she shitting?* tone.

Kara jabbed him in the chest, forcing his attention back to her.

"An *RPA pilot* who is an AMC, and also I can tell you that in thirty seconds this corridor is going to be clogged with U.S. Rangers wondering what we've been talking about out here for so long, especially because you're about the least subtle guy ever hatched. They're action hungry right at the moment and will want to know." She nodded back toward the gathering noise, knowing full well they'd mostly be exiting out the other side of the mess toward the barracks and the rec room up forward.

Major Wilson cursed and then waved. "All three of you, let's go." And he headed off down the corridor.

Kara snagged his shirt before he could move off.

"Now what the fuck, Brooklyn?" Not the Heights. With his prep school and fancy college overtones, he really was Upper West Side and was just playing at belonging onboard here.

Sometimes fate served up a dish even sweeter. She offered her best smile and a sharp salute.

"Regret to inform the Major, but he's going in the wrong-ass direction."

———～～———

Justin watched them turn and approach him with Kara leading the way along the corridor.

She flashed a low hand signal for Justin to fall in beside her as she approached. The Major had fallen behind with Michael, but Kara kept her voice low.

"You ever think about the fact that you're one of the best Chinook pilots in existence or you wouldn't be with the 5D?"

He'd have stumbled to a halt if Kara hadn't been busy moving down the corridor in her typical faster-than-a-quarter-horse-in-the-last-hundred-yards fashion. His legs had to be twice as long as hers and he still had trouble keeping up.

"No. Can't say as I had. Knew you were the best RPA there was or they wouldn't have tagged you for AMC as well. How in the Lord above did you do that anyway? But I hadn't really thought—"

"—the other way around. I know. I just told Major Jerk-Off that you were the very best, then realized that you must be or you wouldn't be here. Pretty wild ride, huh, Cowboy?"

"Saddle up, girl. The ride—"

"—is just beginning. I know."

Justin wondered how many people she ticked off with that sentence-finishing thing. He always hated when a Yankee acted as if he didn't speak fast enough. But with Kara Moretti, it felt more like they were in fantastic sync, like when you shifted from a rough trot to a smooth canter.

He wanted to say something else to see if she'd keep doing it. But his mind was a blank. He'd never had trouble coming up with words around pretty women, but with Kara Moretti—especially this version of her switched over to some hyperintense AMC gait—he didn't know what to do.

Except try to keep up.

———

Kara braced her arms on the ladder's rails, lifted her feet, and slid down a full deck. She opened the hatchway to the hangar deck...and then had to wait for the three guys to clamber down the steep steps to join her.

The white cargo container of the ground control station was tucked back in the corner of the echoing space. The hangar deck filled the rear half of the ship for three decks high. Being capped by the steel underside of the flight deck and walled by the ship's steel hull with only a few gaps in it made a dropped screwdriver echo like a gunshot and a whisper audible down the entire length of the deck. When maintenance was test firing a Black Hawk's T700 turbines, the sound could blow the top of your head off despite safety muffs.

At the moment, the deck was empty. No lights were on, so only the sharp edge of the early morning sun sliced in through the various openings like the aircraft elevator. The light was so bright, it almost hurt, the shadows so thick that they were black and mysterious. The silence was deep enough that even their rubber-soled footsteps sounded clearly and left rippling echoes like waves on a pond.

She glanced down.

Justin wore Army boots, not cowboy boots. For some reason that struck her as one of the oddest things in an already odd day. She'd had Captain Justin Roberts all neatly slotted away in her mind—Texas, macho, clumsy around women. Your basic goofball.

And in the last few hours he'd flown a mission immaculately, delivered and retrieved his customers in difficult terrain, and given her one of the sweetest kisses of her life.

And it had finally worked its way through her thick skull that he'd been assigned to the 5D fresh out of Fort Campbell training. That meant the instructors had really seen something in him. Hell, SOAR only had sixty Chinook pilots out of the more than twelve hundred of the craft out there across the various services. That alone meant the man was damn good at what he did.

And if SOAR only took the best, the 5D skimmed off the absolute top fliers, something the mythical founders of the company, Majors Beale and Henderson, had instituted right from the beginning five years earlier.

Well, she'd always found having a standard to live up to was a strong motivator. And if Beale's copilot had gone on to be the company's first AMC, it was time for Kara to step it up if she was going to hang on to being the second one in the company's short history.

The GCS coffin itself was crowded up against the forward bulkhead of the hangar deck. Heavy cables snaked out of the side, one into the ship's power, the other into the communications array to emerge at the six-meter dish she'd rigged high aloft for communicating with her RPAs. It auto-tracked the Gray Eagle when it was in line of sight and switched over to the *Peleliu*'s satellite feed when the RPA went out of range, like during her dive last night.

At the door of the GCS coffin, Kara halted and looked back at Colonel Gibson. "You're sure about this dude?" She didn't wait for an answer. Kara already knew that there would be few higher stamps of approval than Michael's; she just wanted another shot at Major Willard Wilson. She resisted tagging him aloud as Limp Willy, but it was a close thing.

She keyed the code and then leaned in for the retinal scan. The heavy bolts thunked open and she led the way in, turning on the internal lights.

Justin was last in and stumbled to a halt. He'd seen the outside every day for two months. It looked like a white-painted cargo container, barely worthy of note if not for the heavy locks. But he'd never been in the GCS before, and it was like seeing a whole new side to Kara Moretti.

How much did he know about this woman?

"Not much" was the answer staring him in the face.

One wall was dominated by a pair of long white boxes that he recognized as Gray Eagle coffins. He'd been responsible several times for transporting one of them to an appropriate airstrip, because the MQ-1C Gray Eagle needed a couple thousand feet of runway, more than twice the length of the *Peleliu*. So, when the 5D and the ship were on the move, the ground team would box up the Gray Eagle RPA. Then he'd fetch it, and them, for the move. Afterward, he'd deliver them to some handy Air Force base for launch and recovery.

How odd to fly an aircraft that you almost never saw.

It's what those guys at NASA must feel like. He remembered a trip he and his siblings had made to Florida when they were all kids. His parents had taken the three of them to Kennedy Space Center for a shuttle launch. Rafe only ever cared about the horses, but Bessie Anne had wanted to be an astronaut. Sister who was an astronaut had sounded pretty cool to a nine-year-old. She'd gone U.S. Air Force, but hadn't made it into the program before the shuttles went away.

But he'd remembered that launch and the tour Ma had arranged of the command-and-control center. Granted there had been like sixty gals and guys there, but you could just feel that everything had a purpose and it all had a single focus—launching a rocket into space.

Kara's coffin was like that; it was immersion in an absolutely focused space.

On the first stretch of the wall opposite the Gray Eagle's containers were a long workbench and three much smaller coffins. They were barely two meters long each and as big across as his forearm. These would be the ScanEagle RPAs. They could be launched off a patrol boat or any ship with a little open space. He'd seen Kara use the little craft a couple times for simpler sorties or as a communications relay when the Gray Eagle was over the horizon and there wasn't a satellite channel handy. Even now, one was out on the bench, clearly taken apart for service.

It was the back end of the container that really drove home how different Moretti was. The Gray Eagle's ground control station was a full pilot-and-copilot rig, but Kara's only view of the world was through screens.

And for such a seemingly simple craft, there were a

whole lot of screens. Big ones where he had windows on the *Jane*, secondaries that must include sensor data when active. Then a full set of flight instrumentation and controls.

On top of that was a bank of radios even more daunting than on his *Calamity Jane*, which was saying something. SOAR's MH-47Gs had a whole lot more tech rigged up to them than your average Chinook: terrain avoidance, signal jamming, and advanced threat detection were only the start of what he'd had to learn when he transferred into the 160th Regiment. But the Gray Eagle specialized in signal interception and location, and had the hardware on show to back it up.

He looked over at Kara to see if she'd changed somehow. No and a little bit yes. Still beautiful and with a dancer's upright posture—ballet as a kid that had never worn off, maybe—that could just kill a man. She walked like a confident soldier and stood like one. Her expression didn't look any different as she baited the newcomer over what flavor of soda he wanted from the small fridge beneath the workbench.

But with this high-tech world wrapped tight around her, Kara looked as if she belonged. He supposed it was like how he felt when he settled into the pilot's seat of the *Jane*; everything just kind of fit.

This high-tech dungeon looked good on her, damned good.

"Don't!" She aimed a finger at him and he knew exactly what she meant, though clearly the other two didn't.

Justin couldn't help himself, didn't even bother to try. He just kept smiling at her.

Chapter 6

KARA FORCED HERSELF TO LOOK AWAY FROM JUSTIN. She could see by Major Wilson's face that he'd been inside RPA coffins before. A sweeping glance, and no more. It told her something about his security clearance at least.

His eyes hesitated only twice: once on the poster of an MQ-1C Gray Eagle soaring among the clouds, and once on her Fordham University Rams banner. She made a guess based on his hesitation.

"The Lions suck, by the way."

Wilson's frown was as instantaneous as only a true Columbia University Lions football fan would have.

"And we're going to kick your butts this year too."

He actually growled, but it was hard to argue with Fordham's winning streak. *Reality sucks, dude!* But she kept the last to herself, figuring that she'd pushed him hard enough.

She could also see Justin looking like a kid on Christmas morning, finding a new colt under the tree or something. She still wasn't sure what instinct had made her force Wilson's hand to let her bring Justin along.

It had been a hard-learned lesson to trust that instinct. But once she'd learned to listen to it, she'd graduated top of her ROTC class and eventually ended up sitting in this box in the Mediterranean.

Good little Instinct! She gave it a mental pat on the head and then shoved it aside. She was busy now.

"So, talk." Kara gave it the full Brooklyn *tawk*, spun around her pilot's chair, and dropped into it. At her nod, Justin took the copilot's seat.

The Major dragged over a stool from the workbench; Michael remained standing.

"I can't tell you who I work for and, no, pestering me isn't going to—"

"Well then, I guess we're done here." Kara made to stand up. "C'mon, Justin."

Michael watched her blandly, but she ignored him.

"Goddamn it!" Wilson cursed. "Will you sit still for a goddamn second, Moretti?"

She held out her hands as if intending no offense and dropped back into her seat. Kara had no intention of leaving, not when there was clearly something intense going on here.

"I'm—"

"—with The Activity," Kara cut him off. She had no idea where that shot in the dark came from, but now that she'd said it, it made perfect sense.

Wilson's blink of surprise was the only confirmation she needed.

"The Activity" was just one of the many nicknames for the former U.S. Army Intelligence Support Activity, which had been supposedly disbanded in 1989 and gone through a dozen incarnations since as it was vastly increased in size.

"Centra Spike, Gray Fox, Cemetery Wind…I'm guessing that you won't be telling me your outfit's current name."

"How the fuck?" Wilson exploded.

Justin was smiling, so Kara nodded to him.

"Clue one." Justin slouched down farther in the copi-lot's armchair beside her as if he'd been here a hundred times before. He crossed his booted feet just as if he were wearing cowboy boots out on the range.

She considered being ticked, but then decided that she'd rather have Justin sitting so close in the copilot's seat than Major Wilson. *Bring it on, Cowboy*.

"You won't identify your unit, not even in this location."

"Two," Kara joined in, "arrogant beyond belief."

"Three—" Justin continued without hesitation.

She was really starting to appreciate more about him than just the way he looked and the way he kissed.

"—you didn't even blink entering this container, which is one of the most secure areas aboard the *Peleliu*."

"Four, rude too."

His growing scowl was awesome.

"Five"—Justin made it sound as if the two of them had been tag-teaming idiots forever instead of this being their first run together—"you went directly for her, the 5D's RPA pilot. That points to something very clandestine."

"Six—" Kara hadn't thought of that one, but it was a good point.

Justin was proving that he had a brain despite being from the wrong side of the Hudson River—by about twenty-five hundred kilometers.

"—Colonel Michael Gibson," Kara continued, "knows exactly who you are, and I know that The Activity's primary mandate is actionable intelligence for Tier 1 assets. Which includes: Delta, DEVGRU, and the Air Force's 24th STS. Now, while the Colonel here might be the number one Tier 1 asset warrior there is,

I'm not any of those. Yet you came to me. So can we cut through your Upper West Side ego and get on with it?"

Major Willard Wilson turned to look a question at Michael, but it was clear that he hadn't said anything beyond greeting good old Willy.

"And seven." Kara wanted to crow with triumph as the last piece clicked into place. "You're a support guy. Admin. Logistics and liaison for a field team. Probably washed out and couldn't make the grade."

"It spares the action teams from having to deal with nut jobs like you." But his tone said her last guess had hit too close to home.

They shared a grin for the first time.

"Could get to like you, Major Willard." *Fat chance in hell*, Kara told herself.

"You won't find me banking on that any time soon, Captain Moretti."

"Hey"—she turned to Justin—"he's not as dumb as he looks."

—·ᄿᄿ·—

Justin didn't try answering; he was still trying to catch his breath.

Lord above. The Activity?

Meeting one of them made it feel normal that there were a half-dozen stealth helicopters parked on the deck close above his head. Or that he was sitting inside Kara Moretti's top secret domain.

These guys made the CIA's Special Activities Division look like they were using billboards to advertise their most clandestine operations. The Activity were the ultimate spooks of the military intelligence community. The CIA and NSA specialized in regional and national intel. The Activity pinpointed individual cell phones and could tell you the layout of bin Laden's compound *before* you went busting in the front door.

Saddam Hussein had been captured by U.S. Rangers. Some people knew that Delta had led the Rangers there and then faded out of sight. Only rumor said that The Activity came up with the final two possible hideouts in the first place. But it was the kind of rumor that made perfect sense.

They were an intelligence outfit and their action arms were the very best in the world: Delta and DEVGRU, still popularly known by the name they hadn't borne in over twenty years, SEAL Team Six.

"We…"

Justin could see that Kara was gearing up to go at Wilson again before he even had a chance to start, which wasn't going to achieve anything. You could only humiliate a man so much before it became personal.

He didn't want to kick her; it would be far too obvious. His hand had come to rest naturally on the joystick controller built into the chair arm. A tap showed that it was linked to the one on Kara's chair. He wiggled it hard enough to get her attention.

She glanced over at him, huffed out a sigh, and then nodded ever so slightly, keeping her mouth shut as Wilson continued, apparently unaware of the barely averted broadside.

"…have assets on the ground in the Negev Desert. We have lost communications with them. You are the closest asset available with the resources to locate and extract them."

"The Negev?"

Major Wilson nodded.

"The Activity," Justin said slowly and carefully, "has lost track of ground reconnaissance personnel in the Israeli desert." He didn't know why he had to repeat it to make it real. Because it was too unreal?

Kara rolled her eyes at him. "If The Activity is spying on Israel, it means that we're checking out whether to do some shit against our main ally in the region. They gotta be into something seriously bad."

Justin reached the same conclusion, but it just didn't strike him as…mannerly. No matter how many Taliban, al-Qaeda, and IS bullies he'd helped take down, he could never get over what they did to each other and the populace around them. He'd helped rescue a dozen hostages out of the Somali desert, some of whom had been there for years. Years of their lives lost to some fanatics who Delta Force had made sure were no longer walking on God's green earth.

"So we're going to unleash Delta against our allies now. Between you, me, and the steel walls, what in the world did they do to deserve that?"

"That," Wilson said solemnly, "is what we'll find out after you get our assets' butts back out of there."

Chapter 7

"THREE NIGHTS." KARA RUBBED AT HER TEMPLES AND slumped lower in her armchair pilot's seat. "Three straight nights we've been running at the desert without a peep."

Her Gray Eagle had swept ever-increasing circles over the vast wilderness of the Negev. Overlaps, grids, high-altitude flights hunting for any sign of a U.S. military signal.

The first night she'd only monitored on the radio frequency that Wilson had provided her.

Justin had tried to help, but he only knew choppers. Might as well have sat her down in the cockpit of *Calamity Jane* and said, "Go!" Even if he'd been a jet jockey, it wouldn't have helped much. The RPA was too different an animal.

When she'd looked to Wilson, he simply shook his head.

Michael had raised his hands as if fending her off. "I use your data. I'm no pilot."

She hadn't asked. The next night, when they all gathered for the next flight, she'd had Sergeant Santiago Marquez flying beside her. Wilson hadn't said a word.

Okay, a bit less of a jerk than she'd first thought. A bit.

She kept Justin close, giving him the traffic control sensors to watch. She didn't want any nasty surprise of an Israeli Defense Force F-16 or AH-64 Apache weapons helicopter crawling up her behind unexpectedly.

With the extra help, she expanded to a full spectrum of military radio frequencies on the second night.

On night three, she'd opened to the civilian frequencies with no better luck.

Kara looked at Wilson. "You think these guys are still alive."

"Yes."

"And you think this because…"

"Because they wouldn't go down without a squawk of some sort to let us know."

"Even if—"

"Even if they were under live fire," Wilson insisted. "They're hunkered down hard. They should be squirting a signal of some sort on the hour, every hour of darkness."

"But they're not."

He dropped back onto his stool. "No, they're not."

Kara's scream of frustration was loud enough to hurt even her own ears inside the GCS coffin.

—◠◠◠—

Justin winced; too late to cover his ears. There had to be some way to help Kara find these guys. He'd felt clumsy at the controls. The cameras on the Gray Eagle were its main weapon and were far more advanced that anything the *Calamity Jane* boasted. He hadn't even recognized some of the settings. After two more nights watching Santiago manipulate the cameras, Justin had a bit more of a clue and was even more impressed.

So, time to try using his brain as an alternative resource.

"These guys are the best recon folks out there, right?"

"Yes." Wilson considered for a few moments, then sighed and continued. "The Activity fields two primary types. Knob-turners, the very best signal intercept guys in the business and human intelligence, on-the-ground guys. They collect the information needed by the action team snipers: Delta and DEVGRU. The Activity doesn't recruit the best shooters, but rather the best scouts and spotters.

"Put three of these guys in a room and you wouldn't believe the shit they've done. You put a half dozen of them together and it's freaky what they come up with. They develop their own training regimens, because we can't match what these guys already have. We pass on what prior teams have learned and then let them run with it."

Justin tried to think about that. Such training was designed to shift skills from the conscious to the autonomic subconscious.

When his mother was training a new roper or barrel racer, she made them do the most basic exercises hundreds, even thousands of times. Teens would come in with their hands blistered despite their gloves because they'd spent so many hours casting a lariat at a fence post.

These guys would be like that. Survival wasn't something they had to think about; it would become autonomic, just like making sure a final status message got out.

"This reminds me of a story," Justin started out.

Kara rolled her eyes. "God, you are so Texan."

"Thankee, ma'am."

It earned him the short laugh he'd been hoping for. Between launching her Gray Eagle from Incirlik in time to arrive over Israel at full dark and then flying back after dawn, his and Kara's days in the GCS coffin had been long and their personal time together had been nonexistent.

Justin kicked back in his chair. "I was drinking with this old Navy hand one night, and we got to talking about coming down in the sea." About the worst nightmare for a helicopter pilot. "Turned out he was a submariner, and he started telling me about the emergency alert buoy on those boats."

He did his best to shift his voice so it would sound as if he were the narrator from *Moby Dick* gone old and crotchety.

"We only kick that thar boo-yay loose if we knows we're dead."

Kara laughed, so he must have succeeded. Man, oh man, did that lady ever have a wonderful laugh. Her heart was right in it every time.

He made his voice even squeakier. "See our job in the missile boats is to go out there and get lost for six months at a time. No one is supposed to know where we at. So, if we go down, they never find us without that thar boo-yay. You can bet for dang sure we're gonna hit that if it's the last thing we ever do. Otherwise ain't nobody gonna ever fin' us'n."

"Sounds about right," Wilson agreed.

Michael simply nodded.

Tago looked as if he'd fallen asleep in his chair, but Justin now knew there was no way the sergeant would lose vigilance until he handed *Tosca* off to the ground crew at Incirlik. He was like a gamer on drugs, completely at one with the RPA for the long flight back to the American air base in Turkey. They couldn't exactly move the Gray Eagle team to their normal base inside

Israel. Ironically, they would normally be stationed at Ramon Airbase, the one they now were patrolling—without permission.

"So, why would a submarine stay silent if it was in trouble, other than—" Justin didn't have a chance to finish.

Kara, who'd been slumped deep in her pilot's seat, jerked upright. "Other than if they were hunkered down so close under the bad guys' noses, they wouldn't dare let out a peep."

She leaned forward, and for a second, he thought she was going to hug him right in front of everybody. Instead she slapped his knee harder than he'd whack a reluctant horse.

"Well done, Cowboy!"

He wished he could read her better to know if there had been a hug there. It was one of the strangest things he'd ever done—kiss a woman and then not have even a single second of privacy for three straight days together.

There'd been a few moments, sort of, where Michael and Willard had wandered off to get some food and Tago had rushed off to the head. But they still hadn't been alone because Kara Moretti had been so connected to the Gray Eagle that she was barely in the room.

She was one focused gal when there was a mission on. And he was finding that was something he really appreciated in a fellow officer, even if the woman was frustrating the hell out of his libido.

"So…" He really needed a mental subject change. "If they are tucked down so tight—"

"—then there's no way they'd risk a high-power signal sent to reach my Gray Eagle."

"Why—"

"—doesn't matter. That they don't dare transmit a strong signal is all we need to know."

"We need—"

"—my little ScanEagle. We take it in fast and low, below the Israeli radar sweep. We nestle in so close to Ramon Airbase that we could hear the guys whisper."

"But—" Justin wondered if it was even worthwhile trying to finish a sentence when she was in this mode.

"But"—she smiled at him to prove that she knew exactly what she was doing to him—"we're too far away for my little bird. Michael, you have to get Ramis to move the *Peleliu*. We have twelve hours. I need to be five hundred kilometers closer. They can do that in a high-speed run."

Michael was shaking his head no.

"What the… Why not?"

Michael raised his eyebrow at Justin who grinned back at him.

"Because, Kara"—Justin turned to face her, wondering how much of a clue she'd need—"that's—"

"—RPA thinking, not Air Mission Commander thinking." She thumped him on the arm hard enough to really sting.

Apparently "not much of a clue" was the answer. Damn but she was impressive.

"You're absolutely right. I'm outta here. Gotta find Ramis. Tago, don't crash while I'm gone or we'll both be in a heap of hurt."

And just that fast, the men were left alone in the cargo container.

"That woman is something else." Willard shook his

head. "And, brother, she likes you even more than she hates me—and that's saying something."

Justin massaged his arm and wondered if that was true.

Michael's thoughtful nod made it hard to doubt.

Tago's flinch and the resultant tumbling of the RPA's view of the world confirmed it. Perhaps not in a good way there; his big brother protectiveness of Kara was pretty transparent.

What did that make him?

The RPA lost over three thousand feet before Tago regained control.

Justin knew exactly how the poor little Gray Eagle felt, like someone had just hit his cyclic control—hard.

Chapter 8

ALL DAY THE *PELELIU* HAD RACED SOUTH, THE POOR old ship proving that her bones were still good and powerful. Kara had avoided the many questions from SOAR and Navy personnel alike by retreating to her cabin and doing a face-plant that didn't begin to recover what the last three sixteen-hour days of flying had taken out of her.

When she finally climbed out of the sack, Lola and Trisha were headed for a pre-breakfast run…so Kara headed for the showers. She really didn't need questions at this point, especially ones she suspected she wasn't allowed to answer. She swept through the breakfast line taking anything portable—carefully not looking toward Connie and Claudia at one of the half-filled mess tables—and headed for the GCS container.

Once inside, she pulled down the black case from the top shelf, keyed in the security code, and opened it.

There at the workbench, she ate as she prepped the ScanEagle with the instrument packages she wanted. With only seven and a half pounds of useful payload on the RPA, she had to be very selective.

So, she had to figure out how to put aloft the best package, with no idea of what she needed ahead of time.

A day-and-night camera, but not the hi-resolution gear because it weighed too much, and imaging radar.

She was tempted by the radiation and bioweapon

sensors, but that would only satisfy her own curiosity
about what The Activity might have been hunting.

The rest of her payload was given over to a high-speed
ELINT package. In addition to receiving radio signals
from the team, it would gather any Electronic Intelligence
on a broad spectrum of frequencies and could even provide limited signal jamming of the "enemy" if necessary.

When she was done, Kara tucked the ScanEagle
back in its crate and locked it. Instead of being three
feet square by twenty-five long and weighing nearly
two tons when loaded for flight—like the Gray Eagle's
coffin—the ScanEagle's crate was a foot square by five
long and weighed less than her rucksack loaded for a
10K hike. Despite the military having switched over to
metric, it was still easier to think in feet than in meters.

The four of them now stood out in the fading sunset,
the first one she'd seen in days. They were on the huge
aircraft elevator that moved helicopters between the
flight deck and the hangar deck. The steel platform
stuck five meters out from the side of the ship and was
half again as long. The elevator had been lowered to the
hangar deck position.

No need to go up on the flight deck and expose her
little baby to inquiring eyes. It was a funny juxtaposition
to launch such a tiny aircraft from such a massive ship.

"This little beauty is something few folks get to see."
Kara triple-checked that they were the only personnel
in the area.

Justin hovered close behind her, just like Michael and
Willard. Kara felt as if she were center stage, rather than
standing on the aircraft elevator platform that stuck out
the side of the *Peleliu*.

Justin had helped her wheel out the ScanEagle's launching platform. It was a light trailer with a single center rail. It looked much like a heavy-duty crossbow tilted up at the sky.

She snapped open the case, lifted out the main body, and set it on the rail.

"As far as I know, there are only three other black box ScanEagles and they're all in SOAR. I heard hints that there was one more in use by some wildland fire-fighting outfit. How's that for a crazy rumor, huh?"

Justin noticed that while Willard laughed, Delta Operator Michael Gibson was even quieter than usual. Wasn't that interesting? Justin tried to imagine why a wildfire outfit would need what he was looking at and came up blank.

He'd worked with a normal ScanEagle before. It was as long as a manure shovel and as big around as a horse's muzzle—and about as lumpy. A pair of delicate, swept-back wings stuck out five feet to either side.

In three minutes, Kara had the wings pinned on, the little vertical winglets sticking up from the wingtips like exclamation points. The ScanEagle sported a rear propeller with a diameter no longer than his elbow to his fingertips.

All of that was normal.

But the body wasn't thin-sheet aluminum. He rapped a knuckle on it, black composite laminate. And the body was all strange angles. Even the ScanEagles in the 5D were stealth.

This fascinated Wilson in a way that the inside of the GCS coffin hadn't.

And clearly his interest and obvious attention was being soaked up by a Kara eager to teach willing pupils.

But there was more than that.

And Justin wasn't enjoying it much.

He could see Kara warming up to Wilson.

And Justin could feel that weird edge that some guys had, the ones who only dated married women…or tried to take a woman as soon as they saw she was with someone else.

Worse, she was falling for it. He'd thought her too smart for such ploys and found the bitter taste of disappointment a harsh reality.

Justin considered tossing the guy off the railing—they were still ten meters above the ocean and no one would really miss him, would they?—or nudging him into the propeller that Kara had just started on the little RPA. Then he could spend the rest of his shipboard "visit" in sick bay—assuming the blade didn't catch anything vital.

Instead, he awaited his moment.

Kara warned them, then hit the launch switch, and the ScanEagle zipped aloft and was quickly lost to view in the settling twilight.

"Normally, it auto-launches to a thousand feet up and circles, waiting for me. This time I have Tago scooting her away from the *Peleliu* just as fast as she'll go."

Willard cut Justin off by stepping forward to help return the launcher back inside the hangar deck. Justin bit the inside of his cheek rather than smashing a fist into Willy Wilson's.

They all turned for the GCS coffin.

Justin held the door while waving Willard and Michael inside, and then he shut it in Kara's face before she could enter.

The hangar deck was otherwise empty. The fading daylight, combined with the distant work lights, made soft shadows. Through with her speed run, the *Peleliu's* engines were back to an idle. It was almost peaceful. Justin's pulse was anything but, hammering against his skull so hard he wondered that it didn't echo around the hangar deck.

Justin hadn't put his hands on Kara the first two times. This time he did.

He slipped a hand around her waist and pulled her tight against him. And when he leaned down to kiss her, she turned out to be more than ready; she was unexpectedly eager. Her arms went around his neck and hung on.

What he'd intended as a reminder of their first two kisses and a promise of more to come roared right into full flight.

She pulled him in and took a step back until she landed against the container's door with a thump without breaking their connection. He didn't need more of an invitation to pin her body there with his. Her curves fit against him in wonderful ways that made him think of…nothing. His senses were on full overload, and his brain was not receiving any blood at all.

His hand, with no guidance from his disconnected and dying brain, decided on its own to find out how soft her hair was. The other scooped down to her behind and encountered hard muscle in that ever-so-feminine curve that had been shaped perfectly to fit his palm.

Her mouth was as sweet as her lips, and her hunger was as ravenous as his own.

When she slid a leg up the back of his thigh, he forced himself to pull back until he had a palm on either side of her head against the steel door.

She brushed her hands over his chest.

His entire body vibrated with need for her, but she wasn't looking up at him. She was looking at her hands stroking over his T-shirt and driving him crazier than a stallion separated from a herd of mares by a ten-foot fence.

"He is a little obvious, isn't he?"

Willard.

"Aw shoot! I shoulda known."

"Known what?" She finally looked up at him. Her dark eyes glittered with amusement.

"Captain Kara Moretti doesn't miss a thing."

Kara looked back down at Justin's chest, not so much to admire it—though she could feel that exceptional fitness through the thin T-shirt, right down to six-pack abs—but more to hide her own thoughts.

She hadn't meant to set up Justin to be jealous, though she was flattered that the situation had done so. More than flattered, she wanted another kiss like that one the way she craved a slice of New York pizza or a corned beef sandwich from Fierro Meats down on Carroll Street when she'd been deployed too long between leaves.

"Hey, I've got an idea. Mess up my hair."

"I already did." He made brushing motions at it.

She liked the way it felt, could imagine him doing

that after they'd made love. *Huh! When did you decide you were gonna do it with this tall Texan, girl?* Didn't matter. She was going to. Same unit or not.

"No, Justin, I mean mess it up for Willard. Be quick though." And rested her forehead against his chest. Oh God, she could nestle in right here and never leave.

Instead of just scrubbing his fingers over her hair, he dug his fingers in deep and drove them upward along her scalp. He turned it into a head massage with a delightful scritching by his fingertips.

Then he planted a kiss right on the top of her head and stepped back.

"You now look like a woman who has had something wholly inappropriate done to her."

"Next time I want you to actually *do* something wholly inappropriate." Kara shoved her mussed hair back over her shoulder and then ran a hand down her front, wondering quite when her heart had started beating so fast.

"That"—Justin moved to hold the door for her as soon as she keyed in the entry code—"is something I can promise to deliver at the earliest opportunity, ma'am."

—⁓—

Willy's disappointment was obvious, but then he shrugged and clapped Justin good-naturedly on the shoulder. *Best man won* and all that crap.

Justin managed not to flatten the asshole, instead offering him a friendly smile—the kind a coyote offered right before it tried to eat you. Then Justin turned away and caught Michael looking at him.

It was a whole different look.

Justin wondered if Michael was about to flatten *him*.

But Colonel Gibson had married Claudia Jean Casperson of SOAR and in the same unit that Michael was Delta liaison to. Why would he cut up so stiff?

Duh! Because it appeared as if Justin really had done something inappropriate—without caring if he embarrassed Kara.

Justin tipped his head toward Wilson's back—the man had moved forward to stare at the ScanEagle's flight track on the screen—and tried to indicate that they were baiting him. Or at least that Kara was.

Michael looked at Wilson, then Kara, then back to him.

Finally, he offered a slow nod.

A nod that told Justin exactly how carefully this particular D-boy was going to be watching the way he treated Kara. Going forward from here, Justin knew he was on probation at best. Then Michael turned his silent attention back to the multiscreen displays as if nothing had happened.

Justin wondered if learning to be scarier than a mad bull under full steam was a standard part of Delta training. Even if it wasn't, Justin had no question who would win if Michael Gibson faced such a beast.

No way did Justin want to be ticking off that man.

Chapter 9

"OH BROTHER. THESE MUST HAVE BEEN SOME VERY BAD men." Kara watched the feeds from the tiny ScanEagle zipping low over the central Negev at sixty knots.

"My guys? Why?" Major Willard Wilson had done a whole macho *You win* thing with Justin that had almost earned them both a broken nose. No, not Justin. He was playing the "guy" game; he was simply playing it too well for her taste. Then she had spotted the look that Colonel Gibson aimed Justin's way and actually felt sorry for him. Still, punching Major Wilson, even if he was a superior officer, was a tempting prospect.

"Well, your guys too, just for being associated with you. But I was referring to the Israelis. What evil did these guys do to get assigned to a goddamn nowhere place like Ramon Airbase? There isn't shit growing out here. Just desert and rocks. Probably failed to suck up and kiss ass to some officer about as wonderful and kind as you."

"Ha. Ha. Ha."

Tago nodded that he was ready from his station at the Gray Eagle's controls. He was keeping it high aloft as a communications relay down to the ScanEagle.

The Central Negev showed what might be called a sagebrush about once every ten meters, and they all looked dead. The hard hills had been sculpted by wind and the rare rainfall into tortuous slopes and deep, dry wadis harsh enough to make a moonscape look friendly.

And since it was three hours after full dark, any colors that might be there had gone monochrome green under the ScanEagle's infrared camera gaze. It looked about as welcoming as the home crowd watching the Mets when the Phillies were tromping on them.

To reach Ramon Airbase had taken three hours. Parking an American warship close off the Sinai Peninsula would certainly draw Egypt's and Israel's attention. LCDR Ramis had brought them within two hundred kilometers. The ScanEagle had spent two hours zipping along close above the waves under *Tosca*'s watchful eye, swinging wide to avoid both any shipping lanes and the Egyptian border.

Both RPAs could each stay aloft for the better part of two days on a single load of fuel, so that wasn't an issue. Kara going mad with impatience as she watched mile after unchanging mile was rapidly becoming an issue. She expected premature brain death to set in any time now.

Once the ScanEagle was ashore, another hour sliding down through the Negev had tested everyone's patience. You could taste it in the air despite the powerful air-conditioning in the GCS coffin.

"I'm guessing," she told the others, "that if The Activity guys on the ground were unwilling to use a strong signal, they must be inside the air base perimeter. If they were outside, they could walk up into the hills and send a signal aloft from a steep-walled valley and feel fairly confident that they couldn't be discovered."

"You're going to... Of course you are," Justin answered his own question.

"Of course I am."

———

Justin didn't even know why he asked.

Kara Moretti was the woman who punched through problems. If that meant jumping a stealth RPA into the middle of an Israeli air base to get the job done, that's what she'd do.

But he could see these last hours had really stressed her. All they'd done was exhaust him.

What would be a good distraction, a good brain reliever for her?

"You know, Major Wilson, I'm puzzled by something."

"What's that?"

"How does an Upper West Side guy like you end up in a group like The Activity?" Justin said it straight, but—

"Yeah, Willy Nilly." Kara picked up on the question instantly as Justin knew she would. "I thought those guys had some standards."

Justin knew that nothing at the moment cheered her up as much as razzing Wilson.

"Superior skills," Wilson sneered back.

"Like superior to a gerbil? Or maybe a Yorkshire terrier?"

Justin tuned them out and let himself watch Kara fly as the two of them continued to banter.

All of the flying he'd watched her do prior to this had been very standard, high-altitude, grid-pattern or circling passes.

But now she was in it. Her tiny craft was hugging streambeds, flying so low it had to hop up to clear a barrier guardrail along a road she crossed.

She ducked under a power line hanging so low that even a Little Bird wouldn't try it, and she did it all clean.

"What else have you flown, Kara?" Justin cut off Wilson in mid-whine. Wilson looked thankful for the reprieve, but that hadn't been Justin's intent.

"Gray Eagle, Predator, ScanEagle. Flew Global Hawk a couple times. Why?"

"Well, sweetheart." He couldn't believe that had slipped out, but forged ahead before it would sound in any way unnatural. "You fly like a helo pilot."

"I do?" She was surprised, but didn't bobble the flight for even a split second. Good thing considering that her present flight elevation was a bare wingspan above the rough terrain.

"Like a cross between Trisha and…" He couldn't quit identify it.

"You," Michael said quietly.

Justin glanced over, but the Colonel appeared to be serious. He turned back to watch Kara's maneuvers, and there was little he could have done himself to improve them. The attacks were more aggressive, but the flight was so smooth that they almost didn't show.

"I watch you fly a lot when we're on a mission." Her voice was soft.

Which was almost daily with the 5D.

"You're really amazing to watch fly, Cowboy."

"Aw shucks, lady. Now my head no longer fits in my hat."

Kara went silent and concentrated as she closed in on the base.

Justin could feel the other two guys looking at him strangely, but he didn't turn to see. He was too busy watching poetry in motion as the ScanEagle honed in on its target.

———

Kara ran down the final wadi that twisted and turned its way toward the perimeter wall that encircled the base.

She tried not to think about what Justin had said. She could feel him flying with her, even though he sat in an observer chair. Could feel the way they would have flowed down the narrow canyon if he were the one in control and she were the one watching. It was as if they flew it together and that—

The ScanEagle broke into the clear.

The perimeter wasn't just a fence, but rather a towering wall topped with razor wire and cleared of even the occasional dead shrub for ten meters either side. With the Israelis' hard-learned but absolute paranoia, the entire perimeter probably had motion detectors inside the walls and land mines outside. Of course, since Israel hadn't signed the Ottawa Convention of 1997 banning the use of the evil little devices, any more than the U.S. had, why the hell not.

She wished that the ScanEagle could release one of its tiny kin like a Wasp or other micro aerial vehicle, but they didn't have that capability yet. She'd have to take the ScanEagle over the razor wire.

Kara set up to fly a circuit around the base while remaining a hundred meters outside the perimeter fence, but would bet on having no luck on any frequency. It simply wasn't going to be that easy.

The last three nights had embedded the air base in her mind's eye, no need to look at the maps. Two long runways and a taxiway cut roughly east-west across the desert. To the south huddled a small community of the forsaken Israeli soldiers.

Fortified aircraft hangars, hardened against aerial attack with protective layers of dirt and rock, lined the twisting taxiways close by the airfield. Midfield boasted the largest building of the entire complex. Either side of it was framed by lines of Apache helicopters, fast and lethal craft sold to the Israeli Defense Force by the U.S. If they ever wanted to invade the Sinai again, or rebuff the Egyptians if they were crazy enough to brave the Negev, Ramon Airbase had plenty of firepower on hand.

To the northeast were two clusters of buildings unconnected by taxiways. Farther out, close against the perimeter fence, was the American Camp, mostly trainers and aircraft mechanics. Their fences were even higher than the perimeter fence, even against the Israelis. They had an Olympic swimming pool, bigger than the one for the much more numerous Israeli community. The American Camp was connected to a long and highly defensible perimeter road. The IDF weren't the only paranoid ones out here in the desert.

It had taken Kara some time to get over the inherent disorientation of her job. She was sitting in the GCS coffin, Tago at her side and Justin close behind her at the secondary sensor control panel. He had rapidly proven that he was a fair hand at making sure she saw critical data.

She had reserved a screen for him. He kept it populated with whatever he felt was most critical and correctly chose what she needed almost as often as Tago. She'd be watching infrared, and he'd slip in a visible-light view that showed the nighttime streetlights of an upcoming town to avoid. Or a tactical display showing a pair of F-16s doing a lazy patrol along the Egyptian border.

Willy hovered and Michael watched so silently he might as well not be there.

But Kara was mostly aboard her little UAV, flexing her wings to skim close along the side of a towering mesa or sliding into a winding wadi to catch an updraft and soar upward with no need for additional pilot control; the world's winds supporting her flight.

She often felt she was looking down from on high, not watching screens in a steel box. The disconnect was a deeply evocative experience that was better than sex with, well, most men. Given a choice, she knew which she'd rather be doing. This.

But instead of slipping comfortably along the perimeter fence, she was riding on the swell of heat that had accompanied Justin's kiss—

Dammit! *That man!* He was definitely causing her problems.

Focus back on the view!

There was one more cluster of buildings at the air base. It was to the northeast, close beside the runway and well separated from the American Camp. Two slender access roads of gravel were all that connected it to the rest of the complex.

If there was something nasty going on, she'd wager

it was there. Even one of the hardened hangars wouldn't be as good a bet; too many curious personnel in the surrounding plane bays.

She checked the clock.

One minute to midnight. The Activity team should be trying on the hour—the witching hour.

Well, my little ScanEagle broomstick, let's take a flight.

———

It didn't sound as if Kara had meant to say that aloud. Justin liked hearing the little mutterings to herself that she made as she flew.

If Tago heard them, he gave no sign. He looked so totally absorbed in flying the Gray Eagle as a high communications platform that the outside world didn't intrude.

That man!

Focus back on the view!

ScanEagle broomstick…

She offered intriguing glimpses into her thought process. It was also rather cute because she appeared to be wholly unaware of it.

Then, without warning, she turned a sharp ninety degrees to her previous course, slipped upward on the wind, and crossed the perimeter fence.

Wilson cursed in surprise.

Justin made sure that the Electronic Intelligence package was displayed on her auxiliary screen as well as sending audio to the speakers. But if there was any alert from the tower or security, the ELINT didn't pick it up.

"What the hell, Moretti? That's not the plan we—"

Before Justin could think, he was out of his chair

and had Wilson up on his toes. He did it by pinching with his thumb and forefinger on either side of Wilson's throat. He moved in until they were nose to nose despite Justin's greater height. He kept his voice low and even, the way Dad always had right before he tanned your behind.

"Y'all asked the lady to do a job. Now, I would like to suggest that you keep your trap shut and not disturb her concentration. Are you trying to make this mission fail by interrupting the pilot's concentration?" He resisted the urge to pinch harder and leave bruises. Instead, he pushed away and the man stumbled backward, landing hard into the steel wall.

Wilson prepared to surge off the wall, and Justin braced himself so that he couldn't be knocked back into Kara at this crucial moment.

Michael reached out and placed his hand on Wilson's chest. It didn't look as if he really did anything, but Wilson flinched back and hunched as if attempting to escape a sudden great pain.

"I understand you are concerned about your men." Michael's voice was as calm as could be. "These people are the very best at what they do. I'd recommend that you consider that." Then he removed his hand.

Justin could see now that Michael had grabbed a fold of pectoral muscle in an odd hold that Justin didn't recognize.

Wilson sagged when Michael released him.

Michael nodded for Justin to return to his duties.

Justin settled into his chair and checked Tago and Kara. Neither appeared to have noticed anything occurring in the coffin, and he could see why.

The ScanEagle—despite a ten-foot wingspan—was slaloming between trucks, slewing around a pair of garbage Dumpsters, and actually slipped beneath a building's awning as Kara wound her way through the compound.

It was a crazy ride. He felt dizzy as his MH-47 Chinook-trained reflexes kept searching for some control to jerk the craft aloft and out of such tight quarters. He'd seen Little Birds fly under phone lines and Black Hawks fly under big power lines, but a Chinook wanted some space around her and all of his instincts had been trained to maintain that.

Kara's world was another matter entirely. It was a world of mailboxes and fence posts. But she made it look so smooth.

She wove in and out of alleys and passages throughout a small group of buildings isolated from the rest of the base.

A glance at the Gray Eagle's feed showed no infrared images of guards wandering through the area, but it was still a huge risk. The ScanEagle was radar resistant and quieter than a standard RPA, but it still had a gas engine and a propeller—it was far from silent or invisible.

And then she circled again, and the ELINT screen shimmered with an incoming signal.

—⁂—

"Yankee Four," crackled over the speakers inside the coffin, barely powerful enough for Kara to pick out of the noise threshold of static.

Yankee Four? Wilson had said the team and the mission were named "Ya'akov Blue"—Jacob Blue.

Oh. Four Americans. Exactly the number there were supposed to be, and elegantly communicated. They wouldn't know that the rescue pilot would know their code name.

Kara narrowed the frequency and almost ate a lawn chair at sixty knots during her moment of inattention.

"Roger, Ya'akov Blue." Two could play that game. "Is extract required?"

There was no response.

Tago flashed up a Gray Eagle track of her own ScanEagle flight. He dropped a circle on where she'd received the transmission. She did a loop-the-loop right over the top of the three-story building that she'd been circling and plummeted back toward where she'd picked up the signal the first time.

"Roger, Ya'akov Blue. Is extract required?"

"Immediate!" snapped right back.

Kara stared at the screen, almost too long, only managing to twist the tiny RPA out of the way of a small shack by inches. If the structure had a chimney or antenna, she'd have tangled her bird in it and gone down.

"Roger," she told them and scooted back toward the perimeter fence—and the anonymity of the desert.

"Extract," she called out to the others in the coffin. "I need a solution. Now."

"Circle back. Tell them to listen at 0200," Justin replied. "And they need to be ready to move *very* fast."

She did as he told her, and then scooted once more for the fence after receiving back a microphone key click in acknowledgment.

Not until she was five kilometers outside the perimeter fence and Tago had reported no activity on base

did she set the ScanEagle to do an auto-circle around a
barren chunk of desert sky.

She turned her chair, ignoring Wilson.

Justin sat close behind her; with them both turned,
they were nearly knee to knee. She wished she could
have turned away from the screen for a sec to see what
he'd done to Major Wilson to silence him. She'd wager
it was good. Justin had big, strong hands, the kind that
you'd expect on six-foot-two of cowboy—exactly the
sort a girl always hoped for but never actually happened
in real life.

Had it really been just three days since she was certain she'd never have anything to do with him? *Time
flies when you're having fun*.

"Okay, whatta you got for me, Justin?"

His sky-deep blue eyes made a few suggestions
that were exactly what her body had in mind, if not
her schedule.

"I can be there in two hours—half an hour prep,
ninety-minute flight. The *Calamity Jane* moves over
twice the speed of your ScanEagle. She may not be
stealth, but she's got all of the quieting technology they
could bolt onto her including a radar suppressant skin.
Let me go fetch them."

"You want to land one of the largest helicopters in the
U.S. inventory in the middle of an IDF base?"

Justin just grinned at her. "Land? Nope, not for a
single darned second."

Kara had sent Lola's DAP Hawk as a backup, because
helicopters didn't travel alone in case of mechanical

failure. That wasn't something Justin worried about much anyway. SOAR's mechanics didn't believe in downtime on a craft. They had the highest aircraft availability stats in the entire U.S. military—if you didn't count Air Force One, which boasted a hundred percent with zero failures ever.

He liked the feeling of the most lethal weapons rotorcraft ever developed having his back. Delta Force Colonel Michael Gibson had also loaded aboard with his sniper rifle, which Justin found doubly comforting. Man like that had your back, you *knew* your back was covered.

At 0200, the ScanEagle had gone back over the razor-wire-topped perimeter wall to pass on the operational plan to the trapped team.

At 0210, Justin was hovering close over the dirt five kilometers and ninety seconds to the northwest of the airport. Unlike the impossibly fine sands of Afghanistan that blew up into massive brownouts of dust, this dirt was good, old dirt. It blew around a bit, but it stayed on the ground like dirt was supposed to, a big relief.

Lola hung an extra three minutes farther back; this was the *Jane*'s show.

"Who feels the need for a song?"

Carmen started a rap, which wasn't music by any definition Justin ever had.

Along come the Jane, *flyin' ever so low,*
Tellin' the old IDF, just what they can blow.
Talbot picked it up at the port gun.
And while the old Negev, could really use some snow,
It's not the sort of place, you'd ever want to go.
Justin gave a shot at a chorus.

Here and gone before the morning's glow,
The Night Stalkers come to smash your toe.

He didn't need Danny's snort from the copilot's seat to tell him he'd missed the mark this time. Not that he'd risk an extraneous transmission to Kara even if it had come together. The Israeli Defense Forces were neither deaf nor stupid.

One branch of the U.S. military was about to invade a friendly country's air base to rescue four of The Activity's recon spies. The fact of the U.S. Air Force's residence on the base didn't pertain, as they hadn't been notified by the Army's Night Stalkers. Nor were they likely to be.

At least not if everything went well. Creating an international incident was not on tonight's schedule.

At 0213, Justin tipped down the nose of the *Calamity Jane*. He pulled up on the collective with his left hand to pitch the blades and create as much lift as the twin Lycoming T55 turboshaft engines could provide, dumping ten thousand horsepower into the rotors. With his right hand, he kept easing the cyclic forward, tipping the helicopter nose farther and farther down, converting all that power into speed.

He hit the never-exceed speed in the first twenty seconds, driven down into his seat by accelerating at half-g the whole way. To an observer outside the craft, if there had been one, it would look as if the giant helicopter was moments from diving into the rocky desert soil. Actually she was tipped that far nose down so that her rotors were lifting her almost straight ahead.

Oh two hundred fourteen and thirty seconds, he emerged from the last wadi through the steep hills surrounding the base, running dead level and half a meter above the soil. Moving just under two hundred miles per hour, his first view of the Ramon Airbase opened before him.

At two in the morning the lighting was minimal, except for the perimeter. The main runway was blacked out to avoid being a target until the next flight of F-16s needed to use it.

Exactly what he'd been counting on.

"Weapons free," he called to the crew, "but y'all really try to hold your trigger fingers."

"Shooting locals, bad," Carmen noted.

"Loud noise of shooting locals attracts even more locals," Talbot offered. "Very bad."

He and Danny focused on the flight path they'd chosen. Kara had flown in from the northeast twice now, close to the American Camp and the unknown cluster of buildings where she'd found The Activity team.

The *Calamity Jane* rolled down out of the northwestern hills like a bad flood hauling ass down an arroyo. They were moving so fast that climbing to clear the perimeter fence was barely more than a flick of the wrist.

Once over the fence—with his wheels and the tips of his rotor blades low enough to skim the brush, had there been any—he carved a hard turn, trading speed for change of direction.

Halfway down the paved runway, a vehicle was racing toward him. If all was happening per plan, it was The Activity recon team. It looked like a Humvee, which was going to be a very tight fit inside his Chinook.

He spun around and in moments he was flying at a sixty miles per hour, due west along the centerline of the runway.

Please let this work. There was no time to land, load, balance, and secure the Humvee. Every second spent inside the perimeter fence was one second closer to detection and death.

"Vehicle at two hundred meters," Danny called out.

It had better work or Wilson might get Kara after all.

"One hundred. Initiating rear ramp."

The Open Ramp indicator flickered to life on the console. Justin eased down so that his rear wheels were actually rolling on the runway, barely.

"Fifty meters." Danny.

"Ramp down," Raymond reported calmly from the most dangerous position of this whole operation. Raymond's life now depended on how good The Activity agents actually were as drivers, not as recon.

"Twenty-five."

Justin was suddenly aware of a hundred things at once. The feel of the cyclic control, slick in his hand, smoothed by so many hours of flight. The sharp smell of the cold desert so different from Amarillo. Amarillo might be sparse, but it smelled of life. Ramon Airbase was stark and smelled of runway tar and death so close to the Egyptian border. He could still taste Kara's kiss and feel how her body had pressed up against his.

And he could feel that he had to nose up on the collective a little or he'd be blowing the rear tires that had never been designed to roll at sixty miles per hour down a rough runway.

"Five," Danny called.

The Humvee hit the ramp, causing a scream as the metal lip was compressed down onto the tarmac. The roar of the Humvee's engine filled the helicopter, drowning out the twin turboshaft engines.

The impact of the racing vehicle jarred through the length of the helicopter's fuselage as several tons of vehicle slammed up the rear ramp and aboard.

Justin increased lift on the rear rotor to compensate.

Now the gamble was on the skill of the Humvee driver. He'd had to race at the vehicle's top speed to pick it up, not a move that any of them had ever practiced before. And he had to stop before he drove over the two gunners, the two pilots, and, worse, totally overbalanced the nose of the *Calamity Jane* into the pavement.

Justin was never able to clearly recall the next two seconds of the rescue. When a helicopter took on a three-ton load, it was done carefully, patiently, with strict attention to center of gravity and load-point tie-downs, while sitting parked stably on a solid surface. All three of his crew chiefs were certified MH-47G loadmasters and darned good at what they did.

—and there wasn't a moment for a single one of those worries.

He adjusted for the shifting load with both cyclic and rudders, moving to some state of hyperawareness that he'd only ever experienced during a bucking bronc ride at the Tri-State Fair. Every tiny shift in weight compensated, even anticipated.

And the *Jane* bucked just as hard as the wildest horse. Nose wheels screeched on tarmac for a long moment when the driver tromped on the brakes and threw the Humvee's weight forward. It was a sound that would carry to every resident on the air base.

Then the opposite effect as the Humvee rocked back against the large tires' grip on the steel grating of the Chinook's cargo deck.

The ramp light blinking out told him Raymond was still with them. He must have practically climbed out the ramp gunner's shooting window to avoid being hit.

Justin pulled back on the cyclic only to realize it was already in his lap.

"Carmen," he shouted over the intercom, "he's off center. I'm nose heavy. I can't clear the fence like this."

They were off the ground—by less than a meter. They still weren't climbing.

Over the open mic on the intercom, he could hear Carmen getting the guy to shift the Humvee backward.

"No sudden moves. No big moves. Just back it up like there's an old lady behind you."

The pressure eased on the cyclic. Now he left the nose down to regain speed. It would make Carmen's problem harder, but that didn't worry him; she could handle it. And if the driver was a field agent for The Activity, he could as well…or they'd all be dead.

"Check left," Danny called.

Lights were popping on along the far side of the base. The Israelis would hit the runway lights any moment.

The controls felt almost normal—close enough he hoped.

"Lock it!" Justin called back, and Carmen echoed his shout to the Humvee's driver.

Of course there wasn't time to attach the load tie-down straps. Hopefully the guy standing on his brakes would be enough, but there was no more time to wait.

Justin carved a hard right turn and aimed straight at

the nearest section of the perimeter fence. At the last moment, he jerked back on the cyclic and *Calamity Jane* climbed skyward like the good girl she was.

He nosed over the top as the runway lights flashed on.

He was back down to the dirt before the fence lights fired off. And he was up the wadi into the Nahal Resisim due west of the air base before the outer lights were lit. He doubted that they'd pick out his pitch-black helicopter.

But he was still a hundred kilometers into Israel in all directions except one. And crossing from raiding an Israeli air base into Egypt could start a war, making that an absolute last-resort option.

He keyed the radio for the first time in the whole mission.

"Need a distraction, Kara. I'm clear, but I can't outrun an F-16 or a Sidewinder." He continued to beg the *Jane* for more speed as he slalomed his way up the twisting wadi.

—∿∿—

"Sissy." Kara had to make a joke. She was never afraid during a mission. But watching Justin struggle to control the Chinook in ways that were never meant to happen on a twenty-five-ton helicopter had been deeply…unnerving.

"Roger that." His tone was as dry as her throat.

"Just be glad it's not a Sparrow." That was a nasty missile with an attitude.

"Oh yes, I feel so much better. Ten kilos of high explosive at Mach 2 versus forty kilos at Mach 4. Yes, that's so much better." Man had come within inches of dying half a dozen times in the last minute and he was joking.

Kara wondered how she hadn't noticed him over the last two months. Well, she'd noticed him—what girl in her right mind wouldn't? But she hadn't *noticed* him.

And now she'd better get her Air Mission Commander act together and save him.

A distraction? Like a Hellfire missile into the air base control tower? It would certainly get their attention, but not in a good way.

She had to convince the Israelis, from her steel coffin in the cargo hold of the *Peleliu*, that the U.S. Army had not just invaded their air base. She had to convince them there was an explanation for the noises they'd heard and any possible radar sightings.

She called up the *Jane*. "What's the nationality of the vehicle they stole?"

"And how does that matter to—" Justin cut himself off. "Sorry, ma'am." He sounded so contrite for questioning her. His voice was far more normal when he came back on. "Looks to me like the Yankees are down one vehicle."

That was good news. If an IDF vehicle went missing, the Israelis would probably stage a raid on the American Camp. But the other way around, maybe not.

Would the Americans ever admit to the Israelis that they'd lost one of their own Humvees inside the Ramon Airbase perimeter? Not a chance. It might start a little intramural discord—as only the Americans and Israelis were inside the fence—or a run of back-and-forth practical jokes. Hopefully the U.S. forces would only see it as a weakness to ask if the IDF had taken the Humvee from under the Americans' noses without them noticing.

Therefore, she only had to explain away the noise and radar, and not the missing vehicle.

"Tago, give me back the ScanEagle." Kara had given him the controls so that he could learn to fly it by following Justin's exfiltration from Israeli soil. She could see Tago sweating it even though his craft was a thousand times smaller than the Chinook—Justin was just that good.

Kara wished she could follow him, just to watch him fly. But there was no time. Each second was one second closer to the activation of a wider perimeter. If they escalated to full air defenses before Justin reached the coast, there would be little chance of him slipping away clean.

Tago flipped control back to her.

She took the ScanEagle's engine up to full throttle as she did a flip turn back toward the air base.

"It won't be silent," Tago observed.

"No." Kara looked at him. "It won't." He didn't get it yet. She glanced back toward the only other occupant of the coffin, sitting on his stool. Major Wilson didn't get it either…loser.

She could almost see Justin on that stool instead, if she squinted just right and added four inches to his height, blond hair, and…a cowboy hat. Kara was definitely losing it.

By the time she had the Ramon Airbase back in sight, it was lit up like Shea Stadium for the last-ever New York Mets game…even if they did totally choke and lose to the Florida Marlins, also losing their shot at the playoffs. She'd watched the blue-and-orange fireworks from deep down the third base line and groaned in agony along with every other diehard Mets fan.

Well, if she didn't want fireworks here, she was going to have to get creative.

The tiny stealth ScanEagle was designed to be silent and invisible. Of course the engineers back in Hood River, Oregon, hadn't anticipated someone trying to purposely be seen.

She didn't want the Israelis to get clear photos, but she wanted them to clearly see the craft. So, just short of the perimeter fence, she pulled back on the joystick and sent the ScanEagle soaring aloft.

At three thousand feet, she took it through a hammerhead stall and kicked the RPA into a nose-down power dive.

She gave the propellers full pitch and drove the one-and-a-half-horsepower engine right past redline. Didn't matter if it seized up, not this time.

It was well past the never-exceed speed as she drove down toward the center of the air base. It was dicey to avoid ripping off the wings at this speed, but she rolled out of the dive and aimed straight for the airport control tower.

Individual gunfire was pinging off the bird. There was a hard wobble in her view, which indicated a solid hit.

At two hundred meters out, hating herself for so abusing the craft that had served her so well, she triggered the destruct charge that was rigged in all of the stealth birds.

The ScanEagle shredded before their very eyes.

She'd been told that no piece bigger than a thumbnail would remain. Even the engine block would be powdered by the charges planted on it. She hoped they were right.

Kara's screens blanked with the loss of feeds from the ScanEagle, disorienting her badly for a moment.

Tago flashed up the image from the MQ-1C Gray Eagle *Tosca* still circling high aloft. A high-res camera revealed nothing at least.

Israel could now rest comfortably that they had beaten the "drone"—which would be assumed to be Egyptian or Jordanian—that had been sent to spy on them. Any little bits and pieces would point to American manufacture. But that would be okay, as so much of the world's military was. If it wasn't American or stolen, it was simply left behind from one of the region's recent wars. The tiny bits would make no sense to anyone because the Americans would be right there helping with the analysis.

In their eyes, disaster would have been once again averted by their vigilance.

Kara leaned back and rubbed wearily at her eyes. In her view, she'd just consigned to its doom a hundred-thousand-dollar RPA that had done nothing wrong.

Hands massaged her shoulder.

She wished they were Justin's, but knew they weren't.

Kara didn't have the energy to turn. So she reached up, found the pressure point between Wilson's thumb and forefinger, and drove into it with three fingers on one side and her thumb on the other. She used the leverage to double over his wrist and drive him to the floor. He hit with a very unhappy grunt.

"Three older brothers," she apologized softly, not really caring if he heard her or not.

Then she dropped her hands back into her lap.

Not the man she wanted at all.

Chapter 10

JUSTIN CROSSED OUT OF ISRAELI AIRSPACE WITH NO ONE
the wiser, except for a couple small fishing boats that
he overflew at five meters and full speed in the dead
of night. Somewhere behind would be the DAP Hawk,
though he hadn't spotted it, and far above, the Gray
Eagle would be turning for the long trip back to Incirlik.

"Incoming, boss." Carmen's whisper warned him
over the intercom just moments before a man leaned
over the console between Justin and Danny. "I kept him
out until you cleared the coast, but that's all he would
put up with."

"Hey, buddy." The man clapped Justin's left shoulder hard enough to drive the collective partway down.
They dropped from five meters above the waves to three
before Justin caught it.

"Hey, yourself. Careful there. Three more meters
down, catch a wheel at this speed, and none of us are
going home."

"Sorry, Texas."

"Best state in the nation." Why did everyone insist on
calling him that? Kara didn't—yet another reason to like
her, as if he needed one.

"Been there a couple times…"

Justin mouthed the rest of guy's line under his helmet.

"…got some great barbecue."

"So, buddy…" The man barely resisted another

crashing delivery of bonhomie. "Why don't you just drop us off at Clay Kaserne, then you can be on your way."

"Clay Kaserne?"

"Sure, used to be Wiesbaden Army Airfield. The one in Germany."

"I know Clay Kaserne. It's a twelve-hour flight from here."

"Good, I need a nap. Haven't slept much this week."

Justin knew that any comment about having already been in the air for three hours making for a dangerously long day of flying had just blown out into the wind. Well, you didn't walk right up to an unfamiliar horse; you came at it just a little sideways. And this wasn't Justin's first rodeo either.

"In a hurry to get there?"

"Fastest possible."

"Well, if you were to empty the Humvee, we could—"

"Nope. No one but my men and I touch what we have in there."

Why didn't that sound good?

"What if I could get you there in time for lunch instead of dinner?"

The guy grunted. "It would rock. We're already days late." It was the first time Justin could hear the deep exhaustion in his voice.

"Let me take care of it. I'll get you there."

Again the clap on the shoulder, but not crash-worthy this time. The man wasn't moving off. Clearly he was worried about what Justin might say, despite the encrypted channels.

"*Jane* to AMC Moretti." He hoped she caught the formality.

"Roger, *Jane*. Go ahead." Kara missed nothing and simply made it all so easy.

"Could you find the closest carrier? I need to be there before daylight. We'll need a C-2 Greyhound and a bare deck for a cross-load of cargo."

"Uh, roger that. Head three-four-seven. Two hundred klicks out. I'll let them know."

"Appreciate it, AMC."

"Everything okay up there, Justin?" she whispered. Which was kind of sweet. Made him think of what he'd like to be whispering into *her* ear.

"Roger that. And," he whispered, just as if they were flirting side by side rather than him already flying away from her as he turned toward his new heading, "thanks."

———

Justin had The Activity and whatever secret was hidden inside the Humvee on the deck of the USS *George W. Bush* an hour before sunrise. Per request, the crew on the carrier's deck was minimal.

Instead of landing up forward along the starboard rail, Justin circled to land close behind the waiting twin-propeller C-2 Greyhound. It was parked, tailgate lowered, pilot and loadmasters standing by. As soon as a green-vested deck officer had guided him down, blue-vested deckhands chocked his wheels and white-vested ones double-checked that everything was safe.

Only after they'd all evaporated did Raymond drop the rear gate.

Justin twisted in his seat as the unranked and still unnamed Activity agent backed out of the *Jane*'s cargo bay, down the ramp, and up onto the C-2's ramp. The fit was so tight that Justin would have inched it along, the Greyhound being several inches narrower than the Chinook. By their frantic arm waving, the C-2's load-masters would have preferred that as well. The driver backed onto the Greyhound with all the confidence and speed that most people showed backing out of their garages.

Even if someone on the carrier's deck was watching, there hadn't been much to see. A dark night, minimal deck lighting, and an American Humvee visible for seconds at most.

The two ramps began swinging back up cutting off his view.

Ingrates. Not a word of thanks. Not a—

There was a sharp rap on the pilot's window by his right shoulder. Outside stood the main agent from The Activity. He'd hopped up on the Chinook's aerial refuel-ing probe that was mounted several feet below Justin's window so that they were eye to eye.

The guy stuck his hand in and Justin shook it. "So fuckin' tired I forgot to say thanks. Plucking us up like that was a really sweet job you and yours did back at the air base. Make sure it gets added to the SOAR train-ing. Not many could do that. Name's Tom…" Then he flashed a big smile. "At least I'll answer to that name."

"Justin." He returned the man's crushing grip.

"See you, buddy." And he was gone.

Justin checked in with the green-vested helicopter landing signal personnel who had rematerialized once more straight ahead of him. Since he hadn't cycled down his engines, he took the finger-pointed-at-the-sky signal and headed aloft.

Even as he pulled up off the carrier's deck, the C-2 was firing up its engines. It had already been in position at the catapult when Justin had landed behind it. Less than a minute later, the Greyhound ripped past him, waggled its wings in a greeting, and turned north toward Germany before he had a chance to respond.

He decided it would be better if his curiosity about what The Activity had found at Ramon Airbase was never answered.

Who was he kidding?

He flew with the 5D. It wasn't out of the realm of possibility that he'd find out exactly what was going on. Two months in, and he still wasn't used to that.

All he wanted right now was to get home.

A small flash of reflected sunlight drew his eye upward. High enough above him to catch the first light of the unrisen sun. Kara had kept watch over him as he flew to the aircraft carrier. Now, at long last, she would be turning her Gray Eagle *Tosca* back toward Incirlik.

He liked that she had watched over him.

―⁓―

Kara finished shutting down control consoles. She'd shooed Santiago off to dinner and bed a couple hours earlier and flown *Tosca* back to Incirlik on her own. She enjoyed the peace and quiet. It had been a day of many impressions.

Maybe she'd skip food and simply hit the shower and the rack.

Maybe she'd skip the shower too.

The last radio transmission she'd heard from the *Calamity Jane* was Justin calling in to the *Peleliu* for

permission to land, which had been an hour ago, maybe
two. There'd been no rap on the coffin's door. He'd
probably been as exhausted as she was, but still it hurt.

She slipped out of the GCS coffin and secured the
door. The hangar deck was a world of bright sunlight
and hard shadows. It was always disorienting to come
out of the coffin and reenter the real world where there
was temperature, weather, wind…and people. Except
under extraordinary conditions like the last four days,
her world usually included only her and Tago.

For Kara the world was kept at a radio or long-range
imaging distance.

She was about to duck into the shadows and head for
her berth when she spotted a blaze of white at the other
end of the hangar deck.

A cowboy hat shining in a shaft of sunlight. Its owner
stood with his back to her, his arms crossed, watching
the technicians swarming over his helicopter. The rotor
blades had been folded up, six massive blades each ten
meters long and a meter wide lined up over the fuselage.
There were several mechanics swarming over the craft.

Kara hovered for a moment in indecision. She'd been
focused on sleep…and being ticked that Justin hadn't
come to find her. Three sixteen-hour days had taken it
out of her…yet there he was. Whether waiting for her or
hovering over his craft, he was there.

She meant to turn away but she began walking forward, as if her body was moving of its own volition,
until she came to a stop close beside Justin.

What to say to him? He'd flown like…nothing
she'd ever seen. With the ScanEagle gone, she'd used
her Gray Eagle to ensure his security, done nothing

but watch Justin fly as he wove through the carved mountains of the Central Negev like he was threading a needle with a hundred feet of helicopter. It was… breathtaking. Sort of like standing so close beside him that she could see the slow rise and fall of his chest with his breathing.

"You mess up the poor *Calamity June?* Bad cowboy."

"It seems that I scraped up the ramp a bit by dragging it down a runway somewhere. They also wanted to service the wheels, see the effects of high speed and the unexpected impact load."

Kara looked up at Justin watching the mechanics work on his helicopter. She noticed that Lola's crew chief Connie Davis was right in the midst of them.

"I thought she worked on Black Hawks."

"That and just about every other thing you can imagine. Heard tell if it's a rotorcraft, she knows more than the folks who designed them."

Why were they… "Why are we standing here talking about helicopters?"

"You mean since I've been standing here for seventy-three minutes wanting nothing more than to drag you off and investigate being inappropriate? Can't rightly say, ma'am."

She thought about the GCS coffin close behind them, or any of the hundred other spaces a three-quarters-empty ship the size of the *Peleliu* offered as options. Any of those would have sufficed with any other man. But Justin Roberts wasn't any other man; she wanted him in her actual bed. It was shockingly conventional of her, but it was no less true.

She turned and led the way. He followed without

further comment. Off the hangar deck and through the winding corridors and ship's ladders of the *Peleliu*, there were no strained silences, no awkward moments. They both knew what they wanted, and to hell with the rules, they were going to get it.

As they went along the corridors they chatted about the details of the most recent flight. What could they have done differently to save the ScanEagle? Could the timing have been better? Could...?

Kara hesitated outside the door. She'd never had sex with a fellow officer. Hell, she'd only had sex with another soldier of any rank or branch of the service a few times. It wasn't worth the risk, yet suddenly here she was.

Perhaps reading her emotions, Justin leaned in and spoke softly though this stretch of the corridor was empty at the moment. "You just say so, Kara, and I'll head back down the hallway. You got my word on it."

She studied those summer-sky eyes of his.

He would too. Had used her name so that she'd know for a fact that he was completely serious about that.

She breathed in and found that earth, sun, and man were thick on the air with him standing so close beside her in the bowels of the old steel ship.

It was what finally tipped her across the threshold. She wanted to lose herself in the wilderness that was Justin Roberts. Once inside her berth, she flicked on a small reading light and held the door wide to show that he was meant to follow.

He glanced once to either side, then looked her right in the eye as he stepped in. Not her chest, not even her face, but as if he could see her most clearly that way.

Justin couldn't look away from so much trust. It wasn't the heat, the need, or the desire; those were all mixed in there as well. Rather, she simply trusted him to be decent and honorable. Trusted he would be worth the risk.

Well then, he would live up to that standard.

He slipped his hands to either side of her face and let his fingers slide into the thick cascade of her dark hair. As thick as a horse's mane and as soft as the tip of a horse's muzzle.

Justin wanted to...

He dug his fingers into her hair and fluffed it outward. Reached back in and stirred it around until it was in total and absolute disarray.

"What the—" She batted at his hands, but he didn't stop until not a single hair was still in place.

"I promised to be inappropriate. The proper thing to do was to kiss you until you melted into a little pile of Kara Moretti. So..."

"So instead you mussed up my hair."

He shrugged easily.

She opened her mouth to protest, and that's when he kissed her. He might be all proper and decent, at least most of the time on the other side of the door. But once a woman entered his bedroom, or even more so when he was invited into hers, all bets were off.

He muffled her squawk of surprise with a deep kiss. Keeping one hand dug into her hair, he pulled her in enough to practically devour her—he certainly wanted to. She tasted spicy, alive. She—

Fisted his gut!

Not hard enough to hurt, but hard enough to surprise.

He pulled back her head just far enough to recover his lower lip from her quick nip—not by the hair, but rather by sliding his other hand under her T-shirt and forcing her back with a hand on her breast.

She reached to—

But he'd been in enough tussles with a wild horse to protect his privates.

He pivoted and dropped to the bunk with her lying back across his knees. He kept her head supported, but the rest of her was open to him, gloriously open. A magnificent terrain of hill and valley; breast, belly, and hip.

He leaned down to pin her breast with his lips and cupped her hard through her pants with his free hand.

She hissed and he felt the strength of her response buck through her as she arched against his palm. So he ignored the fist that bounced off his shoulder.

"Damn you, Roberts!" But Kara also rolled to press her breast tighter against his mouth as she cursed.

He drew her in and teased her until she quivered and cursed like a bronc gone mad. She finally got one of her arms wrapped around his head.

All she had to do was grab his ear and she could pull him off her. Instead, she locked her arm about his head and dragged him in even harder. She clamped her thighs so tightly on his hand, he'd have been hard pressed to recover it.

He drove her up. He'd never had a woman who so gave herself to him. She moaned and twisted and pleaded for more in rough whispers.

He flew her body like the best helo ever made. She

rose for him, rose until she soared, and then stayed there as if she'd never come down.

When at last she fell back to earth, he started to wonder quite what he'd done. He'd never used a woman that way, nor been so fascinated seeing quite what he could make her do.

Slowly her body settled, though aftershocks continued. She kept his one hand still clamped between her thighs as she slowly curled into him. She let her arm slide down across his neck, then his shoulder as she rolled, and he was nuzzling the side of her breast instead of attacking the tip.

He still supported her head as she curled up around him.

Justin began to worry about whether he'd hurt her. He hadn't meant to, hadn't ever wanted to do so much to a woman.

But she'd almost gone fetal on him, her face nestled into his side.

He opened his mouth to whisper her name as a question.

Then she nibbled him in the ribs.

Right on his ticklish spot.

The moment she felt Justin flinch up and back, she rolled away from him; she landed catlike on all fours on the deck.

One disadvantage to a Navy berth, there wasn't a lot a lot of room.

One advantage to a Navy berth, that meant that they were very close.

She kicked his boot with hers.

As she planned, he looked down in surprise.

It was going to cost him. She grabbed the back hem of his T-shirt and pulled it up, over his head, and forward down his arms until it was snarled around his two wrists.

Then she stopped. She simply didn't have a choice.

"Justin," she managed against a dry throat.

"Yes, ma'am?"

"You do me a favor?"

"If I can."

"Do not *ever!* stop working out." He was a damned handsome man, but his chest was a work of art. She wanted to relish it, admire it, so…

She attacked it.

Kara shoved him onto his back, straddled over him, pinning his T-shirt-bound hands beneath her, and admired those beautiful pecs. It was clear from his rippling arms that he could throw her off if he wanted to, which he'd think of in a moment. So she had to distract him.

She peeled off her own T-shirt and sports bra, then tossed them in his face so that he stopped staring wide-eyed at her chest much the way she'd been staring at his. Then she leaned forward and rubbed skin to skin, chest to chest. The power of it slapped against her and she dove further in.

He started to explore with his hands. They might be marginally trapped in cotton, but she was sitting right on them.

"Naughty, naughty," she warned him, hoping he wouldn't stop. When he persisted, she used it as an excuse to tease his chest some more. He didn't hiss or buck, he growled—a low feral sound she could feel rippling over his pecs and through her lips.

He finally remembered his strength and pulled his hands free from beneath her, though they were still inside the shirt.

Kara was pushing back with one hand on the center of his chest to give one last good old Army try at controlling the situation, when he wrapped his fingers around her bare waist—both palms to her belly since his wrists were still snarled up.

With that simple gesture, all her desire for a good tussle just slipped away.

She straddled his hips, one hand on the center of his chest, the other slowly slipping along his beautiful arms. He'd shaken her T-shirt and bra aside from his face, though the latter still lay across his throat. She plucked the garment free and tossed it aside, his T-shirt as well, never losing the connection of her hand on his chest. She tossed both onto the growing pile of their clothes.

He slid his hands up her rib cage and back to her waist. As his hands traveled up her body, their rough texture and soft touch made her eyes want to slip closed. But she couldn't look away from his blue eyes.

This time she wanted to protest that those eyes should be focused on her chest, not looking right back at her.

It was too much, too close.

She did close her eyes, and leaned back to guide his hands up and over her breasts. Every callus elicited a nerve sensation that blasted into her brain; every brush of a thumb earned a gasp of breath that pounded out of her.

If this is what it felt like to be touched by Justin, how would it feel to have him inside her?

She wasn't sure if she was ready for that much power.

He hesitated as if sensing her mood.

She opened one eye and peered down at him. He was watching her face intently, both of her breasts cradled in his palms.

"I'm not one of your goddamn horses."

He teased her breasts just right to send a shiver through her. "Must say, I noticed that."

"Stop being so…so…" She didn't have the word that was supposed to land on the other side of that sentence. Aware? Considerate? He was supposed to be a glorious, spectacular, Texas-sized fuck. And then done. *Just a test drive, remember?*

When he'd attacked her, he'd read her mood perfectly. Now that she felt inexplicably quiet, she rather wished he didn't.

But on their own, her eyes slipped closed once more. Of their own volition, her hands slid up over the backs of his. Not to guide—damn, but this man didn't need any guidance—but simply to enjoy feeling his motions as he explored her body.

She floated as he stripped off both of their pants and underwear, never once losing contact with her.

Then he lay back on the bunk, protection on, and she was sliding down over him. Never once did she open her eyes. Never once did she break the feeling of floating, not as he entered her, not as he filled her, not as he sent them both flying ever so high in the impossible sky.

That's a new one on you, Justin.

He really should leave Kara's bed. The potential for

embarrassing her or, worse, causing her difficulties, should get him moving along.

But when they finished making love—for there was no doubt this hadn't been mere sex; he knew what that felt like as well as the next guy—she had slowly tipped forward until she lay on his chest. Her now very-well-mussed hair tucked up under his chin.

Somewhere along the way, their fingers had interlocked. And even as consciousness slipped away from Kara and eased her grasp, he could only marvel at their interlaced fingers: her fine Italian dark ones, his big, soap-white clumsy ones. They were fine on a horse or the controls of a Chinook, but they weren't meant for a woman like Kara Moretti. Though she hadn't complained.

There was so very little to complain about at the moment. Her hair smelled of her. Not shampoo, nothing else but her. Her sweet weight was fully upon him. He wished he could reach for a blanket to pull over her, but that was trapped beneath them.

She was warm and soft against him, was perhaps the most beautiful woman he'd ever lain with, and the sex had been truly off the charts. He wished he could fly half as well as Kara Moretti made love.

He sighed, feeling her resting weight against his diaphragm.

Definition of heaven, found.

—⁂—

Kara woke hours later, curled against Justin who had remained flat on his back. She now lay head on his shoulder and one leg hooked over his hips.

She considered doing some happy girly thing, tracing the fine contours of his chest or maybe trying to tease his body to life so that he could wake once more inside her.

Some evil part of her brain took over. She wrapped her hand around him, marveling once more that all that had fit inside her…and felt so incredibly good. Then she put her lips close to his ear so that it would sound far louder than it was—the compartment walls were made of steel, but they were far from soundproof.

"Alert! Alert! Alert! Fire in the hole!"

Kara wasn't quite ready for the scale of Justin's reaction.

He jerked awake and grabbed for controls that weren't there, planting an elbow hard in her stomach in the process, which caused her to unintentionally clench her fist around him.

Justin offered a sharp squeak in response before she managed to ease her handhold. He looked around wild-eyed and leaped on top of her.

At first she thought that had to be a record recovery time from dead asleep to wake-up sex.

But when he didn't move for a long moment, she realized that he was covering her to protect her from an explosion.

"Easy, babe." She brushed her free hand down his back. Unlike his chest, the skin on his back was rough, scarred. Her other hand was still trapped between them and holding on to him. "Easy. Bad joke. Kara made a bad joke."

He propped himself up and looked around for a moment before looking back down at her. His eyes slowly came back into focus.

Justin blinked a few times as comprehension finally sank in.

Instead of showing the fury she deserved, he cleared his throat a few times, then managed to speak.

"Is there a reason that your hand is where it is during an attack drill?"

"Not really. It wasn't a real attack drill."

"And yet your hand…" He didn't ease back. She was pinned to the bed.

"…is where it is," she admitted.

He eased off her, sat up, and scrubbed at his face.

She removed her hand, wanting to curl up and die for how wrong her joke had gone. A sophomoric tease; a stupid one for a trained soldier.

Justin trapped her hand in his and held on to it before she could curl it against her own chest.

"Need a moment, sweetheart. Just give me a moment."

She was always doing shit like that. Something would be good, so good, and then she'd find a way to fuck it up. She managed to free an edge of the blanket and pull it over her against the sudden chill.

Justin just sat there, feet on the floor, back to her, but unaccountably holding on to her hand despite what she'd done.

His back, barely visible in the shadows of the small light that had been on all night, wasn't smooth and impossibly perfect like his chest. It was rippled with scar tissue.

Justin had struck her as a wholesome, healthy cowboy who she liked against her better judgment. But now, here was another side to him.

Her one hand was clamped in his, as if he was

anchoring himself. There was a sad joke, anchoring to her as if she was so well planted on the ground.

But at his continued silence, she released the corner of the blanket from her other hand and reached out to trace the scars.

A cool fingertip brushed down between Justin's shoulder blades. Traced a line that he knew all too well, one that had burned with heat and pain.

Kara Moretti's bed.

He was sitting on the edge of Kara Moretti's bed.

Not strapped into the seat of a burning Chinook as it shredded from the inside out.

"Humanitarian relief mission," he managed to get out. Closing his eyes didn't help; it only made him see the moment more clearly.

"Shhh. It's okay. You don't need to…" Kara's voice was gentle, soothing, and unsure.

"No, it's something I've had to face. To learn to live with." Though he couldn't turn to face her just yet. Instead he held on to her hand to keep himself firmly anchored in the present.

"The team was keeping the people back as well as they could, but they were so desperate for the food and clean water that they were pushing aboard." He opened his eyes, but it was little better. There on the wall above her small desk were a dozen photos. Family. They looked like family. Kara right in the middle of them with that radiant smile of hers.

He turned to look at her, as much to see her as to stop her hand from tracing over his scars.

"Some crazy jihadist, guaranteed of his place in heaven, food for his family, or who knows, got by security. All we really know is he wore a suicide vest and wanted to blow up an American helicopter. In the confined space, it didn't take much explosive and he wore plenty. My crew and a dozen of the desperate people who had forced their way into the main cabin never even had time to scream. My copilot wasn't as lucky as I was."

He took a deep breath and forced himself to focus on Kara's eyes, on the sympathy there. Sympathy but no real understanding. She might be a soldier, but she didn't fly into battle. He caught himself before he described Rom's last moments. That would be cruel for no point.

"I managed to roll out the door with whole chunks of my seat embedded in my back. Only my armored vest kept the chunks from continuing right out my front. Combat search-and-rescue reached me before I bled out. Spent over a month in the hospital and six months on light duty."

"You came back."

He nodded. He'd owed them. His crew had risked and lost their lives; he couldn't abandon them, even if they were gone. He couldn't turn his back on…their service. He'd done a lot of thinking from that hospital bed, had been on the verge of calling it his last tour. Instead he decided to do everything he could against the people who had sent the crazed bomber. He knew who did that the very best, and he started aiming for SOAR from the hospital bed.

No one had understood, not even his sister flying Air Force, but it hadn't been a choice. Not even a duty to his past. It was need that drove him into the future—a desperate need to protect—because some crazy could just as casually walk into a horse show where his family rode. That wasn't going to happen if there was any way he could stop it.

He stood, releasing Kara's hand with a brief squeeze. "Don't leave. Not like this."

Justin didn't answer. Instead, he pulled on his clothes and boots, and picked up his hat before looking back down at her.

A corner of the blanket covered her hips and one breast, but the other, her arms, and one long leg of the creamiest golden skin were exposed in the soft light.

"You don't want me here right now, Kara. You really don't. Believe me when I tell you that I'm not fit company for woman or horse right now."

She started to protest, so he leaned down to kiss her as softly as he could.

Almost. Almost her kiss, her incredible body, and her sympathy pulled him back down to lie with her.

Then he stood, pulled on his hat, and offered her a nod.

"Ma'am." Did his best to smile with it, but knew it was lame.

He tried to say her name, but it wouldn't come out.

"It will be okay," he finally managed. "I just need some time."

He slipped out of her cabin with no one the wiser. It was the middle of the day shift, so the *Peleliu*'s corridors were deserted.

Once he was well clear of her section of the ship, he stopped and leaned against the wall. He locked one hand around a handy pipe to keep himself upright.

Leaving had been the right choice, the only choice.

Kara had welcomed him to her bed.

She wouldn't have if he had stayed. He'd have taken her, hard, in a desperate effort to purge the images inside his head. He'd made that mistake once and scared the crap out of the poor woman he'd been with. You didn't take this kind of shit to a woman's bed.

It didn't matter if she offered; it was something he would never do again. Ever.

Lying helpless on the ground beside the tortured wreckage of the Chinook, listening to Rom's screams as he burned alive. A crew chief's helmet on the ground close beside him. Blown right through the Chinook's hull by the force of the blast. The scorching so bad, he couldn't even tell whose it was. Despite the head still strapped in but connected to…nothing.

Chapter 11

"WELL, DON'T YOU LOOK LIKE SHIT."

Kara was nursing her coffee and ignoring the Belgian blueberry waffles on her plate.

Now she could ignore Trisha instead.

Good. It took more effort and attention to ignore a person than an inanimate meal. Maybe that would keep her distracted.

"I see that your boyfriend left."

Left? Kara jolted up, ignoring the hot coffee that sloshed onto her hand other than to curse the sudden external pain added to the internal and scanned the room. No white cowboy hat! How could—

"Hold on, Kara. I wasn't talking about Captain Roberts. I was talking about the nameless dude you, Michael, and the cowboy have been locked up with for the last four days."

There, just coming down the chow line. White hat. Tall Texan beneath it. She settled back, aware of Trisha holding one of her wrists and wiping down Kara's hand with a napkin dipped in a glass of ice water. It felt good on the coffee burn; thankfully the liquid had cooled some while she was ignoring her breakfast. She took a piece of ice out of her own glass and took over the job.

"Looks like you've had a busy couple days, in more ways than one."

"I don't think I can talk about that mission." Now

that she'd said that, Kara was pretty sure it was true. She did her best to not make it obvious that she was watching Justin.

He, in turn, touched the brim of his hat to her, then moved to sit with Michael Gibson and the other Delta operators.

"Well, isn't that interesting. Mission, huh?" Trisha drowned her waffle in butter and syrup. She started to douse Kara's.

Kara managed to stop Trisha before the deluge hit. She tried scraping off some of the butter, but it had disappeared down into the holes of the waffle and melted.

"No. You're not going to get by me that easily." For lack of anything better to do with her hands, Kara tossed the piece of half-melted ice into her mouth and gave it a good crunch.

Trisha shivered at the sound.

Ha!

Kara crunched it again. Her middle brother, Joe, couldn't stand it either when she chewed on ice; made for a great weapon when he got out of hand.

"Cut that out!"

Kara did, only because she'd finished that bit of ice. "Can't take the pressure, huh? So much for the kick-ass soldier I always thought you were."

Trisha gave her the finger and backed it up with a grin.

Kara cut into her waffle. Pretty good, even if it had enough butter to season an entire loaf of garlic bread.

"Well, since I can't see Michael getting into a four-way, and with the conspicuous absence of the Chinook and DAP Hawk last night... Holy shit!"

Kara concentrated on her waffle.

"Spook city!" Trisha whispered it just below the general ambience of the room.

"What's spook city?" Lola came up and set her tray to one side of Trisha. Claudia sat on the other side, just as Connie sat beside Kara.

Kara now faced all three female pilots with only the mechanic on her side of the table.

"She got one." Trisha pointed her fork at Kara's chest.

They all turned to look at her in unison.

"What, Justin?" The instant Kara said it, she knew it was a mistake. She was sitting with four women who had all married military men.

"I knew it!" Trisha thumped the fist hard enough on the table to make dishes rattle. "High five, girl!"

Kara didn't feel much like high-fiving her or anyone else at the moment. She just wanted to crawl into a hole. Justin had not only sat in Delta country, but he'd sat with his back to her.

Connie leaned in. "Ninety-eight percent now. I warned you."

―⁓―

"Where's—"

Michael held up a hand cutting him off and then signaled for Justin to look around.

Across from him at their corner table were Michael Gibson and his right hand, Lieutenant Bill Bruce, Trisha's husband. The next table over had a trio of guys that Justin had long since identified as also Delta. Their corner of the officer's mess was a quiet haven in a world of turmoil—the main reason he'd come to sit with them.

Farther out from their oasis of silence, Rangers, Navy, and SOAR laughed, rubbed shoulders, and ate.

In their own island sat Kara with the other women of SOAR. Justin was glad for her. She'd need friends after how he'd treated her this morning. There were things that needed fixing. Needed saying. But he wasn't up to that yet, despite hours of walking the flight deck since he'd left her cabin.

He could still taste her on his lips, smell her on his hands. Her final sweet kiss had been as potent as how she'd bucked and moaned when he drove into her.

He turned back to Michael.

"You do not mention him or his department until you're sure who's listening. Bill has met him before."

Bill Bruce nodded, but didn't speak before returning his attention to his tall stack of pancakes and sausage. Justin had gone for the same thing and started in on his own.

"Because?" Justin prompted before biting down on a sausage.

"The Activity keeps a very low profile."

"Major Wi—That guy wasn't really good at doing that."

Michael nodded. "Willard turns into a jerk around women. But he is very good at getting his team in and out of places. He's gone to meet up with them."

Justin considered. Without Major Wilson's finding the 5D and the team aboard the *Peleliu* in the Eastern Mediterranean—then pushing hard for three straight nights and much of the days—those guys would be either captured or dead. Instead, they were out with their intel and headed back to wherever The Activity came from.

"As to men who turn into jerks around women…" Michael trailed off.

His tone had Bill's head coming up, glancing at Michael, then shifting his focus to Justin. The briefest look over Justin's shoulder toward Kara, then he returned his attention to Justin—except his look had gone dark and dangerous. This was a guy you never wanted to meet in a dark alley—not even if he was on your side. If he was there, it meant that things were going to be very bad very soon.

But Justin hadn't been a jerk.

Or if he had, it was in favor of not being unintentionally cruel to a woman he'd come to like far more than was decent for a fellow soldier.

Now Michael turned his attention slowly down to the meal that he'd ignored from the moment of Justin's arrival.

Bill's attention remained focused on Justin.

Two of the most effective and lethal soldiers there were had just threatened him aboard a United States warship. He wanted to laugh them off, but he was having some trouble holding on to his fork.

───※※※───

Kara's stomach was having some trouble holding on to the few bites she'd managed of her breakfast.

Her efforts to keep her mouth shut hadn't worked. Connie was absolutely right about Trisha's tenacity. When she looked at the other women, she saw some sympathy…enough that it was clear that each had fallen afoul of Trisha's ways at one time or another. But she could see a desire for more information.

"No." Kara aimed her fork at Trisha. "No bloody way, lady. That's all you're getting out of me."

A glint heated up in Trisha's eye and Kara girded herself for battle—one she had no enthusiasm for at the moment, as she'd just seen the cowboy's surreptitious inspection of the room. His gaze had barely hesitated at their table.

Then Trisha flinched as if she'd been kicked under the table, fairly hard. She scowled around the group, and all of the others went to some trouble to look innocent.

Connie was a touch too carefully intent on her hot chocolate, and Kara did her best not to give her away.

Perhaps it was just as well. Kara could feel a dose of anger building up, what Rudi, her closest brother, had dubbed the Dreaded Red Brooklyn Haze. Kara's desire to unleash it on Trisha was building. The fact that she could see the real target's back wasn't helping.

Perhaps detecting the gathering storm, or perhaps having a desire to protect her shins from other women wearing Army boots—Kara wished she'd been the one to think of kicking her on the sly—Trisha evaded.

"I wasn't talking about him, anyway. She got one, I'm telling you."

There was a respectful silence as they all turned to look at Kara.

"I got one what?"

"A black-in-black mission."

"No." Kara shivered at the memory of the black-in-black assignment she'd flown oversight on in her first month with the 5D. Her role in that had been strictly surveillance, but it had been pure hell to even watch.

Trisha and Claudia had been front and center on that one; the latter was lucky to be alive.

Lola was looking back and forth. She hadn't been a part of that mission and was clearly taken by surprise that Kara knew what one was.

"It's—"

"Shut up, O'Malley." Lola Maloney, friend, had just been replaced by the woman in charge of the 5D.

And Trisha did keep her trap shut, grimacing and biting her lower lip.

When Lola Maloney spoke with that tone, it would take a braver person than Kara to face her down. Apparently one braver than Trisha too.

Claudia, who flew an attack-version Little Bird just like Trisha, sighed and shook her head. Lola missed seeing the connection between the three of them from that mission.

A side glance showed that Connie had seen it go by, but she didn't miss anything, so that wasn't a big surprise. Connie had probably just connected a hundred clues and figured out that they'd flown a secret mission into Azerbaijan to fight with the Russian Navy. The woman was that scary sharp.

A new black-in-black? Kara rolled it around on her tongue and didn't like the taste of it. Was that what she and Justin had been in? No, it had been a weird and ugly black op on friendly soil, but no worse than that.

She prayed it wasn't heading into a black-in-black.

She'd flown surveillance on any number of missions and done her fair share of kill strikes over the years, though most of those had been before SOAR. Killing terrorists from a high-flying RPA platform had been the power spot for the U.S. Air Force 3rd Special Operations Squadron. She'd long since lost count of how many CIA spooks had sat beside her handing out targeting confirmations back in the 3rd SOS.

Those were black ops. You didn't talk about them. No news to her that Major Willard Wilson fell into that category.

But black-in-black was divulged to no one. Ever. Committing perjury in order to deny its existence was normal operating procedure.

Kara looked at Lola and waited, doing her best to keep her expression naively neutral, as if she'd heard of black-in-black but never been on one…which wasn't likely. Still, it was the best ploy she could come up with on short notice. She was suddenly grateful that her brothers had taught her to lie straight-faced.

As she waited, she could feel the Red Brooklyn Haze retreating and her focus returning. She wasn't on the *Peleliu* to deal with some Texan Chinook pilot.

She was here to fly with the 160th SOAR.

Lola glanced around at the other tables, but no one was paying any particular attention to them. She huffed out a long-suffering sigh.

Lola grumbled something that sounded French, Southern, and foul. Oh right, she was New Orleans Creole.

She offered a scowl at Trisha before speaking.

Trisha did look chagrined, not a common expression in Kara's two months of experience with the woman.

"What you flew the last three days, and what you did last night — which was very well done by the way — was a black op. Which you" — again the glare at Trisha — "are not cleared for, so don't ask."

"Okay, okay." Trisha raised her hands in self-defense. "I got it. Sheesh. Girl can't even fuck up and get away with it by just being cute in this outfit." The sass and grin was well on its way back to normal. "It always works on guys just fine. Too many women around, I'm telling ya."

"A black-in-black." Lola lowered her voice and they all leaned in. "Well, I just hope to God for your sake that you never do get one of your own." Lola had clearly caught on that Kara had flown one.

The nods around the group were all emphatic.

"Seriously, she's not kidding. They're just the worst," Trisha said in such a way that it just might hide from Lola that Kara had been a part of that one with Trisha and Claudia. Then Trisha grinned. "So, was the cowboy the best?"

Subject change from hell, but at least it was a change. Kara leaned in even farther until they all went quiet. She kept her voice a whisper. "Dream on, O'Malley."

Then she sat back and finally started on her breakfast for real, welcomed by the circle of laughter at Trisha's expense.

"Heads up," Bill said softly, the first words he'd spoken during the meal. It had taken some work, but Justin had gotten Michael talking about some of the more public Delta Force missions. Even speaking in general terms, it was downright impressive what these boys had done.

As they had talked, bits and pieces of their missions fit in with some of the "practicals" during his SOAR training. He'd rehearsed things in training that had been developed by the people in this room, at this table. And they'd done it under live fire.

"You need to send that pickup tactic you did at the airfield in for training." Michael had echoed what the Activity agent had said. "I was watching you from the feed to the DAP. That's new. It's good. It needs to be practiced."

Justin had never had something to send back before. It was an odd feeling to think that the next round of pilots to go through training might be practicing something he'd done in the field.

"Weren't really anything all that new" — he tried to put it off — "I'm just the first one stupid enough to try it."

They had then spent most of the meal devising and discarding ways to make it a less risky maneuver. If the driver had been even the least bit less competent, they'd have nosed down into the airstrip and still been smeared along the tarmac when the Israelis arrived.

At Bill's "Heads up," Justin glanced over his shoulder.

The women all had their heads close together, then burst out laughing. Kara looked terribly pleased with herself.

Justin suddenly felt like a target had just been painted between his shoulder blades.

Chapter 12

JUSTIN WALKED INTO THE BAY OF THE *CALAMITY JANE* as the sun was setting toward the unseen Israeli coast. The *Peleliu* was single-footing her way west. Not fast, but definitely on the move toward whatever her next assignment might be. When they arrived where they were going, Justin wanted to make sure his bird was ready.

He had to take off his hat at the head of the ramp or risk knocking it off. The cargo bay of the MH-47G was one "Justin" high, as his old crew had called it. Carmen had rediscovered that one recently, coming up with it on her own, which had both hurt and helped with the old memories.

Inside he could walk about safely enough, but not with the extra three inches of cowboy hat. The cargo bay was head high, a Humvee wide as he'd proved the night before, and long enough for a pair of them though it would certainly cramp the two crew chiefs at their forward miniguns.

He'd expected some maintenance personnel to be aboard. His crew was out for some practice time on one of the Black Hawks; the 5D was big on cross-training.

But the only one there was Sergeant Connie Davis. She was so unlike Kara it was hard to equate them as being in the same service. Connie looked like the pretty girl next door, not the genius mechanic of the entire regiment. Her husband, a massively built crew chief called Big John for a reason, also flew on the Black Hawks and was as gregarious as she was silent. It was generally acknowledged that he was the second-best mechanic in all SOAR. Hell of a couple.

"So, is she back together?"

Connie preceded to rattle off the maintenance, inspections, and impact of his unusual flight on the *Calamity Jane*'s mechanical well-being. He considered himself well versed in the components of his helicopter, better than most pilots, but he was still barely able to follow the list she read off from some mental file; she used no paper references.

"I'm takin' it that all in all I didn't bust up my sweet ride none too bad."

Connie stared at him for at least a count of ten, then nodded. Maybe she figured that was the most complex information a pilot could be expected to process.

He liked that quiet bit of sass, so different from Kara's, but still there, deep and strong.

"I've been thinking about something Michael said." He watched her and saw that he suddenly had her full attention. Yes, Michael commanded that kind of respect. Something Justin wouldn't mind having himself some day. Not the respect itself, but being worthy of it. And to start that process, he'd have to track down Kara and soon. But not yet.

Besides, Connie waited.

He posed the problem of the chaotic weight shifts he'd experienced while picking up The Activity team.

They discussed wheel chocks, ones that could be slammed onto the cargo deck at a moment's notice to stop an on-boarding vehicle. The problem was if the vehicle jumped the chocks due to its initial momentum, then its weight would be trapped too far forward.

Then he suggested a net, and they began discussing stress loads on hull-frame anchor points. It was a different problem because the *Calamity Jane* wasn't an upgraded MH-47D, but a purpose-built MH-47G. His Golf had monolithic framing—rather than individual components riveted together, large sections were machined as single pieces. It cut the helicopter's weight by almost fifteen percent, which was a huge payoff in performance. They debated those differences back and forth for a bit.

They spent most of the shift working the problem, and he was pretty pleased with the results. It was also his first time working with Connie, and he came to appreciate quite how skilled the woman was at what she did. She was as focused on the machines as a quarter horse was on the home stretch, perfectly made for her passion.

There was a change, as abrupt as a wind shift ahead of a squall line. He almost looked up to see if there were clouds gathering, but he was still inside the *Jane*, still on the *Peleliu*'s hangar deck.

Then he spotted the cause. Kara Moretti stood at the foot of the ramp, arms crossed over that lovely chest, watching him.

Connie tapped her tablet computer to save their notes and calculations.

Then she looked at him. It was an appraising look. One that speculated whether or not it was safe for her to depart. It struck Justin that as a DAP Hawk crew chief, Connie would have as exceptional facility with weapons as she did with machinery. The Direct Action Penetrator was the most lethal helicopter ever designed, exclusive to the 160th SOAR. And Connie flew on the only stealth one in existence.

Her look took on new significance.

He offered a careful nod and a soft "ma'am." He would be careful with Kara.

Connie acknowledged his intent and then departed, pausing by Kara to rest a hand on her shoulder before walking off.

Now, Justin wondered, just what defenses was he going to have to round up to survive Kara Moretti?

—~~—

Kara was startled by the sympathy from Connie, though she tried not to show it.

Connie didn't say a word as she passed, but she'd passed some kind of a silent warning on to Justin. That much was clear.

Kara didn't need someone else to fight her battles, but Connie clearly understood Kara's inner turmoil of the moment and had let her know she'd be available if Kara needed someone to speak with afterward.

The silent kindness heartened her, far more than her mere inclusion in the circle of the women of the 5D. And coming from the quiet Connie Davis made it all the more powerful.

Justin started toward her, until she held up a hand.

The hangar deck was the biggest open stretch on the ship for running laps. Even with her coffin in one corner and the massive Chinook in the other, it was a quarter-mile around the deck's perimeter. As night shift was ending, runners were starting to hit the deck. Running the hangar deck was the most common workout on board ship other than free weights.

Already a dozen Rangers, several SOAR, and tight group of Navy were working their way around the deck's perimeter.

SOAR ran loose, some pairs, some singly.

Navy hung together, jostled about but in a cluster.

The Rangers could be spotted miles away, three neat rows of four Rangers each. As more showed up, they fell in behind and made another neat row. They started up a chant that was already echoing louder off the steel walls than the runners' feet pounding the deck. The Rangers could make the deck ring so loudly that it shook the coffin until she thought she'd lose it and go completely bonkers.

Instead of letting Justin come to her, she walked up the ramp and into the cool darkness and sound-buffering structure of the helicopter. The few interior work lights that Justin and Connie had been using barely lit the cavernous interior.

"It's more comfortable and quieter up in the cockpit." He waved her forward.

At least the man knew she was here to talk.

"Goddamn horse-whisperer tricks," she muttered at him as he let her lead the way forward.

He laughed dutifully, but not much spirit behind it.

She chose the left-hand, copilot's seat; no way was she going to sit in Justin's position. She considered it, putting him at a disadvantage, but her heart wasn't in it and she didn't want the reminder of sitting right where his body spent so many hours.

"Pretty comfy," she noted as she settled into the chair. It was well padded and plenty wide. She'd sat in Black Hawks, which were markedly less cozy. The Little Birds that Trisha and Claudia flew forced you to rub shoulders while flying together, and not an extra ounce of the tiny craft was wasted on comfort.

"Armchair pilots," Justin agreed as he settled into his own seat, "that's us. Though it does grow old after the first dozen hours, doesn't it?"

She hadn't thought about that, but it was one of the things that her slender Gray Eagle had in common with the massive Chinook: long-endurance flight.

A Little Bird had to land every couple hours for a refuel. A Special Ops Black Hawk could go three hours and then do a midair refuel for another three. At three hours a Chinook was simply warming up. It could cross the U.S. with only two four-minute refuels. Though it would be crazy to try the twenty-hour flight with only one set of pilots. Her Gray Eagle could go for thirty if she had to; Kara had flown a few missions like that where handing it off to a relief pilot simply wasn't an option.

Both of their craft offered comfortable seats for their pilots, and she knew only too well how little that helped on the longer missions.

"I was about to come looking for you."

"So that y'all could round me up?" Kara gave it a Texas twang. "I don't round up so easy, you know."

Justin grinned at her. "Y'all's accent sucks. But it is easier to understand than that straight Yankee you normally sling around."

She didn't smile back and he didn't appear surprised.

Instead he stared straight ahead out the broad wind-shield. The open fantail of the *Peleliu* offered a broad view of the night ocean—the green phosphorescent wake stretching for a long way behind them.

Parts of this cockpit were familiar, and parts of it were so foreign, much like Captain Justin Roberts. His response to her body was so gloriously male, but his response to her, and hers to him, was territory she'd never experienced before.

The Chinook's dashboard had broad glass displays the size of a laptop screen ranged low in front of both pilots. Where she had larger screens, they had a sweep of bulletproof glass laminate that afforded a wide view. A panel of radio gear separated the two seats, which was all familiar.

Where she had a few simple settings for her craft's electrical and engine systems, the Chinook had a broad switch panel mounted in the ceiling. And for the Gray Eagle her simple joystick was mounted to the right, with fire controls for the four Hellfire missiles she could carry, and throttle control to the left. The Chinook's joystick standing between her knees had far more but-tons than she had fingers, and another button-covered control that almost looked worse where her left hand would naturally fall beside her.

This was a terribly complex machine that Justin flew into the fray of battle.

Like his aircraft, Justin was turning out to be much more complex than she had first thought.

She looked back over her shoulder and down the long cargo bay where just last night a Humvee had roared aboard *at full speed*—a vehicle that fit with only inches

to spare. Had it barreled forward, it would have killed
the crew and the pilots before crashing the helicopter.

And five years ago, a bomb in a cargo bay just like
this one had killed Justin's entire crew.

Maybe she understood a little more of why he'd left
her this morning so abruptly. That he flew at all wasn't
just a surprise—it was a miracle.

"How did you get back on the horse?"

—∿∿—

It wasn't a question that Justin had been expecting. He'd
been rehearsing different ways to explain how dangerous he was when the black memories washed over him.
He had tried losing himself in a willing woman just the
once, only to terrify her. He'd almost worked out how
to explain that…

But it wasn't the question Kara was asking.

He rested a hand on the controls. Slowly whirled
the cyclic around, odd without the power-assisted back
pressures to give him a feel for the flight. It was loose,
felt disconnected without the feedback.

"Sometimes you get on a horse because you refuse
to give up."

"Was that what you did?" Her voice was so soft, he
almost looked over at her, but he couldn't. There was
too much he didn't want to see, too much he didn't want
to show.

"No." It wasn't. He'd… "Other times you get back in
the saddle because you have no choice."

He could still hear them. Mariko Hosokawa had the
most beautiful singing voice. It was she who had started the
tradition of music in flight, one Justin did not participate

in until he'd healed and once again sat in the right-hand seat. They hadn't been lovers, but now he wished they had been. The mutual heat had been there, but she'd been on his crew and was therefore inviolable. He missed the whole crew, but she'd left a hole in his heart.

"I owe a debt," he managed with his eyes closed, his hands still light on the controls as if he were flying them to safety before the suicide bomber could blow his crew and his aircraft off the face of the planet.

There was the softest of sounds beside him and then a fingertip traced along the back of his left shoulder. Despite the T-shirt he wore, Kara traced the worst of his scars where the seatback had not wholly protected him from the initial blast.

He couldn't speak.

Justin thought of himself as a brave man, but he didn't dare try to speak.

Not with what his heart was feeling for Kara in that moment.

Like blessed water, her warm fingers traced the scar as if offering a benediction.

They didn't go to dinner.

Instead, they sat and held hands above the central radio console that divided their seats, Justin's clasp alternated between a desperate hold as old memories took him and a clasp so soft that Kara wanted to cry over the conflicts inside the man.

The morning light drove away the stars and filled the sky outside beyond the fantail of the *Peleliu* with a thousand shades of orange, then blue.

When Kara led Justin from the helicopter, he still hadn't spoken.

They exited the hangar deck, now silent with everyone at their meal or their duty stations. Passing the officers' mess, neither of them turned aside.

Instead, she led him back to her quarters where they had parted so poorly in the middle of the previous night.

With the door secure behind them, Kara finally turned to look up at Justin. His blue eyes watched her, almost numb.

What could she say to this man? Kara had lost aircraft before, in addition to the sacrifice of the ScanEagle at Ramon Airbase. Each had entailed a pile of paperwork, an investigation, and then she'd been cleared and issued another bird. Justin had lost his crew and nearly his life as well.

For the first time she understood all of those pilots who said she wasn't a real one. Yes, she had the technical skills and the stresses were immense…from her little white box with its big comfortable chair.

But she didn't—

She wasn't—

Kara didn't know how to go forward from here, but the look in Justin's eyes told her that it was up to her. The poor man was barely functioning.

So she took his hand, that big, powerful hand that could make her feel so much, and rested it with his palm against her heart.

Together, they stood in silence and listened to her heartbeat—she in her ears, he in his fingertips. They stood without moving until his eyes began to once more show hints of the man who was so alive he took her breath away.

To solve one thing, she'd now created another she didn't know how to handle. Kara Moretti was great at seducing handsome operatic tenors until they were near to going mad. She didn't know what to do with the incredible intimacy that was building moment by moment between her and this man. If he started to cry or something, she knew of no way to handle it.

"You forgot your hat." Which had to be about the dumbest thing on the planet to say at a moment like this.

Justin looked upward at where the brim should be. "Seem to have. That'll make it right hard to take it off before I kiss this lady." He returned his attention to her face.

Kara knew from experience she could have her pick of men; that was her body's doing. Of course she'd usually piss them off pretty damn early in the game and they'd be gone, but she could have her pick.

This didn't feel like that at all. Whatever Justin's initial reaction when they first met, he was no longer looking at her the way most men did. She glanced away from the unbearable intensity of Justin's gaze, but couldn't bring herself to break the connection of his palm over her heart.

Using the broad width of his hand, he slowly turned her and pulled her in until she was leaned back against his chest. His arm now clamped her in place.

"I have an awful need, Kara," he whispered into her ear. "You'll be wanting to tell me now if the answer is no."

Kara knew they were about to cross some line. It would

be only their second time together, but "affair" was on the verge of being thrown out the nearest porthole.

She couldn't say no.

—∿∿—

Justin waited with his nose buried in her hair, his hand across her chest now pinning her back against him. He couldn't get close enough; it was impossible to get close enough to this woman.

Her pulse accelerated beneath his palm. He felt her rapid breathing where her shoulders pressed against his chest.

She slid both hands up onto his forearm that crossed in front of her, that pinned her, but he couldn't seem to let go. She gripped his arm tightly with both hands and he readied himself for her to peel his arm off and regain her freedom. It would hurt like a bandage ripped off a fresh wound, but if that's what she wanted...

Kara went very still, holding on to his arm and leaning back against him.

And then she nodded once, as if her answer was too big for a mere word to encompass it.

Something inside of Justin snapped. Such a simple gesture, like the single rattle of a surprised snake building toward a stampede of the full herd. Such a little beginning.

Yet she was choosing trust.

To trust *him* of all stupid things.

To trust the man who had killed his entire crew by acting as if he was in a friendly country, which they supposedly had been.

There was something in him that needed to take, that

needed to conquer, to prove that he was somehow still alive when so much inside him was dead.

Still Kara Moretti waited in his arms.

There were some things a man of honor couldn't betray. The trust of his former crew that he would not give up the mission. The trust of Kara that whatever he needed, she was able and willing to give.

The feelings shifted inside him. The emotions were no less intense, no more kind, but they shifted. Like a crack in a wall that he dug into with both hands and tried to pull wide.

He wrapped his other arm around her waist and pulled her in so tightly that she probably could barely breathe, and yet he couldn't ease up.

Another deep breath, another powerful round of Kara's heady scent of soap and woman. He kept his face buried in her glory of hair until there was no other world.

He had thought to take her with his hands. To keep her pinned against him with the arm that she hung on to and use her with the other until she cried for release. Begged him to stop. Felt some small piece of what tore at his soul cry from her lips so that he wasn't quite so desperately alone at that deepest layer he showed to no one.

Yet Kara trusted him.

He did keep her tight against his chest with the arm she hung on to.

But with the other, he slowly coaxed her body to life. Relished the fullness of her breasts against his palm. When he slid his hand down inside her waistband it wasn't to drive, but to entice. He asked her body to lift for him.

To lift with him.

When she lay her head back against his shoulder and shivered with the power building in her, he could only watch and marvel as he led her upward. The long line of her neck pulsing as she swallowed hard. Not in fear. Not in terror. But in gathering strength for the climbing moment that would soon swamp her.

When her fingers dug into his arm, when she finally released with a low moan that shook her whole frame, galvanizing her with its release and then making her near boneless in the aftermath, Justin could only ride with her.

His pulse had climbed with hers, his heart pounding against where her back still pressed against him. His breathing grew short and fast. They were in more perfect sync than any horse and rider; they rode upward together.

And when she released, when her soft cry was muffled where she'd turned her face into his neck, he could feel that crack inside of himself let go.

A shell of pain, the solidest armor ever created, that had encased him for five years now fell away as little more than brittle dust. Kara hadn't slid past his defenses, nor had she demolished them. Being with her had made them as irrelevant as if they'd never been.

Justin now stood on the other side of a threshold, having flown across some chasm so wide he hadn't even known there was another side to shoot for.

His knees gone, he settled back onto Kara's bunk and pulled her into his lap as the last of the shudders ran along her trim frame and generous curves.

She nudged his arm upward enough for her to curl

into him without letting go of it. Rested her ear on his chest as if she were nestling against his heart.

Which, he supposed, was true.

How little he knew of this woman.

And how much she had changed him in this moment.

He didn't know what else to do but hold her. And that was something he would gladly do for the rest of his days.

The rest of his days…

The fact that it was a crazy thought didn't make it any less true.

—⁓—

Kara hadn't known what to expect.

Justin had been so hurt, but she didn't fear him. His power, had he been any other man, would have been terrifying in his present state of mind. So, she had done her best to brace herself for whatever he had planned or needed, but had still been wholly unprepared for such fun.

She curled against his chest unable to believe the gift he had just given her. The most incredible sexual experience ever, while still fully clothed no less.

But it had all been about her.

Well, fair was fair.

She took one more deep breath that felt as if it cleansed her down to her toes and pushed herself up out of his arms and looked at him.

Something was going on behind those deep blues of his, and being a guy, he wasn't going to say a thing about it of course.

She had an answer for that and slid from his arms,

surprised at how reluctant she was to do so. Once clear of him, the effect didn't diminish. She wanted to climb right back in there.

Instead she offered him her sexiest smirk, which was pretty easy considering how loose and liquid her insides felt at the moment.

"You"—she pointed a finger at his chest—"no touchee. You do, this girl stops."

And then she began to peel in front of him. She took her time, felt like a Grand Avenue stripper, but she was okay with that for this audience of one…especially when she saw Justin's eyes go dark with need and his hands clench. She'd never done anything like this before, and probably never would again, but she really wanted to give him a special treat as he'd just given her.

When she began to undress him and he tried to help, she slapped his hands aside and forced him to be passive. To let it happen to him, just as he had done for her.

She touched and teased until he was wholly in her control. To achieve that with such a man was a pretty heady tonic. She'd never understood the whole rodeo, race car, ride-a-stallion thing that guys were so into. She did now, in this moment.

As Justin lay on her bunk, quivering at her slightest touch, moaning in a dark and dangerous tone when she ran a finger or her lips over him, she knew what that power must feel like to a man.

It was ab-so-lutely, goddamn glorious.

True to the rules, he didn't touch her as she sheathed him and then took him inside her. But his powerful hands nearly shredded her blanket and sheets as they looked for something to hold on to.

She rode him, and rode him hard, until they were both sweaty and the strain overpowered them. His explosion rocketed through her and gave her the most amazing ride imaginable.

The rushing waves robbed her of enough air to laugh, but wasn't it just a hoot that she was using the cowboy's own lingo.

Chapter 13

JUSTIN DID HIS BEST TO APPEAR NORMAL IN PUBLIC, but how was a man supposed to do that when he had Captain Kara Moretti embedded in his nervous system?

He'd fly a night mission into Libya—

They'd been doing that a lot for the last few weeks. The *Peleliu* had been called west from Israel as yet another faction shattered the delicate balance of the post-Gaddafi power vacuum.

—and he'd feel himself smiling as Kara guided him from her perch in the sky. He could feel her six miles above, inside her ground control station a hundred kilometers offshore, and way deep in his system.

Last night he'd slipped the *Calamity Jane* into the backstreets of Tripoli out near Tajoura, well beyond the Second Ring Road. It was far enough from the U.S. embassy not to draw attention from any of the various militias. Michael and a small team of Delta operators had rolled out the back of Justin's Chinook in a slightly battered blue Hyundai Elantra sedan. The ambassador, semipermanently exiled to neighboring Tunisia, needed an assessment of the security of certain assets in the abandoned U.S. embassy that Justin didn't want to know about.

Tonight he'd gathered the Delta team back up just as quietly from the middle of Asfah Road southwest of the city. No flying pickup this time; he'd landed right in front of the car, which had then driven aboard. Carmen had it positioned and strapped down in less than ten seconds using the adjustable harness that he and Connie Davis had designed. They were aloft fast and clean.

And Justin had flown back to the *Peleliu* counting the minutes until he could once again be in Kara's arms. What had begun as a desperate need was now an insatiable one.

He had thought about calling his parents to tell them that he'd found "the one." It would probably shock them no end. His lady friends since the bomber had been few and far between—and never lasted long.

But *he* wasn't ready to admit that, not even to himself.

How could a bossy, funny, outspoken Italian beauty from—the good Lord help him—Brooklyn be "the one"? He was in so much trouble.

Her greeting once they were all secure back aboard had been predictable and fantastic.

"Y'all sure are good at the tactical strike," he whispered into her hair when he could breathe again. Sex had been hard, fast, and with an imaginative twist that had nearly made him go blind.

"Why, thank you, Captain Cowboy." Kara climbed out of the bed and started dressing by the small light they always left on so that they could see each other. Closest they were going to get to candlelight aboard ship.

Or firelight.

He could sure imagine this golden-skinned beauty lit by a campfire and a Texas-sized sky of stars.

The curves, and nerves, of her body were something Justin had become finely attuned to. But like an unbroken wild horse, there was something going on inside, close below the surface but out of sight.

It puzzled him, though he'd figure it out when it was time. She looked almost as good in her Army gear as she did out of it. He liked the juxtaposition of competent soldier and sensual woman.

"Don't sleep through dinner." She leaned down to give him a kiss that rapidly had him thinking about things other than food, despite what they'd just done. "Jeez," she remarked and grinned down at him while she straightened the bra and T-shirt he'd messed up some. "And I thought I was the one-track hound of this team."

Then she was gone.

With the way she'd left his body buzzing, sleep was no longer an option, so he stood up and dressed. Taking his time, though he was sure they were fooling no one, he wandered into the chow line about ten minutes behind Kara.

She was nowhere to be seen. He double-checked the room, even if he couldn't imagine how he could miss her despite the crowd.

The stewards had put on a spaghetti feed and it was causing mayhem. Rangers were taking a bowl of spaghetti that would feed, well, an entire Brooklyn Italian family, and then covering it in sections with different sauces like a battle map marking areas of control. They were cycling back into the line for more, pushing ahead of him when he blocked the path to more sausage marinara or pesto meatballs.

The smells were deliriously good, but that didn't explain where Kara had gone. None of the SOAR women were present. Maybe they had decided to have a sunrise picnic somewhere.

He actually had the ladle for the sausage marinara dipped into the serving bucket when he caught a whiff of something. It was so clear that he realized it was the first aroma he'd been aware of other than Kara in a fair while. It didn't take long to locate the source.

A bacon-and-ground-sirloin tomato sauce. He breathed it in again and ignored the Ranger jostling him to get more garlic bread.

There. In a quiet corner of the steam table was a small tureen of Texas-style spaghetti sauce. Right down to the Worcestershire and chili powder. He ladled it onto his pasta, added a fistful of the sharp cheddar from the handy bowl that no one else had touched, and topped it with a sprinkling of scallions.

Then he went over and dropped his tray across from Bill and Michael.

He dug in a fork, unable to wait till he actually sat down, and the flavor exploded into his mouth. He sat and leaned in to inhale the aroma as he chewed.

"You planning to wear that or are you gonna eat it?" Sly Stowell, one of the Navy's chief petty officers, dropped his own tray next to Justin. He drove monstrous hovercraft parked down on the *Peleliu*'s amphibious deck.

"Don't you be joking about this food none, Sly. That's Texas spaghetti sauce on a Navy ship in the Mediterranean. I'm either dreaming or I'm gonna marry the cook."

"Gonna have ta fight me for her, boy."

Justin inspected Sly. He was broad of shoulder and looked as tough as any Special Ops soldier despite being Navy.

"I wouldn't suggest it," Bill advised, actually breaking his silence.

"Why not? Other than I'd get some incredible food if I win."

Bill contemplated a piece of his garlic bread at length before responding. "First, Sly beat the shit out of every Ranger aboard in a wrestling match a few months back."

Justin had wrestled more than his fair share of bull calves, angry steers, and rowdy cowhands. He and Sly traded friendly grins that said a wrestling match might be in their near future.

"The main reason…" Bill finished the piece of bread with a crunch and left for another iced tea. When he returned, he continued the conversation right where he'd left it. "His wife is chief steward and almost as scary as the rest of the women she hangs with." He tipped his glass to acknowledge the empty table in the center of the officers' mess.

"Trust me." Sly started twirling up his pasta covered with shrimp and scallops and other things that had no business being on pasta. "I'm married to her, and I can promise you that she is *just* as scary. I tried messing with one of her recipes once." He shuddered. "I'm lucky to be alive here today. A missile can only kill you. A chef with her knives… Look out, son, and keep your legs tight together."

―⁓―

"So, a soon-to-be inductee in the Married Special Operations Forces Club…" Gail Stowell drawled in a soft Southern accent as she joined them at the stainless steel prep table in the main galley.

Kara jolted as if someone had just stung her with a cattle prod.

"I knew it," Trisha crowed and slapped the chief steward on the back.

The woman was as slender as one of her knives…and a raving lunatic.

"It is all over you," Gail informed her.

Kara didn't know whether to pound her head against the steel table or be sick on it.

She'd arrived in the officers' mess close enough to the end of the meal that the women were already leaving. They had scooped her up and led her down a deck to the large galley kitchen that was being cleaned up from the last of the service. A few of the crew were finishing the scrubbing, but most were eating and laughing at another prep table on the far end of the kitchen.

While Kara struggled to recover, Gail ducked into the crew's neighboring mess hall and returned with a big bowl of spaghetti with meatballs and a sprinkle of parm on top that smelled almost good as Kara's mom's recipe. Gail set it down in front of Kara and sat on a stool with a pleased sigh as she surveyed her quieting kitchen.

Kara looked down at herself to see if she was wearing Justin's underwear on the outside of her pants or what.

"She doesn't know." Connie made one of her rare pronouncements. She took a piece of garlic bread from the basket that Gail had also supplied.

"Know what?" *Know what?* "I'm so not talking about this." *Justin.* "You." She pointed at Trisha. "I am not falling for your tricks."

"Have I said a word? For once I'm minding my own

business, and look what I get for being right." Trisha did her best to sound deeply and morally offended. Maybe if she'd left out the "minding my own business" part, she'd have stood a chance.

"Wait." Kara tried for a breath, but it wasn't working. "Right about what?" she asked Trisha. She turned to Connie. "I don't know what? I—"

Claudia had sat on the stool next to her and slid an arm around Kara's shoulders, offering a sideways hug. "Shh, honey. It will be okay. Honestly it will. And if it feels like you're choking or want to kill him, you're absolutely on the right track. I almost murdered Michael before I married him."

"She's the one I want to murder." Kara aimed a finger across the table.

"Oh, I'm so scared." Trisha did a lousy job of cowering.

"I'm—" Kara stopped because something terrifyingly unlike a hiccup had caught in her throat. *Deep breath. Drop into the zone. Fly through.*

Her self pep talk wasn't working.

Ride it out.

The fact that Justin's metaphor helped more than her own completely negated any bit of calm it earned her.

She grabbed the edges of the table and braced herself. There were way too many assumptions flying around.

Fine! She'd fix that.

"I like him." Though she couldn't seem to let go of her death grip on the table. "He's an amazing man."

The women nodded, though she'd guess by some of their rather mushy expressions that they were thinking of their own husbands.

"Really good with his hands." She'd play that angle.

Several of the women sighed.

"But there's no way I deserve him."

They all startled in unison and turned to face her.

Where in the hell *had that come from?*

But she didn't deserve him.

She sat in a steel coffin aboard one of the most powerful ships in the Navy. He flew into the heart of Israel and rescued people from the middle of allied Air Force bases. He'd been blown up, lost his crew, and climbed back aboard to fly into SOAR.

Several of them started to speak, doing one of those group stumbles and stops. After their second attempt, Gail raised a hand to cut them off.

"Stop it. Just go away. We need to let the woman get some calories." Spoken like a true chief steward. Then she grinned. "By the size of the smile on your face when you first came in here, I think you have a need for those calories."

Kara wanted to cut and run, but didn't dare under Gail's commanding gaze.

Trisha tried to say something, but Lola grabbed her by the ear and dragged her out, going, "Ow! Ow! Ow!" for which Kara would be eternally grateful. Later.

Claudia gave her shoulders a final squeeze, and Gail sent off the last members of her lingering crew and followed them out.

Soon it was only Connie at the table, along with Kara and her confusion.

"Quite something when it catches up with you."

Justin looked at Michael across the dining table and

nodded. No question what the man meant because Justin was feeling it right down to his bones.

"Was there a moment for you?"

"Top of a tree," Michael replied without elaborating.

"I was chewing her out for rescuing my sorry ass from near certain death," Bill put in, pointing upward toward the flight deck. "Didn't even know her name yet. Cutest damn thing I'd ever laid eyes on."

"Best damn barbecue anywhere." Sly got a round of laughter as he pointed down toward the belly of the ship. "What about you?"

"I can't really say." *First time he saw her?* Not the moment when she'd given herself to him with such perfect trust. Perhaps when she'd reached across the cockpit of the Chinook and traced a finger along his scar that so few were allowed to see.

The others were waiting for him.

"Doesn't make it any less true though. Does it?" Justin already knew the answer to that.

All three of his dinner companions shook their head in agreement.

Michael passed him the salt and Sly went for more garlic bread.

"It doesn't matter, you know."

Kara really didn't need some Connie statistic about the inevitability of Trisha's prodding. She wanted to be like Kirk to Connie's Spock: *Never tell me the odds*.

"Whatever we say doesn't matter. You'll know when it's time." Connie stood up to leave.

Kara grabbed her sleeve to halt her departure. "What

if I don't? Because no matter what you all say"—she barely managed to resist one of Justin's lazy *y'all*s—"what we have is great sex. Nothing more."

Connie's smile was slow. It was a rare thing—she was mostly deadpan to the world, even around her husband—which made the expression all the more stunning when she did let it out. Pure brain; she really was part Vulcan.

"Believe that as long as you can. The *it's just sex* concept was a comfort to me while it lasted." She moved several steps farther away before turning back. Now her grin was suddenly as wicked as one of Trisha's.

"What?"

"Well, I should, being me, point out that you are in a statistically bad grouping. So far, the women who fly for the 5D—going all the way back to Emily Beale, the first woman to make it into the 160th—have each and every one married Special Operations soldiers within or closely tied to the 5th Battalion D Company. I just thought you should know that."

Kara considered heaving a meatball at her, but threw her balled-up napkin instead.

Connie's grin flashed briefly once more before she departed, leaving Kara to fetch the napkin from where it had fluttered harmlessly to the immaculate floor of the empty kitchen.

Chapter 14

"A SAILOR'S LIFE IS A VERY ITINERANT ONE." Lieutenant Boyd Ramis had called them all into his cabin up on the hangar deck shortly after dinner.

Justin felt an incredible sense of déjà vu. The first time he'd sat here, he'd been so hopelessly naive. Fresh out of SOAR training, he'd thought that he knew what he was doing. They'd been in the Arabian Sea at the time.

Then Kara Moretti had walked into the briefing room, and his world had tilted worse than a pinball machine in a typhoon. Twenty-four hours later he'd been flying a raid deep into Somali territory and rescuing hostages during the peak of a tropical storm. Since then he'd flown in a dozen different countries, both friendly and a bit less than.

He'd also taken a lover who now sat in exactly the same seat she had before, close beside Captain Claudia Casperson. Once again the blond and the brunette sat side by side on the couch in Ramis's topside office. How Justin's emotions had traveled such a distance in such a short period of time was beyond him.

"Once again"—Ramis managed to sound both noble and put-upon—"it is up to the hardworking Navy to travel to a remote destination with no reason given. I have been informed that there will be no operations while en route."

Justin glanced around but saw no more clarity on anyone else's faces than he felt on his own. A herd of longhorns on a cattle drive had more sense of where they were going than anyone here did. He saw Michael's unending patience and did his best to emulate it. Experience had shown that Ramis would get around to the point only when he was good and ready.

"We are to transit the Med once again, this time via Sicily, Athens, and Cyprus…"

In his peripheral vision Justin saw Kara start to look toward him and then stop herself. Only four people in this room knew about the trip into the heart of Israel; even Ramis hadn't known that's where they went, though it wouldn't be a hard guess. That the *Peleliu* was headed back in that direction only meant more trouble.

"…which we are told to take at a moderate rate to 'avoid unnecessary equipment wear and tear.'" Ramis was plenty smart enough to not buy that for a single second. "The transit that we made in four days going west is projected to take eight going east. We already have notified teams to shift all of your aircraft down onto the hangar deck."

At least there they'd be out of sight. But that meant a week trapped aboard without a single flight. There was only so much ground training and vehicle maintenance that could be done.

"All except Captain Roberts's *Calamity Jane*."

That snapped Justin's attention around—his thoughts had been on the verge of wandering over to Kara and her easy smile.

"Captain…" Ramis addressed him directly but was clearly speaking for the rest of the room. "Your crew is presently installing jump seats on your cargo deck. You are hereby cleared for the four-hour flight to Camp Darby, outside Livorno, Italy. You and any SOAR flight crew and officer-level action personnel who would like to are hereby cleared for a one-week leave. Departure in thirty minutes."

An image flashed into Justin's brain so hard that it almost hurt.

Kara Moretti in a scant bikini on an Italian beach.

Or riding a horse over Texas grassland in a denim shirt with the tails untucked and tied together, exposing her slender midriff. He'd buy her a proper Stetson, though she'd probably want it in pink or something equally silly. Still, it would look so good on her.

"Yes." Kara did a fist pump. With deep familiarity, he could pick out her words through the burst of excited talk. "Brooklyn pizza, here I come."

New York? He'd blown through a couple times with Mom when he was a kid, but never liked it much. The city was filled with crowds tighter than an Army barracks and more noise than a battle zone. Because of that, he and the Big Apple had never much taken to each other. If that's where she wanted to go, he'd go.

But New York? Really?

Chapter 15

KARA FELT LIKE A SCENE FROM ONE OF THOSE COWBOY-comes-to-the-city movies when they landed at JFK airport. The New York girl and six-two of cowboy lover at her side.

It was clear she wasn't the only one imagining that. Several of the civilian flight attendants had flirted with Justin though she was right there beside him. Hitting baggage claim had the same dynamic. Kara was used to men's gazes tracking her across a room—her feeling was let 'em look and dream 'cause they were never going to touch. But it was strange that this time so many of the women were tracking the man beside her.

She wasn't quite sure how it had ended up this way. Justin had flown them across the Med to Camp Darby, he and his crew singing off-key Christmas carols for way too much of the four-hour flight. The fact that it was May didn't seem to factor in even a little bit.

From there most of the various crews transferred over to the airport in Genoa before scattering to different flights. There she and Justin had simply gotten on the same plane without ever really discussing it. It was early afternoon by that point in the travel, the middle of their "night," so she'd been too tired to think of protesting.

Not that she minded.

Not really.

BY BREAK OF DAY

Though while she'd taken boyfriends home before, this felt different.

"You sure about this?" she asked as they boarded the A train out of JFK and toward the city. Justin eyed the jam of evening commuters with caution.

"A bit less so than when I was back in the airport. Awful lot of folks here, moving fast in a mighty small space. Always took a cab."

"That's like fifty bucks. Subway is way cheaper, trust me." And he'd followed her aboard. The subway train ride had started out by the airport and was going against the tide of the main evening commute. They'd easily found seats and had their duffels propped on the floor between their feet.

New York had really fixed up the subway cars since she was a kid. They were clean, with a minimum of graffiti, and a transit cop looking bored as shit stood two-thirds of the way down the car. While they were here, she'd make sure they went at least once into the city proper during commute hours, just to mess with Justin's head.

It was an evil thought. Normally she did her best to avoid that exact situation, but watching Justin's face in the packed crowds and seeing him learn to ride the surges of the subway along with the shifting masses crammed into every car could be worth the price of admission.

"Your hat does make you stand out a bit, Justin."

"Reminds me of home and family. It also keeps you from losing me in the crowd. I get lost in this herd and I'm not ever gonna be finding my way. I reckon that alone makes it worthwhile."

"I don't have any plans on losing you." Which was an odd thing for her to say. But nobody looked like him or moved like him, perhaps not in the whole city. The hat was just the icing on the cake.

"I don't plan on losing you either, Kara." His expression was oddly serious.

She was about to comment on it when they reached her stop. She almost lost Justin right there. He was moving at a leisurely pace, standing and shouldering his duffel. By the time he reached the door, well behind her, the surge of people loading from the platform had him being all polite and holding back. If she hadn't noticed and rushed back to snag the door as it closed, he'd have been whisked off into Manhattan proper.

"Gotta be quick on your feet now, Cowboy. You're in the big city."

"Yes, ma'am. I can see that now. Or I could simply change my tactics." He grabbed her hand and held it as they walked along the mostly empty platform.

It was an odd sensation. They certainly hadn't held hands while walking around on board the *Peleliu*. Except during sex, they'd held hands only that once while sitting aboard his Chinook helicopter.

Kara had never been big on it. In high school and the neighborhood, guys used hand-holding to stake their claim. Even worse was when they hook their arm around your neck until it felt like you were in a permanent, vicious headlock. Signaling not only "this one is mine," but also gaining some kind of strange validation among their friends that they had a girl attached to their side, as if they could grab one any time they wanted.

Yet Justin made it feel like the most natural

thing—aside from their heavy packs, the exit gates, and the narrow stairs that climbed the three stories up from the subway. On the sidewalk she was walking along the so-familiar streets holding hands, which made the neighborhood feel completely new and strange. They moved like a walking roadblock to the natural flow of traffic on the sidewalk. She'd always looked down on couples that did that. She'd wondered if she should pay a kid to walk out ahead of them with a "Wide Load" sign to clear their path.

Justin, despite his hat, didn't gawk like some hick. Of course, this was just Brooklyn. Most of the buildings were only three or four stories, all tucked together side by side and leaving no gaps between them.

"I have been to the city before," he told her when she asked, then he'd shuddered. "To think I could be out on the ranch right about now is a sad, sad thought." But it was his teasing voice, so she didn't feel too bad about that. Besides, a ranch, no matter what size his might be, would be just as foreign to her.

She knew the first place she had to go and led Justin the roundabout way home to reach the family pasta shop.

"Kara!" Mama's shout was ecstatic as she hustled out from behind the counter.

"Mama!" Kara fell into her embrace. There. Now she was home.

—⁓—

To give them a moment of privacy, Justin inspected the shop. The two embracing woman completely blocked the single long aisle. Along one wall were packages of biscotti, olive oil, dried pastas, and dozens of other dried ingredients. It was a tiny grocery store dedicated to making pasta dinners.

Down the other side of the shop ran a long glass-fronted cabinet. Trays and trays of fresh pasta were lined up: spaghetti; lasagna; little dumpling things; the big, round tube ones; and a dozen others he couldn't begin to name.

At his end, close by a cash register that might have been built during the war—perhaps the American Civil War—were great tureens of sauces: green pesto, bubbling red sauce with and without sausage, a whole container of meatballs each nearly as big as his own fist, and a half-dozen other sauces, some red, some yellow with butter. They filled the air until the shop was thick with flavor. He did notice that there was no Texas-style, but what did they really know here in New York? He pitied the poor people their uneducated ways. *And wouldn't Kara beat the crap outta you if she heard that sentiment.*

The heavy plank flooring, plaster walls, and beaten copper ceiling might well date back to the Civil War.

It was like a barbecue shop for New Yorkers—the perfect Italian comfort food.

Though the Rolling Stones playing on the oldies station was a misfit.

A man who shared Kara's skin coloring and age was eyeing Justin carefully as he dished up a to-go container of the marinara for one of the half-dozen customers being jostled by Kara and her mother, not that they seemed to mind.

But the cousin—no, he had the same eyes—the brother definitely minded. Not the jostling or the people, but the tall, blond Texan who stood a hand taller than any of them—even not counting his hat.

In the midst of a happy embrace, Kara's mother was inspecting him over her daughter's shoulder.

"And who is this?" She turned them both until they faced Justin, but she kept a hand around her daughter's waist.

"Mama, this is Justin. Justin, this is Angela."

"Mrs. Moretti." Justin put on his best manners, belatedly tipping, then removing his hat. "It is easy to see that you're kin, but it's not so easy to tell you aren't sisters."

And he wasn't totally whistling in the wind. Angela Moretti was a few inches shorter than her daughter and her curves were softened with age, but she was still a stunning woman. Though the dark eyes didn't quite match Kara's; he suspected Kara had her father's eyes.

"He is a sweet talker, Kara. And it's Angela to you. And you—" She turned on her daughter, then cuffed her an affectionate blow to the side of her head, then pulled her taller daughter over so that she could kiss the spot.

"Ow! Hey! What did I do?"

"Why did you not tell me you were bringing home a beautiful man when you call from Italy? Huh? You pick him up on the plane, the airport, or the subway?" She sent Justin a broad and friendly wink to show she meant no offense.

"When I called, I, uh, didn't know he'd be able to—"

Mrs. Moretti turned back to face Justin and cut off her daughter mid-explanation.

"You watch this one close, Justin-who-she-doesn't-even-know-your-last-name." Another saucy wink. "She's slippery. You fall in love with her, and then she breaks your heart like a boiled cream sauce."

"Mama!" Kara cringed.

Which Justin found rather cute. Apparently nothing impacted Kara's innate confidence except her mother.

"I would be Justin Roberts, Mrs. Moretti."

"Polite and pretty. Too good for my Kara. You think I don't know the truth about your heart." Now she was back to her daughter. "Carlo's always asking about you."

"Sure, me. And Nadya. And Katarine. And anything else that has two legs with nothing betwee—"

"Yes. Yes. But he asks special about you. See, you broke his heart and he isn't ever again the same."

Kara attempted to silence her mother with another hug and offered Justin an eye roll in apology.

Actually he found himself quite enjoying this view of Kara and her mother.

However, the brother's scowl had darkened even further. Him Justin was less sure about.

"We'll see you at home." Kara made good their escape. The shop was always busiest right before dinnertime, and between them and their duffel bags, they had quite jammed the flow of business.

They stepped out onto the bustling street as a light May rain spattered down, leaving little dots on the dry sidewalk. A glance upward said they would have to hurry or they'd be caught in a downpour.

"You might have introduced me to your brother. I think he already hates me."

"Didn't I? Shit! He's Joe—middle brother. Al Junior's my big brother. He's a cop like Papa, and Rudi, just a year ahead of me, he's the black sheep—left the force to go back to law school. Don't worry about Joe. He hates everybody I bring home, so don't take it personally."

"Like your mama loves every one of them."

"You have no idea." Kara shook her head. "There were times I'd come home from a class or ROTC and find three old boyfriends sitting around the kitchen table eating Mama's cookies and drinking a soda."

"Sounds like you had quite a following," Justin continued right over her as she spluttered over that. "So, did you always break their hearts?"

Kara pointed. "Best pizza in the neighborhood. I'll take you tomorrow. Best pizza in Brooklyn makes it best on earth. When they start selling pizza on the moon, it will be the best in the solar system."

"Evasion, Moretti."

She stopped and looked up at him, shading her eyes against the increasing spatter of raindrops. "Always, Cowboy. So don't be giving me yours. I'm hell on hearts."

He laughed and leaned down to kiss her just as a flash and a hard thump of thunder rattled the windows. The heavens opened in a proper East Coast–style downpour and she didn't care. The sizzle and thump wasn't only in the sky. She actually moaned beneath his kiss. She never moaned, but there was no question it had been her. Kara clung to him as the raindrops grew from orzo to gnocchi sized.

Around them, New Yorkers scattered under a ragtag collection of umbrellas, raised collars, and newspapers refolded over their hair.

Her face remained dry in the tiny zone of safety beneath the brim of Justin's hat. She let his kiss sweep through her until her knees were as weak as her hair was wet.

Chapter 16

"Kara!"

She wished people would stop shouting her name when she was busy swooning.

Then the voice registered through her Justin-induced haze.

"Papa!"

She moved to hug him but he kept her at arm's length.

"You're soaked through, girl." He wore his J.C. Penney's suit from his work as a detective at the 78th Precinct. His umbrella had kept him dry on the walk home from his shift.

She pushed his arm aside and splatted herself against him. "Oh, you're all warm too." The May rain certainly wasn't. She snuggled in and rested her head on his shoulder as he patted her back. He smelled like home. His cheap suits and stale coffee. The lingering hint of the inevitable salami sub that Nonna made for him every morning, heavy on the mustard.

"You're kissing cowboys in the rain, *mia piccola*?"

Kara stepped back and grinned at the outline of her damp self on his dark suit. He wore his silver tie that she'd bought him for Christmas years ago. "You were in court today?" She reached out to loosen the tie.

He batted her hands away and gave her one of those stern looks that still made her feel like she was twelve.

She loved coming home so much. "Yes, I am kissing

BY BREAK OF DAY

a cowboy. And, trust me, Papa, ain't nobody more surprised by that than me. But can we get out of the rain before I introduce y'all?" It slipped out before she could stop it. "I'm gonna be drowning here any second."

She glanced back at Justin who was either on the verge of running in panic or about to laugh in her face; she couldn't quite tell which. Maybe both. To forestall his escape, she hooked an arm through each man's elbow, as Justin had already shouldered her duffel on top of his, and she turned them for home.

"'Y'all' is a surprisingly useful word." She addressed her father. "English has no *voi*." Which sounded like a lame excuse even to her.

"'Course English does, little lady." Justin squeezed her hand tighter in the crook of his elbow. "It has a perfectly fine one, and you used it just right. Even if your accent is still all Yankeefied."

Papa gave a snort that was about as close as he ever got to a laugh.

Kara hoped that was a good sign. Unlike with other men she'd brought home, she discovered that she cared whether or not Papa liked this one.

———※———

Justin stood on the polished wood of the front entryway and did his best not to drip on the floor. A tropical monsoon's worth of water was running off his and Kara's clothes, forming a widening puddle.

Alfonso Moretti Senior had a grip like a cop…or a farrier who could bend horseshoes without needing his anvil. It was a crushing handclasp even by Justin's standards. The look in Mr. Moretti's eye said that he had rid

Kara of more than few of her male suitors with that grip and a dose of that evil glance.

He smiled and offered a sharp nod when Justin returned as good as he was given.

While he was standing there trying not to drip, the front door slammed into his back.

"Shit! It's wetter than a baptism out there." A younger version of Alfonso Senior shoved in the doorway. He was still in uniform right down to his sidearm, billed hat, and jacket with the NYPD emblem on the breast and sleeve. "Hey, Kara. Didn't know you had leave."

He gave her an absent peck on the forehead. "Hey, Papa." He shoved by his father.

Justin wondered if he was somehow invisible.

Then, just as the man stepped through the inner entry, he glanced back at Justin with a look that said, "Oh brother, another one? What this time?" The last of the look rested above Justin's head then he was gone. His father followed him into the house.

Justin had to admit that Kara's assessment about his cowboy hat being out of place in New York City might be an accurate one, but giving in and removing it now was out of the question.

A second man had slipped in behind the first one — who hadn't introduced himself but must be Rudi. This last one could have been Kara's fraternal twin. He was as short as her, not that any of the Morettis were particularly tall, but Kara and Rudi had clearly inherited their stature from their mother rather than their father.

"Hi, Kar." His voice was also soft and Justin decided that he liked him right away. Rudi gave her a real hug, not an idle peck. They were sweet together. By the way she wrapped her arms around his neck and held on, this was clearly the favorite brother.

"How's my favorite lawyer?" Justin could just over-hear her whisper to her brother.

"To avoid incurring liability, I must inform you that I am your favorite law student." It was clearly a thing between them.

Their embrace made Justin miss his sister, actually his whole family. He was half tempted to turn around and find his way back to the airport to go see them. Except he was more likely to see Bessie Anne at some foreign air base than back in Texas; the Air Force kept her on the move.

Unlike his older brother, this younger one inspected Justin carefully when Kara finally let him go. He offered his hand and an honest, if cautious shake along with his name. "Rudi."

Then Justin and Kara were alone once more in the tiny foyer. "Can I stop meeting people now?"

Kara patted his arm. "That should cover you until dinnertime, which will be as soon as Mama and Joe get home from the shop." She grabbed his hand and dragged him through the inner door.

In the pouring rain, he'd only had the slightest impres-sion of the outside of the house. A long city block with a line of four-story houses made of brownstone, just like in the movies. Each had a front yard about as big as a horse stall and a stone stoop of a half-dozen steps from street to porch. More people lived in this block than were ever on the ten thousand acres of the Roberts family ranch. Again the urge to go kicked at him, but he brushed it off.

Inside, they stepped into a living room that wouldn't fill the front hall of his family's ranch house. But it looked cozy with a couple of couches, several armchairs, a low table scattered with magazines, and a TV screen not even two feet across. Of course, in the ranch's rec room, you'd never sit this close to the screen unless you were a young one down on the floor with a coloring book, so you needed something bigger.

Besides there could be a whole passel of folks when there was a big televised horse race or a Bowl game. A whole lot more than could fit here. But he'd wager that during a game this room was a cozier, livelier place to be.

He kept looking for the doorway to the next room until he realized there wasn't one to the side. The bay window looked out on the street and the room was the full width of the house.

Close in front of him a narrow set of stairs led upward; beneath it another set led down. To the back he could see Mr. Moretti emerging from what must be the master bedroom wearing a button-down shirt and jeans. That would be the whole floor. It was a very vertical house.

Kara led him up the stairs.

"Nonna and Al Junior with Marta—that's his wife; she's a singer in a band—live on this floor."

"She…what? You're brother doesn't exactly strike me as the type."

"I know. You'd expect a traditional Italian girl…" She raised her voice and turned her face toward the room she'd indicated.

He came out of his room wearing jeans and an NYPD T-shirt.

"…for the big lummox," she finished without lowering her voice.

"Too bad, Sis. Now you're not the only 'wild one' in the family." He thumped down the stairs and Kara ignored him except for sticking out her tongue at his back. Al Junior flipped his middle finger at her over his shoulder without bothering to look back.

Justin had never flipped someone off in his life. Had stuck his tongue out at his sister more than a few times though.

"She sings this hot, indie rock, makes you want to dance or have sex or both. Has her first tour coming up. Beautiful Irish redhead, so no gawking."

Justin could hear the pride of her sister-in-law in her voice and knew that it would run through the whole family despite the unlikeliness of the match.

"And that's"—Kara pointed at the other end of the hall—"the guest room where Mama will try to put you." She went to lead him up the next flight, but he turned aside. He set her duffel by the stairs and then, exploring along a narrow hallway, he reached a small bedroom with an open door that faced onto the street. The bed had a pretty quilt, but no personal belongings. He set his wet duffel in the corner, careful not to rest it against the wallpaper.

"You are not sleeping here." Kara stood in the doorway, fists on her hips.

"Kara, I—"

"You did not follow me to New York City to sleep in a different room."

He hadn't, but that didn't change things. He took off his hat and set it on the dresser—an old oaken piece of curved wood with an age-faded mirror above it.

Kara glared at it resting there.

Justin stepped over to her and rested his hands on her hips. When she opened her mouth to protest, he simply kissed her. She thudded the side of a frustrated fist against his shoulder, but then clenched his sopping wet T-shirt to keep him in place. There was no denying what was between them no matter where they slept.

"Now go change." He turned her about and gave her a slap on the butt to get her moving. Just like a high-spirited horse, she glared back at him, but gathered up her duffel and headed upstairs.

The door across the hall had opened, and a tiny woman, wrinkled and gray-haired, tilted her head sideways to look up at him.

"Looked like quite some kiss, young man."

Justin looked down at her. Kara's maternal grandmother he guessed, based on her features. Nothing to do but brazen it out.

"Your granddaughter is quite some woman, ma'am. Would be a waste not to make it the best kiss I know how."

The woman laughed, her voice light but still strong. "You know how to handle her. Most men, they know nothing. She is a girl of high spirits, but her heart, that she is unsure of. I know mine though. If I were a few generations younger…"

He leaned down and kissed her on the cheek. Not as he'd seen in Italy, those air kisses, but an actual kiss.

She slapped lightly at his chest and then rubbed her fingers together. "You're all wet, *bambino*. Go change your diapers. I think maybe I will like you."

And then her door closed and Justin was left to drip alone in the hall.

He headed off to find a towel and fresh clothes.

———

"He is so pretty, Kara." Marta made a sighing sound that Kara's brother had better never hear pass her lips. He might have married a singer and went to all of her gigs, but her big brother wasn't the most understanding sort. Marta continued to dice onions for the sauce.

"Good manners," Mama noted with a voice that said she certainly hadn't missed how pretty he was. She was unwrapping a Tupperware container of lasagna noodles she had brought home from the shop.

"Justin is—" Kara tried to turn the conversation somewhere, anywhere else.

"One heck of kisser," Nonna put in from her perch on the other side of the counter where she now directed rather than cooked.

They all looked at her, and Kara wondered what form of hell she had walked into. "Nonna!"

"Old, *bambina*. Not blind or stupid. I see how you hang on to him when you kiss. Like a woman who is—"

"Nonna!" Kara cut her off, looking to her mother and sister-in-law for some reprieve.

Marta began to snigger as she tossed onions into the hot cast-iron skillet. "Paybacks are hard. How much did you tease me when I started dating your brother?"

Kara grimaced. *Every chance I got*, was the answer.

"Now what we all want to know, *bambina*. If he makes a kiss look so wonderful, how is he the rest of the way?"

Kara felt the flush of heat roar up to her cheeks, and Nonna smacked the counter with her palm.

"Good for him, *bambina*. Good for you. You want a man in your bed who can make you feel that way."

Kara glanced at her mother and sister-in-law. They both turned away from her. It was bad enough to think about your parents having sex, but your grandmother? It was more than any of them were ready for.

Maybe if Justin found his way downstairs to the kitchen, they would stop talking about him.

"Hey, when's dinner?"

Mama looked at the ceiling and swatted Rudi affectionately as he came off the stairs. "Every day the same. It doesn't matter when I cook, you know it will be done in thirty minutes when my darling boy shows up with an empty stomach. Get the antipasto tray from the refrigerator and take it back up to your papa. You boys be nice to Kara's young man."

"Don't worry, Mama. Papa and Junior already got that covered." Rudi took the tray and was eating a rolled-up piece of salami before he hit the stairs back up to the living room.

"Maybe I should go rescue him." Kara tried to head out.

"Maybe you should shred this cheese for the lasagna first." Her mother handed her several balls of fresh mozzarella.

"So, Nonna"—Marta tossed some green peppers into the pan, evoking a fresh sizzle—"how good a kisser is he?"

Kara groaned. She'd been right the first time; no chance of reprieve.

—w—

"I must admit, most of the sports in my part of Texas have to do with horses." Justin knew he was in dangerous territory here. He had met enough Yankees and Mets fans in the service to know better than to ever mention the Astros or the Rangers. And he'd wager that bringing up the Dallas Cowboys and going for a change from baseball to football wouldn't help matters much either.

The game on the television was in the sixth inning, the Toronto Blue Jays down by a lot to the Yankees. No one was paying close attention to it, even though that's where their focus remained as they spoke.

"We have a good minor league team in Amarillo though. The Amarillo Thunderheads, though they were the Amarillo Sox all while I was growing up."

"Like the Red Sox?" Rudi asked, returning with a big plate of individually rolled-up meats alongside olives and some kind of bright green peppers Justin didn't recognize.

"Same spelling, but not as good."

"You think the Red Sox are any good?" Joe, Kara's middle brother, jumped in as if looking for any angle of attack.

Justin opened his mouth, then realized that he was about to praise the Yankees' main rivals, the Boston Red Sox. He'd always felt a kindness toward them just because of that same *s-o-x* spelling. He closed his mouth again.

"I see you're a smart one, Justin." Mr. Moretti spoke. "Don't let my boys rattle you none. Though if you said something nice about the Phillies…" He left the threat hanging.

Justin didn't really follow baseball very closely. Was he supposed to praise or despise the Philadelphia team? Despise, he decided. New Yorkers looked down on everywhere outside their city limits.

"I'd never do such a thing, sir."

Mr. Moretti grunted in a pleased way that didn't seem to have much to do with one team or another. He ate one of the pickled peppers.

Justin tried one, biting it cautiously in the middle. It exploded with liquid that dribbled down his chin and burned where he'd just shaved.

"You have to bite pepperoncini off close to the stem and eat them whole, son. Can't take just a part and end up with anything good."

And it was clear that Mr. Moretti wasn't talking about pickled peppers either.

———

By the fourth knock on his bedroom door, Justin had pretty much given up on sleep. Marta, Angela, and even Nonna had each wanted to "just make sure he was comfortable."

Marta had delivered a glass of warm milk.

Mrs. Moretti had brought him a delicate china plate of some chocolate cookies called *baci* that went very well with the milk.

Nonna had actually giggled like a far younger woman when he offered her one. How was he supposed to know that *baci* meant kisses in Italian? He'd been given a plate of "kiss" cookies and offered one to a woman fifty years his senior.

Now the fourth knock repeated and Justin wondered

if it was Alfonso Moretti Senior showing up with his .38 Special, Al Junior with a Taser, or Joe with a butcher's knife. Only Rudi had given him any sign of friendliness. Apparently Kara's approval was all Rudi needed to know.

"Yes, come in." He wanted to hide beneath the covers.

"Kinda terse greeting for a cowboy." Kara slipped into the room. Her flannel robe was nearly floor length, but the backlight from the hall revealed that it was a light material, and plenty of her shape was silhouetted to fire up his imagination and other parts of his body.

"Kara, go away," he whispered to her, knowing it wouldn't work.

She stepped in and closed the door behind her.

A streetlight shone through a gap in the front curtains that he hadn't found the energy to get out of bed and fix.

Kara pulled a string at her throat and shrugged. Her robe shimmered down to the floor, leaving her naked and him breathless.

All through dinner and that evening, they had been so close, yet unable to touch. Well, not unable; she'd seemed willing enough. But Justin couldn't find it in himself while his every word or gesture was being weighed and considered. He'd been poked, prodded, and scored like a prize cow at the Tri-State Fair in Amarillo.

Now she shimmered. The sliver of light rippled over her as she moved through it, offering momentary views of curve and shadow, of muscles and a gleaming smile.

Against his own better judgment, he shifted back and held the covers up for her as she slid into his bed. And then he did as had been suggested: he made the best love to her he knew how.

Chapter 17

Kara flinched.

She was in Justin's bed in the guest room. She'd meant to merely use his body, then sneak back up to her own room. But he had made the night shine and her body burn. When he at long last had thoroughly had his way with her, for there was no question about who'd taken the lead last night, she'd slid into a contented slumber in his arms.

Kara enjoyed being the dominant one in bed, guiding and controlling. But last night Justin had found some weird corner of her soul that wanted to be pampered and coddled, and that she didn't recognize at all in the morning's light.

Now she was alone, except for Nonna looking down at her.

And smiling.

"Your grandfather needed me just so much."

"What? How much?" Kara immediately wished she hadn't asked.

"So much that he make me smile the way you now smile, *mia cara*. For forty-seven years he make me smile that way." Her smile grew wistful. "It is good when a man needs a woman so fiercely." She brushed at the corners of her eyes and turned quickly back for her room.

"Nonna?" But she was gone.

Kara clambered out of Justin's bed, slipped on her

nightgown, and made the bed before slipping up to her own room.

A Post-it note was stuck clearly for all to see on the middle of her own bedroom door.

Gone for a walk. J.

Like that would fool anyone. It certainly hadn't fooled Nonna. Still, it was nice of him to make the effort to protect her honor.

She grabbed some clothes and headed for the shower. The water ran hot, if with a familiar lack of force. She got herself wet in the first thirty seconds, then soaped with the water turned off. As she was getting ready for the ninety-second rinse off, she remembered this wasn't a shipboard Navy shower and she could take her time. That was one of the hardest things about long hair—getting it clean within the water conservation rules at sea.

Even serving at Clovis in the New Mexico desert, they'd had a more generous water allowance. Kara had always remembered how much she'd loved Mama's long hair and how she'd wept the day Mama cut it shoulder length. Papa had not looked much happier, though Mama had.

As soon as Kara shifted over to Special Operations at SOAR and learned that they allowed longer hair, she'd gone for it. Anywhere but the 5D, she'd have had to trim it back. Justin's deep appreciation of her hair was yet another reason to keep it long despite the logistics issues.

Justin.

He was starting to get on her nerves, though her nerves weren't complaining.

When they'd been granted leave, he'd come home with her. He'd done it without asking, as if it was the most natural thing. Maybe it was for him. Not caring a bit about it being her home and her family, just caring about sex and sating his own desires.

Except that sounded nothing like Justin and a whole lot like her. She'd followed her fair share of boys right into their kitchens and their bedrooms—and to hell with what the parents thought.

Justin had chosen the guest bedroom and tried to turn her away.

Damn the man for being decent. What was up with that anyway?

She slapped off the water, wrapped her hair in one towel, and began rubbing herself down with another.

Kara hadn't asked him home, though she'd been pleased when he came with her. *Admit it! If he'd gone to Texas, you'd be on the phone every night to see what he was doing.*

And if it was distance she'd wanted, she'd done a lousy job of that last night.

Kara dragged on fresh clothes and found her old hair dryer tucked in the back of the sink cabinet. As she bent forward to hang her head and hair upside down, she had to admit that Nonna was right.

The man put a smile on her face. Even now, the bastard. Here she was wearing a perfectly decent frown, but with her head upside down and her hair hanging down, her mouth was curved upward like a smile.

He didn't have any right!

Any right to what? Make her feel like she was loved?

She caught her comb in a snarl of hair at that moment and almost ripped off a chunk of her scalp in her surprise.

Loved?

No way in hell had this soldier signed up for that.

Her hair was only half dry, but that was just tough. She chucked the dryer back under the counter still running, then unplugged it and heaved the cord in after.

Kara caused herself a surprising amount of pain with the comb before she'd tamed the multiple snarls. At one point she was almost angry enough to pull the shears out of the drawer and chop the whole damn mess off.

But she resisted, managed a decent ponytail, then headed off on a search-and-destroy mission.

Target?

Justin soon-to-be-bloody Roberts.

Justin was on his cell phone when Kara walked into the kitchen. Her hair shone. With a bit of a jolt, he realized that this was the first time he'd seen her in civilian girl clothes. A light blouse hid more of her shape than an Army sand-colored T-shirt, but it told more of the woman within. Instead of khakis and Army boots, she wore formfitting jeans and running shoes. She was always breathtaking, but now she was pure woman and it stunned his brain to mush.

For a moment, he forgot about the voice buzzing in his ear. Then he held out a hand to her. She stepped forward and took it.

Then with a practiced flex and twist she had it twisted against the small of his back and leveraged it to crash his face down on the counter.

He managed to hang on to his phone. "I'll have to call

you back, Ma, but it will be great to see you. Give my love to everyone. Bye now."

Justin found the off switch, then hooked a foot behind Kara's knee and swept her in the direction that would ease the pressure on his arm.

She was stronger than he expected, even after their various tussles between the sheets, but he was able overpower her. She went for a cheap shot that he barely managed to block with a thigh.

He finally latched an arm around her waist and her arms. Hooking a leg around hers, he managed to fall back against the refrigerator for support.

She pounded her head back against him, hard enough to shatter his nose if she'd been taller. Instead, her head bounced off his chest.

Kara kept squirming until he shook her. "Cut that out, Moretti. Hell of a 'good morning' for a man you made love to only a few hours ago."

His comment seemed to take the wind out of whatever was happening.

He picked her up by the waist and set her on one of the kitchen stools. Then he backed off quickly just in case she was going to go for another poke at him.

"Now…" He blew out a breath when she didn't attack right away. "What in the name of the Lord Almighty was that about?"

"You bastard!"

"Ma and Dad might argue with that." He shot for a little lightness until he figured out what was going on.

"I'd still be right."

"So much for the power of humor." Maybe he'd just wait her out.

"You made love to me."

Justin debated, but Kara wasn't moving. Somehow this was normal in her family, right out in the kitchen. In his family there would never be this conversation to begin with. And if there was, it would be held out in the back corral with no one but the horses to overhear.

"Yes, to answer your question, I made love to you last night. I'm surprised you didn't notice."

Kara folded her arms on the counter, rested her head on them, then screamed in frustration.

"Could I at least know the offense I committed?" Justin did his best to sound reasonable but rather suspected that he sounded totally pleased with himself. Kara Moretti could certainly please a man thoroughly. "We have made love many times as I recall."

"No. No, we haven't." She didn't raise her head. "I wasn't making love. I was having the best goddamn sex of my life, Cowboy, but Kara Moretti, I can assure you, doesn't 'make love.' Ever!"

Justin felt as if he'd just been punched by an Abrams M1 battle tank.

"Oh," Nonna remarked from the doorway. "Why do I think I walk in at just the perfect moment?"

"Go away, Nonna," Kara snarled at her without bothering to raise her head.

If her grandmother felt any surprise, she didn't show it. "Don't you mind me. I'm going to be quiet as a mouse. I need to make lunch for my son-in-law and his boys." And she moved right into the kitchen.

Once she was past Kara, Nonna winked encouragement at Justin, an encouragement he certainly wasn't feeling at the moment.

He and Kara—

They'd— "And stop winking!" Kara snarled without looking up.

Was it possible he was so wrong?

Nonna raised her hands as if in shock, but her smile didn't fade in the slightest as she began slicing bread and fishing items out of the refrigerator.

Kara looked up and glared at him for a long moment.

He did his best to kept his churning emotions off his face.

Then Kara turned on her stool to face her grand-mother. "Please tell me this gets easier."

Nonna shook her head, then reached out to pat Kara's cheek.

Justin already knew the answer to that one. It didn't.

"Not in love. Not no way. Not ever!" Kara snarled at her grandmother as if he wasn't even in the room.

———————

The words tasted bitter in her throat. They caught and burned.

Kara wanted to be sick, to curse, to cry.

Instead her chest simply knotted up so tight she couldn't breathe. It knotted until it hurt like she'd been shot—sucking chest wound. The "sucky" part was right at least. All she could hear was her pulse pounding in her ears and her lungs' lame attempts to catch a breath.

She couldn't turn back to face him, couldn't stand to see the look she knew would be on Justin's features. Kara was searching for some nerve—she'd never been a fan of cowardly until this moment—when Nonna spoke.

"I do not know." Her voice was cold and hard in a way

Kara had never heard. "Do I smack you like a spoiled child? Or do I hold you in my lap like a broken *bambina*?"

"I'm too big to sit in your lap anymore, Nonna."

"I still do not know which I should do to you."

Kara closed her eyes and turned back toward Justin, taking several deep breaths so that she had some chance of being calm when she told him, "Not no, but hell no."

Up the stairs she heard the front door open and close. Kara opened her eyes.

She and Nonna were alone in the kitchen.

"Where's Justin?" She looked out the back window that opened onto the small fenced backyard behind their house, but it too was empty.

Nonna just shook her head.

Kara jumped up to bolt for the front door, but Nonna's hand on her arm kept her from running to see where he'd gone.

"You have hurt him, Kara. Like with a knife. He will need some time."

"But—" She didn't understand.

Nonna pulled Kara into her arms and hugged her with surprising strength for a woman in her late seventies.

"He loves you so very much, *mia cara*. Now you must decide how you feel about him."

"He—" It was all she managed before her knees let go, she missed the stool, and she sat abruptly on the kitchen floor. "What?"

—⁓—

Kara sat a long time as Nonna's and then her own words sunk in. If that Texan idiot thought he was in love with her…and then she'd said…about it just being sex…

This time "sick" was the obvious choice of reactions, and it was only with iron control that she managed to keep from barfing up right there on the kitchen floor. The bile burned, but she kept it down.

When she made it to her feet, she drank a glass of juice to clear the foul taste.

Nonna gave her a silent hug, offering no words of comfort where they could find no home, and then handed her the bag lunches for Papa and her brothers. Then she waved for Kara to take them upstairs.

They were all leaving for work and school.

"Thanks, Kara." Al Junior took his and went.

"You look terrible, honey." Papa gave her a hug and was gone.

Joe would already be at the store and get his lunch there.

Rudi gave her a hug before taking his lunch. He was almost out the door before she noticed what was over his shoulder.

"Wait."

Rudy ducked down his head and moved faster.

Kara managed to snag a strap and bring Rudi to a stumbling halt. Al Junior took one look over his shoulder and kept moving. The expression on his face said that he was glad to have made good his escape. Papa didn't look back at all, very determinedly didn't.

Rudi didn't turn to face her.

"What are you doing with Justin's duffel?"

He tried to tug free, but she jerked back on the strap. Then he mumbled something.

"What?" She jerked it hard enough to spin Rudi and slam him up against the doorjamb.

"I'm taking it to him. He said he couldn't wait, couldn't stay. He asked, so I packed it and I'm taking it to him."

"Where?"

"C'mon, Kar." He whined out the nickname only he was allowed.

"Where, Rudi?" she shouted in his face. "And, remember, you couldn't get by me when we were kids and I'll put Special Operations up against lawyer training any day. Now—" She forced herself to take a deep breath and slow down. It was barely past eight in the morning and she'd already done so many things wrong today.

"Please, Rude. Where did he go? He doesn't know the city, at least not this part of it."

"Papa told him to go to the Marriott by the Brooklyn Bridge."

"Shit! Why'd he do that? That's like the most expensive place around."

"Why would he care? He's rich."

"No he's…" Kara trailed off. She didn't know that about him. She knew he was great in bed and was one of the best pilots she'd ever seen in any craft. But his family… She knew their names and that they were close. Some worked with horses, sister was Air Force. Not much else.

"Crap, Kara. Don't you know anything about the guy you're shacking up with? Papa did an Internet search, didn't even have to hit a search with his NYPD credentials. High-end horse breeders. Their family helped found the American Quarter Horse Association, which impressed the shit outta Joe though none of the rest of

us knew what it was. But you know Joe and the horses."
Rudi shrugged.

She knew. One of the lines Joe always gave for not
having found himself a girl was that he couldn't afford
betting on the races *and* a girl. He always concluded
by saying that the horses were cheaper and generally
more fun.

"Apparently quarter horses are the biggest category of
races in the U.S., especially in the South and Midwest. If
one wins a race, Joe said there's something like a thirty
percent chance it comes from the Roberts' ranch or one
of their studs. This dude's way high-end, Sis. What did
you do to him?"

"Uh, can I just say it wasn't real nice?"

"Crap, Sis. You gotta fix this. I can see how it's
hurtin' you. You gotta fix this."

"Don't know if I can, Rude." But she lifted Justin's
duffel off Rudi's shoulder and put it on her own.

"You gotta try, Kar." Then he hugged her hard and
headed off to keep the courtrooms of Brooklyn safe.

Kara stepped out into the light morning mist. It was
damp and chilly. She turned back for a coat and the door
closed in her face. Through the beveled glass she could
see enough to know that Nonna had shut the door.

Then the dead bolt clicked into place.

Kara's keys were still hanging on the hook in the
foyer where they always hung—next to her coat on the
other side of the locked door.

Chapter 18

JUSTIN TOOK ONE LOOK AROUND HIS TWENTIETH-floor room of the Marriott with a view out over the Brooklyn Bridge. If he sat in here, he'd go mad. So he went downstairs and bought shorts, a T-shirt, and some decent running shoes because he couldn't wait for his duffel to show up.

He thought about going for a run in the city, but Brooklyn was so damn crowded he didn't know where to begin. The deep Somali desert, Ramon Airbase in Israel, Tripoli—those he understood. New York was like a city gone mad. Vertical. So many people crowded in that he couldn't think. Couldn't breathe.

Finally he went to the hotel's fitness center and hit one of the treadmill machines. It was mid-morning and he owned the place. Everyone else was off to their business meetings or whatever.

He started running fast. At one mile he goosed it and at two he increased the incline and goosed it again. Without a forty- or fifty-pound training pack he could run a half marathon before he felt it.

Some part of him acknowledged that he couldn't do it at this pace, but he couldn't make himself slow down. Didn't matter that the sweat was burning his eyes; he hadn't thought to grab a towel and he wasn't going to stop.

So, he did something he almost never did, especially

not in public. He pulled off his T-shirt, exposing his back, and used it to wipe at his face from time to time.

Justin was nine miles out at a dead run when he hit the wall. It was too much, so he cycled down, first to trot, then jog, then walk. Until finally the machine ground to a halt and he stood there with no more idea of what to do than when he'd started.

He turned around and jolted.

There on a chair behind him rested his duffel bag.

Beside it sat Kara Moretti with her knees pulled up to her chest, her hair down and mostly hiding her face. But he could feel those wide, dark eyes watching him.

His heart ached with the need to go to her, but he couldn't do it. Not after what she'd said. He stepped off the treadmill and sat down on the trailing end, facing her.

They sat in silence a long time before she spoke.

"How was I supposed to know?"

Justin shrugged. He'd simply…known. He'd thought that was enough somehow, dolt that he was.

"You never said you loved me."

He hadn't. Didn't make it any less true.

Again they lapsed into silence. Someone came in, looked at the two of them, then opted for the swimming pool next door. Wise choice.

"I hate that you're mad at me." Her voice broke. Kara's voice never broke.

"C'mon, Kara. You're not the one I'm mad at."

"Then who?" It came out on a choke and a gulp. Her face remained mostly hidden by her hair.

"Duh! Who else is sitting in the room?"

She tipped her head to the side until one red-rimmed eye studied him in the clear. She'd been crying while sitting silently behind him, and the thought almost ruined him.

Then she shook her head, which totally blocked her face.

In frustration she grabbed at her hair and tossed it back over her shoulders.

He waited, feeling the chill of cooling sweat. The T-shirt clenched in his hand was clammy but he wasn't about to fish another one out of the duffel; it was still too close to Kara.

"I don't get it. Why are you mad at yourself?"

Justin scrubbed his hands through his hair, wishing he could reach inside and fix the mess there. "Pretty obvious."

"Not to this girl."

"C'mon, Moretti. Use that amazing, intuitive brain of yours."

"My what?"

"The attack on Turkish OKK. Blowing up your ScanEagle to cover my retreat. Those kinds of tricks don't come from training. They're the reason you fly with the 5D—because you're that damn good."

"I am?"

Justin looked around the room for help, but it was just them and a few dozen fitness machines. "You are," he finally answered. "Though that's off to the side of the current conversation."

"The one about you loving me and being angry at yourself for it?"

All he could do was nod. Why did Kara Moretti knock all of the words out of him? He had no clear answer to that one either.

"You're angry because…" He could see her testing

the idea. "You fell in love and you thought I had gone there with you."

That was only part of it.

"Because…no."

"What?" He needed her to explain, because he certainly couldn't.

"Give me a break, Justin. These are your feelings. Why am I the one trying to explain them?"

He shrugged. "I've just beat myself up for nine miles and I have no idea. I'm hoping that you do. All I know is that I have this overwhelming gut full of anger. When I started, I thought it was at you. By the time I was done, I knew it was at me. I just don't have a fucking clue why."

"Wow! The cowboy swore. In front of a woman no less."

Justin could feel the heat flaming his cheeks, and wiping them with a soggy T-shirt didn't help. He went over to his duffel, dug out a fresh one, and pulled it on. He retreated back to the treadmill and sat down once more facing her. "Sorry."

―∿∿―

Kara was the one who was sorry. Sorry that he covered that beautiful chest of his. Sorry that he was so ashamed of the scars on his back. They made him more human, more believable…and much more complicated than anyone she'd ever slept with.

She had arrived at the fitness center early in his run.

When he hadn't answered his hotel room door, she'd thought about where she'd go if she had a load of anger to work off. Geri's Gelato came to mind first, but she hadn't had a chance to introduce Justin to that particular indulgence yet. Second choice was a workout. Hotel fitness center, easy once she thought about it.

For over half an hour she'd watched his back and thought about how those scars had shaped the man, reshaped his life.

"If your Chinook hadn't been destroyed and your crew killed, would you still be in the Army? Or back on your horse ranch?"

"Well, I think that's another conversation off to the side."

Kara shook her head. She didn't think that it was, though she didn't know why she thought that.

He shrugged in that way of his, signaling his easy acceptance.

There was another trademark of the man. He took life as it came to him, rather than fighting it every step of the way. She wondered what he'd look like when he was truly angry, and was actually a little relieved that she had missed that. It had certainly left an impression on Nonna though.

"I was near the end of my first tour with the 10th of the 10th—10th Combat Aviation Brigade of the 10th Mountain Division—when it blew. I was due to muster out halfway through my rehab. But I couldn't."

"You don't make SOAR just because you're stubborn as one of your mules."

"We don't have mules, but I can think of a few of our horses that make your point. No, I was a different kind of flier after the attack. Discovered that I was just as careful, more so, but all that naive crap about somehow being the one in control was stripped away. You ride a bronc and think you're the one in control, the next thing you know he's putting you into the fence. Same with a Chinook. I learned to work *with* the helo, not merely be some urban cowboy dude flying a machine."

Kara wished she knew how it all tied together, but couldn't find the pieces. There were so many of them.

Justin waited with all the patience in the world. He'd never yelled at her, not even when she slammed his face into the counter. Instead, he'd gathered her up in his powerful arms and sat her down.

"I think your patience is one of your problems."

His smile quirked, but it was a sad one.

"Seriously, if you'd shouted at me, you might have gotten some message through my thick skull."

"What message should I have shouted?"

"That you're crazy in love with me and that I'm going to have to figure out how to deal with that."

Justin sighed. "No. This is my problem to deal with."

"Cowboy!" she shouted at him and clambered to her feet.

He rose to face her.

She strode up and poked him in the center of his chest. "I'm the object of you being crazy in love with someone. I think that makes me pretty involved."

"Yes, ma'am." He snapped her a salute that she instinctively returned. "What are you planning to do about it, ma'am?"

There was a laugh. "Hell if I know, Cowboy."

━━⁕━━

Justin didn't know if he was pleased or disappointed that Kara didn't try to join him in the shower. It was better that she didn't, but he didn't want her any less for all of what was going on.

She had remained exactly where he'd left her, sitting by the twentieth-floor hotel window staring out at the Brooklyn Bridge and the city beyond.

"What do you see?"

She startled and turned toward him, then her smile came to life. "I see something very delectable."

He should have taken fresh clothes into the bathroom with him. When he began to dress, she offered a pout, but turned back to the window before he even shed the towel from around his waist.

"I was just thinking about you being here with me rather than going to see your family. With how close you are, that means something. Means a lot."

"Why are you more impressed that I'm not seeing my family to be with you, than that I'm here to be with you?"

"Family matters."

"And you don't?"

"Cut that out, Justin. You can't keep making me face things I don't want to. I'll go crazy."

"You mean crazier?"

It earned him the scowl he'd been hoping for. Her emotions were right on the surface, and he loved watching them cross over her features.

He picked up the phone. "Have you eaten?"

"You're not ordering room service."

"Why? Their menu looks good."

"So not! You're in Brooklyn, the land of amazing food. Come on, we'll get a bagel and coffee."

"I thought you were Italian."

"I'm from Brooklyn. Sue me."

They didn't hold hands, but he liked how close she stayed as they walked to what she claimed was the best bagel shop this side, or any other, of some place called Ratner's.

She relaxed more and more throughout the morning as she toured him about the city, came more to life as time passed. Maybe there was hope for him yet.

Chapter 19

"This is your idea of outdoors?"

"Yeah. What of it?" Kara watched Justin as he surveyed the Brooklyn Botanic Garden. He'd complained of feeling claustrophobic in the city. Weird thing was they'd been standing on the Brooklyn Heights promenade at that moment, up on the cliff overlooking the East River with Manhattan as a backdrop—one of the best vistas in all of New York.

The Botanic Garden was fifty acres of woods, a tropical hothouse, and a wide selection of planned gardens. There were several places where you couldn't see the surrounding city buildings at all. At the moment they were on a path deep in the bluebell woods. Shade trees of oak, birch, and beech shadowed over an acre of bluebell flowers in riotous bloom. A light vagrant breeze kept them stirred into constant motion.

"Sorry. Other than a couple of camping cabins, we don't have much past the barn on ten thousand acres. And our ranch backs onto the Lake Meredith National Recreation Area. You can ride back into the hill-and-canyon country for a couple days and not see a soul. I'm in mind of a hundred acres or so that are so thick with bluebonnets in the spring that the bumblebees are stumble-drunk on the nectar and can barely fly."

Right. She'd forgotten what Rudi had said about Justin's family being wealthy. It was hard to remember when it was just him sitting there in the shade of his fool cowboy hat.

"How is it you seem so normal?"

"Man, do I have you hornswoggled. You should ask Ma about that when you see her tomorrow."

"Tomorrow?" Kara stumbled to a halt on the path.

"Sure, she's coming to New York."

"Your mother?" She reached for a park bench.

"Yes."

"Coming to New York?" She sat.

"Yep," Justin agreed far too amiably and settled beside her, stretching out his long legs as if there wasn't a thing the matter in the world.

"Tomorrow?" Kara managed to gasp out. The field of bright bluebells now waved back and forth like an ocean until she felt vaguely seasick.

"Seems I might have already said something about that."

Kara glared up at him. "You're enjoying this, aren't you?"

"Can't see why I shouldn't. I was on the phone to her when you put my face into the kitchen counter."

"You were? Sorry 'bout that. I seem to recall that I was upset."

"I may have noticed that myself. You seem less upset now."

"Other than your mother coming."

"Other than that."

Kara let out a scream of frustration that sent the pigeons that had been sidling up to beg for crumbs running for cover. They scowled back at her as they went. And with their deep pigeon brains running at full speed, it was barely five seconds before they were turning back to beg for more crumbs despite her hands being empty.

Justin reached into his jacket pocket and pulled out one of the bagels he had stowed there. He unwrapped it and tossed some bits of bread.

"No! Don't!"

"What? You are filled with a whole lot of commands, Captain Moretti."

She simply waved her hand to indicate the walkway in front of them. Where there had been four pigeons a moment before, there were now forty. More were flapping in from other less-promising tourists.

Justin kept tossing out bits and crumbles until the birds' cooing was so loud she couldn't even think.

"Your mother?" was all she could manage.

"Flying in tomorrow. I'd like you to meet her, if you're over hating me." His easy smile softened any protest she might have construed from his words. "If you still despise me or feel yourself prone to making jokes about our hats, I'll leave it up to you to reconsider."

"I don't hate you. I just—"

"Don't know what to do with me. I know. I think we have trampled that ground sufficiently for the time being."

"Is she flying here to...meet me?"

"How much would it scare you if I said yes?"

She elbowed him sharply in the ribs in answer, causing him to bobble his next set of bread crumbs all over his sneakers. The pigeons descended, pecking for every crumb that might have slipped between shoelaces.

"Hey, guys! Cut that out. It tickles and these are brand-new."

Kara was…dating, she could handle "dating" for a descriptor…a cowboy who talked to pigeons.

"Ma is by pure coincidence flying in to speak at the next New York Quarter Horse Association meeting. She's coming out a day early to see me and, if it doesn't make your brain explode or some equally New York Italian event, would very much like to meet you."

"Did you tell her that…" Kara couldn't say it.

"That I love you? Dang!" He tipped his hat back on his head and looked winded. "Don't think I've said that part before. Whoo-ee but that changes a man's view of the world, saying it aloud. I didn't have to say it in so many words as it was pretty obvious. Still, takes a man's breath clean away. Sorry it just sorta slid out into public like that, but you heard it first from me."

"Actually"—Kara covered her face—"I heard it from Nonna first."

Justin nodded soberly as he tossed the last of his bagel out to the eager flock, now a veritable sea at their feet. "She's a smart woman. I like her a lot."

Kara loved her. But that didn't mean she wasn't going to kill her grandmother for stirring up everything this morning. It was a real problem; Nonna was still sharp as all hell, but now that she'd retired from the shop she'd founded, she had far too much time to meddle.

—∿∿—

Kara and Justin waited on the edge of the parking apron in a corner of the Teterboro Airport—a forty-five-minute taxi ride from Brooklyn. Small planes zipped down the runway every sixty seconds or so. Inbound and outbound, its two runways felt far busier and more alive than LaGuardia or JFK, though both had three times the traffic, all of it monstrous jets.

Kara liked this airport; it felt more personal that all the glass and steel of the big terminals. She and Justin had taken a taxi, walked through a gate, and were standing among the parked and tied-down planes waiting for...oh God, Justin's mom.

Every third or fourth takeoff was a little business jet similar to the one rolling to a stop on the apron in front of her.

The neat Citation M2 jet looked as if it had been branded with a giant hot iron, "RQR." Below that were the words "Roberts Quarter Horse Ranch."

Kara did her best to not cower before the tall, blond woman who climbed off the plane—she had apparently piloted from Texas to New York on her own.

Kara didn't know what she'd expected, but "mothers" in her neighborhood all came in variations on her own. Even the Jews and the Greeks tended toward moderate statures, raised voices, and waistlines that showed visible signs of a passion for food.

Annie Roberts was none of those, which made her even more surprising. She was only a few inches shy of Justin's towering height. Light skinned and slender. The same wheat-blond hair that Kara had so come to appreciate on Justin slid in a wide, wavy cascade over the woman's shoulders. The blouse and slacks weren't "country"—Kara recognized high-end designer elegant when she saw it. And the toes of her cowboy boots were stitched works of art that Kara deeply craved even though she'd never been much of a shoe person.

"Kara, this Annie Roberts. Ma, this is Captain Kara Moretti. She's the Air Mission Command for my company."

"Which means what in English?" Her accent was even thicker than Justin's, but it fit her and her lighter voice well.

"It means," Kara answered for him, "that when he's in the air, he has to do what I say."

"And on the ground?" Annie asked in a way that had Kara grinning despite her nerves.

"That's still a matter of some negotiation, Ms. Roberts."

Annie's laugh was as bright and sunny as her son's as she turned and flicked a finger against Justin's hat brim. "Y'all are in the city now, Son."

Kara cheered and sent a told-you-so smirk to Justin.

"Just trying to keep the natives in line, Ma." He tugged the brim back into place to declare his staunch support for his state.

"Yeah, right." Kara pumped a fist in victory.

"I'm not the only one who can't hide being country." He kicked the toe of his mother's cowboy boot with the toe of his own. Their hug was far less effusive than the typical hug in the Moretti household, but no less sincere for that.

"So." Justin's mother turned to face Kara.

Kara felt suddenly small and dowdy, wearing her favorite worn jeans close beside a gazillion-dollar private jet in front of these two amazing specimens of human genetics.

"Justie has never been one to trip and fall over his tongue about a woman before."

"I believe that may have been my doing."

Annie Roberts did that same silent question-with-her-eyebrows thing that Justin did.

"I was planting his face into a kitchen counter when last he spoke to you." She barely resisted adding a "ma'am." Justin's mom was wholly daunting.

Again the sparkling laugh. "Well, if you can keep Justie in line, you're a better woman than I am, Captain Moretti."

"Kara."

"Annie."

Maybe Kara wouldn't feel *too* self-conscious about how much she liked this woman's son.

Liked sounded as if she was fooling herself, but she wasn't going to think about that at the moment.

----~~~----

Justin wondered how he'd eaten quite so much. The big bowl of minestrone soup would have been enough. But the homemade pizza with all fresh toppings had been stunningly good. And somewhere along the way he'd consumed at least two sides of spaghetti with Nonna's red sauce that she only made for special guests.

"You really should consider my offer, Joe." His mom and Kara's middle brother had been talking horses for much of the meal. "I'm glad to fly you down to look over the operation."

Justin had long since given up any attempt to control the dinner conversation. The Morettis had shifted from being cautious of Annie Roberts to full embrace, faster than a quarter horse could shift his gait. The Morettis also had a talent for all talking simultaneously that left his head spinning.

"I've never worked with horses, Ms. Roberts." Of them all, only Joe had retained the honorific. "Only ever bet on them."

"I know plenty of racers and ranchers who know far less about horses than you do. My older boy, Rafe, could help you fill that gap of experience right quick."

"Ma"—Justin rested his hand on hers—"his family and his job are here."

"Oh, I beg your pardon. Justin was always the thoughtful one. Most of us Robertses simply leap into the middle of the ring without asking no mind or pardon. Still, Joe, you should think about it. My daughter has leave next month…" She trailed off suggestively.

"If she looks anything like you, Annie"—Kara leaned excitedly into the conversation—"he's toast."

Justin gave up and joined the fray. "Spitting image. Rides like a pro too. We all thought she'd go pro rodeo before the Air Force tripped her up by offering a steed she couldn't turn down. She captains an AC-130 Spooky gunship like you can't imagine."

"Total toast!" Kara cheered.

—◇◇◇—

Justin's look across the table stopped Kara cold. If a younger version of Annie Roberts would spell doom for her brother Joe, what did that mean about Justin?

Last night he'd come home with her for dinner, but slept at the hotel. What was even more irritating was that it had gained him respect and support from her own family. She'd complained to Nonna that it felt like everyone was ganging up on her.

Nonna had laughed in that way of hers that always

made things better. "Oh, *mia bambina*. They only try to wish the very best for you. They love you with all their hearts; that is how we Morettis are made."

At least it made her feel better until she was well clear of Nonna's influence and sleeping alone in her own bed. Then it still felt like they were all conspiring against her.

And now the way Justin was looking at her across the table told her that Joe Moretti wasn't the only one who was toast here.

Was that the stage that came between dating…and that other word?

Kara Moretti.

Totally unable to look away from the handsome, blond cowboy with the dazzling blue eyes he'd inherited from the woman close beside him.

Yep. Toast seemed to cover the bases just fine.

Crap!

—∾—

"It was so wonderful to meet you, Kara." They'd taken Annie back out to the airport. It was still predawn, but her first meeting was for breakfast in Syracuse, a four-hour drive most of the way across the state or just a quick half-hour flight in the sporty, little family jet.

Annie was as fresh and lively at six in the morning as she'd been stepping off the plane after a three-hour hop north from Texas. She had a terrifying energy that Kara was rather glad Justin lacked. He was more steady, whereas his mom was part steamroller—beautiful and charming, but at least fifty percent steamroller.

It was clear by watching them prepare the plane for flight that he was also very familiar with the little jet.

Kara had ducked her head inside while they were pre-flighting the exterior. Clearly this was Annie's traveling office, with a wide variety of personal and very feminine touches that Kara would never have thought of. But seeing them, she wished she was the sort of person who would have the means and reason to do so. It wasn't avarice or greed; it was the perfect juxtaposition of woman and businesswoman that she appreciated. She was also amused to spot a fancy tooled-leather western saddle—a real showpiece—hanging on a support clearly made for the purpose and a white straw hat that matched Justin's sitting on the empty copilot's seat.

Once the plane was all ready, Annie led her aside, leaving Justin standing by the steps.

"I really can't believe he didn't sleep with you last night." If Annie Roberts was anything, it was plainspoken. Straight to the point.

Justin and his mother had both stayed at the hotel.

"If you want my advice, don't let him get away with that again. He learned his manners from his father—bless the man. I love him to death, but if it had been left up to him, we'd still be courting. Robertses are not the fastest men in the herd."

"I'll remember that."

Justin wasn't the one dragging his feet; at least not his emotional feet.

"He is quite the gentleman." Kara wasn't sure she'd ever used that word about a man before. "Can't say as I'm real used to that. They aren't what you'd call common in Brooklyn."

"He *is* a good boy." Annie wrapped Kara in a surprising and powerful hug. It felt as if Justin had inherited his hug talent from his mother. Annie Roberts made her feel very safe.

"He is, Annie. Your son does you full honor. You should see how protective he is of his crew."

Annie's grin was as huge as only a proud mother's could be. "You're gonna have to do me a favor, Kara."

"What's that?"

And in that instant Annie Roberts's face completely shifted. The impossible composure was gone and a deeply fearful woman looked at her for a moment. A flash of fear so deep yet so brief that Kara would have doubted seeing it if she hadn't felt its impact.

"What is it, Annie?"

Her smile wavered back to life. "Try to keep my boy alive, Kara Moretti. Please try really hard."

Kara could only nod. She'd seen hints of the expression on her own mother's face every time the family went to work. Being a policeman wasn't generally dangerous, but all it took was one psycho domestic disturbance or one wound-up, drugged-out asshole… It wasn't the amount of danger, but that it was always there. It was why Mama always asked if Kara still worked from her box—Mama didn't call it a "coffin" of course.

"I'll do my damnedest, Annie. Really I will."

Annie mouthed a "Thank you" and suppressed a sniffle.

"I'll try for both of us." Kara hadn't meant to say that; it wound her one loop tighter to Justin.

"Good girl." Annie hugged her. "Now, happy face for the menfolk. Can't be letting on how much we worry." And in a flash the radiant Annie Roberts stood once more before her. But Kara now knew what lay beneath that perfect surface she presented to the world and to her son, and liked the woman all the better for it. They wandered back to Justin arm in arm as if they'd been best friends since forever. "Do you ride? I already know the perfect horse for you."

Kara winced. She never even had a chance to mention that the closest she'd ever been to a horse were the mounted police patrols in Central Park before Annie rushed on.

"She's the sweetest little three-year-old. Y'all come down and we'll go out riding. I'll round up some of the girls, and we'll talk about nothing except men the whole time. Or better yet, we won't talk about them at all just so they don't get swelled heads." Annie poked her son in the chest. "Now I'd best scoot; I am the guest of honor after all." She winked broadly to show how much being front and center didn't bother her or feed her ego.

She embraced Justin, whispered something in his ear, and then clambered aboard. Moments later the jet roared to life and was taxiing toward the main runway.

They watched until she leaped into the sky with a roar that rippled down the field. She waggled her wings, banked west, and was gone in moments.

Kara still couldn't catch her breath from the whirlwind of emotions the woman had left behind. Justin looked equally battered.

"Is she always like that?" They turned back for the parking lot as a turboprop roared aloft with far more noise than the quiet little jet.

"Yes, except when she's even more like that. Once Ma gets an idea in her head, there's no slowing her down."

"What did she say to you?"

Justin looked interested in the fuel truck parked close by the terminal building.

"C'mon, Cowboy. Give."

"She, shall we say, suggested that I should take you back to the hotel and…" He faltered to a stop leaving no question at all about what his mother had said to him.

Kara considered both Annie's instructions to her and her own emotions. Being "toast" didn't sound bad at all.

"I think your mother is a very smart woman."

Chapter 20

JUSTIN ABSOLUTELY AGREED THAT HIS MOTHER WAS A VERY smart woman. And as much as he was tempted to simply drag Kara into the nearest hotel—never mind the ride all the way back to his room in the city—he'd noticed her flinch even if his mother had missed it.

He had a whispered conversation with the cabbie before climbing into the backseat of the car.

"What was that about?"

Justin kept his mouth shut.

"C'mon, Cowboy. I'm not going to ask again, and you know I don't fight fair."

The cabbie snickered and pulled out of the airport and into traffic.

Justin did know that. She'd found a ticklish spot on him that once and had used it on occasion until he hadn't been able to breathe right without wincing in remembered pain for a long while afterward. How was a man supposed to maintain any dignity while curled up the fetal position on the cold, hard steel plating of a Navy warship's deck, trying to protect himself from five-foot-five of naked Italian on a warpath? As far as he'd ever found, Kara Moretti didn't have a single ticklish spot... though she had several that made her purr like a very happy cat lying in the sun.

Which put him in mind that maybe this was a stupid idea and they really should be headed back for the hotel, any hotel. He needed to distract her and fast, or the cabbie would be getting more of a show than Justin was comfortable with. New Yorkers might do it in the back of a cab, but he was more of an open prairie kind of guy.

"So, are you planning on taking Ma up on her offer to go riding? It'll be a hoot. Sis, a couple aunts, and the ranking women of the American Quarter Horse Association; they're a formidable group."

"And way the heck outta my league. I'm from a cop family in Brooklyn, for crying out loud."

"Did you think my mother cares a single whit about that?" That finally seemed to distract Kara.

"Humph," was her only response.

"Trust me, sweetheart. You'd fit right in and they'd love you to death."

"And bury my bones out on the wide prairie."

And there was the image back at him, burying himself in between her legs out where they'd be the only souls in a half-dozen square miles of grassland.

Kara was slouched down in her seat until her knees rested up against an ad for some Broadway show about wicked witches that hung on the back of the front seat. Her arms were folded tight across her chest.

"Ma wouldn't let them bury you. She's already half adopted you."

"Collects stray puppy dogs too, I bet."

"And such a sweet thing you are." He stroked her hair as if petting a pup.

She growled deep in her throat and made as if to snap at him.

The cabbie announced that they were at their destination barely in time to save Justin's hide.

"What the—" Kara ducked low to look out his window at the store's sign. "You gotta be shittin' me, Cowboy."

"Nope! Not for a second. I can't have you goin' to Texas lookin' all citified."

"I'm not going to Texas tomorrow."

"I'm offering to buy, sweetheart. It will be a treat to buy you your first pair of cowboy boots, to corrupt your New York soul with proper footwear. You're not gonna be turning me down now, are ya?" To preempt further argument, he clambered out of the taxi, gave the cabbie a couple twenties to wait, and led Kara inside the shop.

——

The smell was the first thing that hit Kara. The shop door swung open, and the smell of fine leather as thick as the scents of Mama's red sauce wrapped around her. It was so rich that she didn't know whether to breathe deeply or try to cough it out.

Justin stopped at the threshold and took it in deep. His chest expanded, then he let out a long sigh of contentment. "Add in a couple horses and some straw, and that's the smell of home come to life."

Rows and rows of cowboy boots lined the walls. Short ones, tall ones, simple and ornate. A girl came up to them looking all blond and outdoorsy in jeans, a form-hugging tank top, and a well-worn pair of shit kickers.

"Hi there, folks!" At least it wasn't *Howdy*, but the *Hi* was somewhere between a *Ha* and a *Hey*—and certainly had no place within a thousand miles of Paramus, New Jersey. "How y'all doin'?"

"Jes' fine," Justin drawled in reply. "I need to get this

lady into some proper footwear. Hoping you can help me with that."

"You betcha!" If the girl thought Kara was one bit charmed by her batting eyelids and sassy hand-on-hip pose, she was grossly mistaken.

But Justin was acting as if she was merely being friendly. For some reason Texas-friendly didn't look all that different from New York come-on, but Kara was learning to trust that even if the salesgirl didn't know the difference, Justin did.

It was a classic Paramus strip mall kind of place. The walls could be covered with discount shoes, kitchen supplies, or pet food, and it would be the same store—except it wasn't. She'd never seen so much leather in one place since she'd watched *West Side Story* as a kid.

Six shelves high of cowboy boots lined the walls. They weren't just brown and black. There were blues and reds. There were smooth ones and textured ones. Big ones, little ones…it felt as if she'd gotten lost in an adventure of Dr. Seuss does the O.K. Corral.

There were so many different types that they all started to blur together. If it had been a normal shoe store, she'd have been able to sort it all out: sneakers, slippers, high heels, flats, boots—though none like these. Here she had no way to discern one from the next as they ranged shoulder to shoulder, or rather ankle to ankle, down the walls.

"Oh, I know that look, darlin'," the girl cooed at her.

Kara considered planting a fist to prove that she wasn't anyone's *darlin'*, especially not this girl's, but she refrained.

If the girl knew the prior look, she'd certainly missed the latest one that threatened her perky little nose.

"I can jes' see that this is gonna be your first Western boot. What I suggest is don't be thinkin' too much. I'm gonna let y'all just wander about for a few minutes and kinda get your bearings. Don't focus on what's different; just watch for what catches your eye. If a girl knows a fine pair of heels at a glance…"

Kara wouldn't know a fine pair of heels from a hole in the wall.

"…a real woman knows a fine boot. Y'all jes go wander and give a hoot if ya' got any questions." She waved them off with a flap of her hands and then went to see to another customer who had wandered unsuspecting into the store's honey-trap door. "Hey there, y'all."

"Is she for real?" Kara looked up at Justin.

"Kansas, over to the Missouri side." Justin had kept her hand in his and now led her deeper into the fields of leather. "Sounds almost as good as home when I'm this far afield. Her advice is good; let's just wander."

As they browsed, Kara noticed that one boot or another caught her eye. A few were pretty enough to pick up, but she already had something in her mind's eye, and none of them were up to that standard.

"I don't see anything here as nice as your mother's boots."

"Won't either," Justin acknowledged. "Those are custom, handmade Lee Miller's. The guy is so good, he doesn't want any new clients. He won't even take on a friend of a client."

"Or a son?" Justin's boots were good, but they were nothing like his mother's.

"Well, he might." Justin looked down at his own footwear. "But these are just everyday boots, not for going-about-fancy like Ma's."

"If I'm going to get cowboy boots—did I really just say that?—they're going to be going-about-fancy ones for dang sure, Cowboy. And, remember, you said you were buying."

"Fancy ones for my Kara it is."

She wasn't so sure about the *my Kara* part of that remark. She didn't belong to any man, even if she'd just broken bread with his mother and was now wandering about a boot shop holding his hand. She took some comfort from the fact that they were still in New Jersey.

He turned her and led her to a central display that she'd missed earlier.

When her eyes focused, she could only gasp.

—⁓—

"Pretty!"

At Kara's totally girly coo, Justin knew he'd hit a home run. He'd never heard her bubble like that over anything. That cowboy boots had done the trick for his Army gal shouldn't be a surprise, but it was.

However, there was no question about the woman's taste. "Lucchese Classic hand-tooled, they're about the best boots made short of a custom."

"Don't care. They're pretty." She reached out to stroke a hand over the fine leather. He was pleased when she bypassed the exotics like lizard, snake, and croco-dile; he'd never been a fan of such. She'd toyed with a buffalo-hide boot stitched in a floral pattern, but that too was soon bypassed.

He half expected her to go for a high, all-black urban boot. Or short, sassy ankle boots—though he'd have tried to talk her out of those. But that wasn't his Kara.

His Kara.

He couldn't believe he'd said that aloud. What loco idea had ever made him think that he could possess such a woman? He could have "owned" any number of tall, blond airheads going right back to Francine Freeman, the high school cheerleader. He could have found himself a biddable wife a hundred times over. Even Mariko Hosokawa would have been a fine companion and a gentle lover.

Kara was elemental. She made her own path—and beware any fool that crossed it. She was the one who'd ride right straight into the fray beside Martha "Calamity Jane" Cannary with a six-gun on her hip and a lever-action Winchester rifle in her saddle scabbard.

And he was taking his life into his hands by calling her *his*, as if a man could in any fashion own such a woman. Not that possession was ever his goal, but he wanted her beside him like he'd never imagined he'd want anything in his life.

"These." Kara held aloft a pair. "I gotta have these." She wrapped her arms around them and hugged them to her chest.

They were neither pure black nor wildly ornate. The base boot was soft black leather. The hand tooling was on the toe, heel, and cuff in a mahogany brown, partly floral and partly soft geometric. Beautiful, intricate work.

"Let's see how they look on you, sweetheart."

The girl rematerialized with the perfect timing that spoke of long retail experience. "Oh, I just love these.

Someday I'll own a pair of them." She kept bubbling as she helped Kara find the right size and slip on a pair.

"I thought they'd be all stiff or something."

"Oh no!" The girl sounded horrified. "Not a Lucchese. They're like bedroom slippers to rule the world with."

"I like that." Kara seemed very pleased by the allusion.

Justin would just bet she did. Kara saw herself as a quiet, patient sort used to working alone in her quiet coffin. She was also a highly skilled RPA pilot, as good an Air Mission Commander as he had yet to fly with, and a lover who demanded the utmost from both herself and him.

Then she stood up in the Lucchese boots and stomped the floor a couple of times to settle them in place. She didn't walk up the store aisle—she strutted. The two inches of boot heel did some really splendid reshaping of her calves and behind. Her long hair flounced off her shoulders as she walked around the shop until she found a mirror.

"Jesus, Mary, and Joseph! Justin, these are awesome!" Kara called across the room, startling several of the others in the shop. "How did I not know about these?" She ran back across the shop and threw herself at him.

He almost took out the salesgirl and the entire Lucchese display behind him before he regained his balance. She wrapped her legs around his waist, hooked her chosen boots behind him, and kissed him hard. He lost himself in the kiss, hard with pressure, soft with lips, and rich with power. It staggered him to the core, that blast of joy bigger than the fire from a five-inch deck gun. He allowed himself to fall into it for a long moment, to just revel in the taste and feel of the woman clutching on to him.

When he finally released her, it was like a part of him tore away. Probably a chunk of his heart.

One thing for damn sure, if there'd been any doubt about how much he loved this woman, that was long gone.

"Now where?" Kara was practically bouncing on the cab seat. "I've got to take you somewhere special for getting me these boots." She kept reaching down to brush her hands over them, not sure if she'd ever owned anything so beautiful.

"I had somewhere in mind." Justin did one of those way-too-pleased-with-himself guy grins.

The cab was already in motion.

She tried to focus on the gift, not the scale of it. Justin hadn't blinked for a moment as he handed over his credit card. All of Kara's wardrobe put together cost less than these boots. She'd never have even picked them up if she'd seen the price. Who paid over two thousand dollars for a pair of boots without batting an eye?

Someone like Justin Roberts. And she had the feeling that if he'd been broke, he'd have hocked a month's Army pay to get her these boots. With him, the money wasn't the object. The gift was.

So she curled up against him in the back of the cab and let him lead where he would. Tucked inside his arm was one of the best places she'd ever been.

Time flowed strangely there, as if she'd dozed, though she knew she hadn't. As if she'd been dazed by a blow to the head…or to the heart. Justin kept filling her thoughts in a way that neither Carlo nor any other man ever had.

Carlo.

She hadn't thought of him, asked after him despite Mama's prompting, or even checked if he was in town.

It was odd.

Whenever she was on leave and he was in New York, they always got together. Pizza and too much beer was a tradition that went way back. Massive amounts of flirting, though no action except for the occasional steamy, drunken good-night kiss.

And she hadn't even thought of him.

She thought of Justin though and floated timeless in his embrace…until the cab pulled off the highway.

First they were on something named Valley Road. Then Mountain Park Road plunged them out of suburbia into dense trees as if Scotty had beamed them out of New Jersey. The next sign said Weaseldrift Road.

"Where in the hell, Cowboy? What part of the planet are we on."

"Don't rightly know," he drawled at her. Then he pointed to a small sign set into a stone pillar where the cab was turning in: Garret Mountain Equestrian Center. "But it's the right sorta place."

"Equestrian? Horses? Hell no, Cowboy."

"They aren't real cowboy boots if you haven't ridden in them."

"But I don't want to muss them up."

"They aren't just for show, Kara. Like the salesgirl said, they're for using. A couple scuffs gives them character, makes them something a real person wears, not some barhopping, line-dancing cowboy." He made little quote signs around the last word.

Hadn't she thought that's what he was at first? Showed how much she knew. His boots were well used and his hat worn proudly. The goddamn man radiated who he was—unadulterated Texas male.

"You trying to reshape me in your image?"

At least he had the decency to look surprised and then confused.

"Cowboy boots. Now riding lessons. Next thing you know, it will be a hat like yours—and you can just forget all about any such stupidity."

"Yes, ma'am," he replied with deadpan seriousness. "It would look darned cute on you though."

She sent a sharp jab into his ribs, but he'd anticipated her and her fingers bounced off hard muscle.

—m—

The horse looked at her—looked down at her—and Kara wasn't the least bit pleased about the whole idea. Justin had done his sweet-talk thing, and they now had the only two Western saddle-trained horses in the whole place. Her horse, Ivory, was mostly white with gray spots on her rump, dark legs, and a dark mane.

"Dapple gray," Justin had informed her.

Her head was about the size of Kara's torso. And the beast just knew that she had beautiful, dark eyelashes and wide, warm hazel-brown eyes.

"You probably have a stone-cold heart, are known for bucking rookies into blackberry bushes, and will try to bite my ass when I'm not looking."

"Aww, don't hurt her feelings." Justin brushed his

hand over the horse's nose. "She a total sweetheart; you can see it in her. And on a horse it's a greenhorn, not a rookie." Then he waggled a warning finger at the horse. "But if you do any messing with Kara's behind, I'm gonna get jealous. That's my turf."

The horse looked at him blandly.

"You know how a dog likes to be rubbed behind the ears?"

"Sure." Could she reach Ivory's ears?

"Horses like this." He reached out and scrubbed Ivory's cheeks hard with his fingertips. The horse leaned into it like a giant puppy. "You try."

Kara was surprised at how coarse the fur or hair or whatever was. But again, the massive head leaned into it with as much unconscious strength as Justin had. Kara hadn't even thought about throwing herself at Justin in the store; she simply had, knowing she'd be caught.

Where was the cautious Kara she knew so well who gave herself to no man? Had sex with, sure. But around Justin she simply gave without thought, not a familiar place to go.

"Horses are suckers for treats." He pulled out a pocketknife and an apple, splitting it into quarters. "Make your palm flat, fingertips together and straight, and keep your thumb tucked safe to the side." He dropped a quarter apple on her palm and guided it forward. "She won't bite you on purpose, but she can't exactly look down at what she's eating."

Ivory snapped it out of her hand with a muzzle just as soft as her cheek had been coarse and crunched happily. Justin gave Kara another piece, checking her hand position.

Then he moved over to feed his horse, an imposing red—more a brown than a red, but Justin insisted on the designation and she wasn't about to argue with a cowboy. If Ivory was big, Red was ginormous.

"Sixteen hands high if he's an inch," Justin had said admiringly when they'd first brought out the horse, as if that meant something. He looked noble and lively, and even with her new boots, Kara couldn't see over his back because he was so tall.

"Time to saddle up, sweetheart." Justin showed her how to hold the reins and the pommel. "Always climb aboard from the left side. Way to remember it is which side you would wear a sword on."

"How should I know. I'm not a lousy jarhead Marine." Though she'd dated one for a while and he'd let her wear his sword once. It was easy to imagine it on her left side.

"You don't want your sword interfering with how you mount. So left foot in the left stirrup, grab the horn and the cantle, push off with the right, and up you go. Don't kick Ivory's behind as you swing your leg over or she's likely to try running off with you."

Before Kara could protest that she wasn't ready, Justin's strong hands wrapped about her waist and let her float up into position. He made a few adjustments to the saddle before shifting over to his own horse.

It was as if she could see the whole world from up here. She looked down at Justin's hat, which was a new perspective on him. Though the ground looked pretty far away seeing as she was sitting atop a very large animal. As Ivory shifted her stance to accommodate Kara's weight, the saddle seemed to shift and ripple beneath her. Kara resisted the urge to grab on to the horn with both hands; cowboys never did that in the movies, but lame girls always did. She wasn't a lame girl and kept her hands calm, one holding both reins, the other resting on her thigh—ready to grab the horn if need be.

She admired how effortless Justin made it look to mount. This was clearly as natural to him as riding the subway was to her. He stepped his horse sideways until their knees brushed and he leaned in to kiss her.

"Kara Moretti astride a horse wearing Lucchese boots. Who would have thought you could get even more beautiful than you already are."

Kara was not going to swoon at a compliment. She was far too nervous to swoon. But her nervous system considered it.

One look at Justin astride the tall red and the concept of swooning took on a whole new meaning. It was as if she'd never seen him clearly before. This was where he belonged—in the saddle, out in nature on a sun-dappled morning, ready to ride off among the oak and maple.

Then he led them forward and all thoughts of anything beyond survival were swept away.

—⁓—

Justin had helped train hundreds at the Roberts Quarter Horse Ranch. The young ones generally did better because they weren't set in their ways yet. Most adults were stiff, awkward, thought they were driving a car, or just couldn't relax in the saddle which always made a horse twitchy.

But every now and then an adult student simply had the intuitive feel for what was right. What happened then was always a wonder to watch. With a confident hand, a horse behaved, which increased the new rider's confidence in a feedback loop.

Perhaps it was all those hours Kara spent dodging through harsh air currents, perhaps it was just in her nature, but Justin never had a student go so easily from walk to trot to cantering down a trail. Ivory had a smooth-footed pace, but that wasn't even half of it. Kara simply let herself ride. She looked so natural that he was half tempted to try a gallop, but decided not to push her on her first time astride a horse.

As in so many things, Kara was a natural. With her hair banner-flown behind her, she moved with the saddle as easily as she moved in his arms.

And with an equal impact on his libido.

They'd only hired the horses for an hour because more than that would be cruel to a new rider's legs. And that was a good thing. If he didn't get her alone in short order, he was going to be one deeply frustrated cowboy.

———•~~•———

Justin wasn't more than two steps into the hotel room when he was attacked by a short, Italian whirlwind who smelled of heaven and tasted of pure sin. Keeping his hands off Kara Moretti for three days in a row had been torture and he never wanted to do it again.

She pinned him against the window with a twenty-story drop just a thin sheet of glass away. But she'd been very strategic in her attack. His T-shirt was gone and his jeans were around his ankles, held there by his cowboy boots. She was fully dressed, and he was naked and couldn't even walk.

But his hands were free and he didn't resist the entice-ment to run them up her still fully clothed body as she slid down his unclothed one. Womanly hips, a waist that he tried to trap because it felt so wonderful against his palms, but still she continued down. Generous breasts filled his palms but still she slid down until all he could manage was to dig his hands into her hair.

That's how she took him. Pressed against the glass with his back and butt exposed to lower Manhattan, his hands lost in a tangle of hair so thick that they could get lost there and decide to never leave, and his heart completely gone into the morning sky.

His pent-up need for her exploded from him as she hummed happily, sending vibrations racing up his ner-vous system.

When his knees finally let go, he slid down to the carpet, taking her with him. He managed to free his hands from the luxurious fall of brunette and gold, but all he could manage was to shift her so that he could lie with his ear resting on the center of her chest.

Her happy hum continued as she wound a leg and her arms around him. They lay unmoving long enough for the sunlight streaming in the window to warm them.

"Justin?" His name blended with the quick double beat of her heart through her soft blouse.

"What does it feel like?"

He opened his mouth and then closed it. How could he describe what it felt like to have her teeth lightly scrape him, the soft, moist heat of...

No. She wasn't asking about the sex.

He opened his mouth a second time, with little better luck because now he knew exactly what she was asking.

Kara had gone still with waiting for his answer. Wanting to know.

"I think of you all the time."

"I do that too. Give me more."

He went to prop himself up on his elbows.

But she'd wrapped her arms around his head upon her breast and kept him anchored there.

"When I make love to you, or you make love to me…" He broke off when he felt her hesitation. "Because trust me, girl, what you just did wasn't merely sex."

"No. It was toast."

"What?"

"Doesn't matter. What does it feel like?"

She still didn't say the word. This time he forced his head up to look down at her.

Her dark eyes were wide, tracking back and forth across the ceiling as if searching for an answer that she couldn't find. Finally her gaze settled on his face.

"It feels like flying. When you're riding the curve of a storm or a battle and you know you've got it licked. No way it can buck you off. You've got it so clean because you're in that perfect flow and synchronicity no matter how wild the ride. I've watched you fly, Kara. It doesn't matter if you do it from a chair or in the sky; you know exactly what I mean."

Her expression shifted again, every emotion clear. Uncertainty, doubt, then fear. That was one expression he'd never expected to see on her face.

"What are you afraid of, Kara Moretti?"

She rolled her head back and forth against the carpet. "I don't know." It was barely a whisper. Then her eyes focused on him once more. "But I do know one thing."

"What's that?"

Kara didn't answer, but instead closed her eyes and pressed up where his one hand had come to rest on her hip.

He began tracing over her clothes, under her clothes, working her body with his free hand and his mouth until she lay naked and shuddering on his other arm. He had replaced the boots after helping her shed her pants; it was a wonderful combination—soft leather and soft woman.

"What one thing do you know, Kara?" He stopped, held her on the edge of a cascade reaction that he could never tire of evoking from her limitless responses to his attention.

"Kara?" He nibbled an ear.

She forced her eyes open, though it clearly took effort to come back from the place he had her teetering.

"What one thing do you know?" he prompted her again.

She rested a hand on his cheek even as she shuddered with the effort. "I may be the AMC." Her breath came shorter and shorter. "But on the ground, I'm going to do my best to follow your lead. I'm afraid of several things, Cowboy. But you aren't one of them."

Justin brushed his lips over hers in a sweet kiss as he slipped into her and offered her the release her whole being was begging for.

Chapter 21

IT WAS ALMOST DINNERTIME BEFORE JUSTIN CHECKED out of the hotel and they headed back toward the Moretti home.

Kara was sore in a dozen places, every one of them wonderful. Justin had a cat-ate-the-canary grin that shone brighter than the Manhattan skyline on Christmas Eve.

They walked hand in hand, and she ignored the grumble of the early commuters today just as she had three days before.

"Three days." She spoke in surprise.

"I was just thinking that myself."

"How come shit happens so fast?" She didn't even recognize herself. Holding hands with a cowboy—while wearing totally awesome cowboy boots—and totally happy to be doing it. Far past the *toast* stage and headed well into four-letter land.

"I suppose that we're simply two right fortunate folk."

She squeezed his hand in agreement and did her best to erase her smile when some street punk sneered at her expression. Kara gave it up as a lost cause and left the goofy smile in place even though it was making her cheeks hurt.

"There is one other thing it feels like, Kara."

"What's that?" Oh, being in love. Rather, him being in love with her. *Being in love*—that still only applied to him, right?

He stopped her in the middle of the sidewalk, ignored the surge of commuters as only a Special Operations cowboy pilot could, and kissed her. Kissed her until her toes curled inside the soft Lucchese leather. Until she wanted to drag him down on the sidewalk and to hell with the street punk's sneer and the crowds threatening to trample them.

Justin released the kiss, but not his one-armed hold that held her so tightly against him.

"It feels like a kiss?"

"What? No. I did that simply because I wanted to."

Kara could feel the goofy smile go right over the top.

He started them walking again before he continued. "Being in love feels like you'd rather die than ever have the feeling stop."

Kara caught her boot heel and stumbled on a crack in the sidewalk, might have fallen if not for their interlaced fingers. Though when she glanced back she couldn't see the break.

If that was being in love, then she was way past "toast" and right on over into "totally screwed."

Justin's phone rang as they approached the Morettis' front door. By chance, Al Junior and Senior, along with black sheep Rudi, were approaching from the other direction at close to the same moment.

Justin pulled out the phone but didn't recognize the number.

"Roberts."

He heard a sound that had always reminded him of a chicken the moment its neck was wrung. He tapped in the current encryption code to unscramble the signal and tried again. "Roberts."

Kara hadn't missed what was happening and moved in closer to listen. It was against protocol, but he leaned down and tipped the phone out so that she could hear.

"Your present location, Brooklyn, New York." The operator's all-business tone didn't make it a question. "Report Fort Belvoir, Virginia, Pence Gate at precisely 2315 hours tonight. You will be directed from there. A rental car will be reserved and waiting for you six blocks due east of your current position. GPS locator on Captain Kara Moretti's cell says that you are in probable contact. Is this correct?"

"Yes."

"She is also required. This is a secure message. Need-to-know only. Acknowledge."

"Acknowledged."

And the line went dead.

He barely had time to exchange a glance with Kara before her father and brothers reached them.

"So, you come to stay with us now?" Rudi addressed him, but didn't wait for an answer before turning to tease his sister. "You gonna make him stay in the guest room again?"

His father smacked Rudi on the back of the head, which only made him grin.

"I was hoping to stay. However, that is no longer possible." He held up the phone still clutched in his hand before tucking it away. "I apologize, but I'm afraid that I've been called back to service and have to leave immediately."

Mr. Moretti looked genuinely disappointed. He

reached out and took Justin's hand, but offered no bone crusher this time, instead a single firm shake.

"We will miss you. You are welcome back for as long as my daughter will allow it."

"Thank you, sir. You're most kind. And I regret that Kara is also called back. We just need to pick up her belongings."

"Hey, that's not right. Sis was supposed to be here a whole week, not three days." Rudi sounded genuinely upset.

"Get a grip, Rudi." Kara punched her brother's arm, hard. "It's not his doing. I'm the one who got a new job title last month; I'm important now. And I can still beat the shit out of you." Then she kissed him on each cheek before turning to face Justin. "Give me two minutes."

—⁂—

Kara scrambled up the two flights to her room and began jamming the stuff she'd scattered all over the room into her duffel. She looked longingly at the comfortable single bed. She'd hoped to have Justin in here with her tonight.

It wasn't about making love here, for she could no longer deny that's what they were doing. It was about holding and being held. Almost as if at twenty-seven, taking Justin into her childhood bed would be when she finally became a woman.

She paused at the window as she picked up a bra and a blouse that had landed there rather than going into the wash as they should have. No time now.

Down on the street below, the groups had shifted. Mama and Joe were home from the shop. Marta arrived from a rehearsal in a short yellow dress that offset her flash of red hair. It was a regular Moretti convention down there on the sidewalk. They had all gathered and were obviously waiting for her and Justin's departure. But he and Papa stood off to the side, apparently having a serious conversation.

"They're talking about you, *bambina*." Nonna had arrived at Kara's elbow without making a sound. Kara slid her arm around her grandmother's waist.

"You'll have to tell me how you sneak up like that someday, Nonna."

"When you need to know, dear, you'll know how. So why should I waste good teaching on you now?"

"I have a grandmother with stealth technology in her bones. Be careful the government doesn't label you top secret. What do you think they're saying?"

Nonna pulled Kara close and kissed her cheek. "You don't have to reach my age to figure out that one, Kara."

"'I'm aware'"—Kara tried to lower her voice like Justin's—"'that we haven't known each other long. And while Kara and I are not yet ready, I hope that someday I may have your permission to ask for…'" Kara sighed.

"You always were smart…when you let yourself think about it."

"I'm going to have to kill him, Nonna. It's the only solution."

"Either that or say 'Yes' when he asks you his question."

Kara finished packing, shouldered her duffel, and kissed Nonna good-bye.

Killing him sounded easier.

Chapter 22

THEY WERE IN A LATE-MODEL TOYOTA HIGHLANDER, and Kara had slept most of the drive down from Brooklyn to Fort Belvoir outside of DC. She looked so cozy in the tipped-back front seat that Justin had wanted to curl up with her. But that wasn't an option, so instead he'd driven and thought about her.

He thought a great deal about his conversation with Kara's father.

As soon as Kara had disappeared inside, Mr. Moretti had tipped his head and led Justin a little way down the sidewalk.

"You strike me as a smart young man. You also strike me as a man of integrity, a view also held by your mother. I value what a mother says about her son, especially when she is talking of other things and I can listen to the words between the words."

"It's easy to see why your daughter is an Air Mission Commander. She's like a detective; she can see what matters." Justin paused. "It appears I just used her abilities to compliment myself, but I really meant the compliment for your daughter."

Mr. Moretti nodded his understanding. "My daughter, she's smart enough inside her head. But her heart, it's an idiot."

Justin tried to protest, but her father's sigh spoke of a long history of observations.

"Her heart is a good one, but it's… How would you say it?"

"Like a young colt who hasn't yet learned that hay is for eating and runs about the corral tossing it in the air like a toy. But—"

"No. No." Alfonso Senior stopped him with that half laugh of his. "Do not apologize. You describe my Kara's heart perfectly."

Justin felt disloyal, but her father seemed so pleased that he bit his tongue.

"She is discovering that her heart has another use. Be patient. She'll find her way to you."

Justin wondered quite how many strange conversations he was going to have about Kara today.

At the beginning of the trip south from Brooklyn, she'd prodded him about his conversation with her father.

He'd like to know why she'd looked so pleased by his refusal to answer. But then to ask his own question about what his mother had said to Kara this morning… He took the tactful route of silence and she finally slept.

He woke her twenty minutes before their appointed arrival time. Now, they were parked ten blocks from the Pence gate and waiting for the dashboard clock to creep to 2310.

"Any idea what's at Fort Belvoir?" Kara voice was still thick with sleep.

"The only thing I know about it is that Fort Belvoir is the center for nearly all Army Intelligence operations."

"No shi—Oh shit!" Kara began muttering more curses under her breath.

"What?"

"Major Willard Wilson. If it's that asshole who has

interrupted my leave and taken me away from my family, I'm gonna cut him a new orifice, and it won't be anywhere comfortable."

"Or..." Justin had a sudden thought and couldn't decide which option he liked less. He started the engine and drove the last ten blocks, then pulled into the narrow lane that was barely labeled "Pence Gate, Fort Belvoir" at precisely 11:15 at night.

"Or?" Kara asked as they eased up to the guard station.

"The Activity would certainly be a part of Army Intelligence. Perhaps the guys we rescued in the Negev Desert are based here as well."

They glanced at each other and then looked back toward the gate. During their moment of inattention, Colonel Michael Gibson of Delta Force had materialized in the road before them where he was now lit brightly by the Toyota's headlights.

"Oh shit." Their voices sounded in unison.

Justin would have laughed if he could have, but his throat had gone completely dry.

―⁓―

"Get out of the vehicle." Michael moved up to the window of the SUV. "Take anything that's yours. The guard will turn the car in at Dulles International Airport."

Kara hadn't unpacked so much as a cough drop, so she stepped to the back and shouldered her duffel.

Justin came up beside her and pulled out his own.

"You forgetting something, *Justin*?" It felt odd to say his name. She hadn't realized how little she used it. But it only seemed fair to give him a clue.

He looked down at her with that puzzled frown of his

and then jolted as if she'd pinched his butt. He hustled to the back passenger door and pulled out his hat.

"You're makin' me forget who I am, sweetheart." He pulled it on and tugged it into place by the brim.

"Need your hat on if I'm gonna get your name right, Cowboy. Now, we're on Army soil. Time to clean up your act."

"Yes, ma'am, little lady."

"Sheesh. Texans! Really sad."

"Now don't you be insulting Ma and how she went and raised—"

"Will you two cut it out?" Michael had come up beside them. "Are your belongings now out of the vehicle?"

Justin handed him the keys, which Michael pitched over to a waiting guard. In seconds, the Toyota was gone and Michael led them forward and guided them into a small but very substantial-looking guard shack.

In moments every single one of their electronic devices had been unearthed—from their cell phones to her e-reader to Justin's electric razor. Each underwent intense scrutiny. Which puzzled her for a moment until she recalled this was U.S. Army Intelligence's main base.

Between the Army's nineteen agencies and the Department of Defense's twenty-six—and those were only the ones that were listed, which did not include the Activity—this was probably the most paranoid eight square miles on the planet. The people who worked here would also be the ones with the most knowledge about what was going on in the world, which meant their paranoia was heavily fact-based.

She glanced up at Justin as he waited patiently for the guards to finish inspecting his gear. *Let's get out of here*, she wanted to say to him. *Let's get as far away as humanly possible. Let's get on your horses—God help her—and disappear into your massive Texas ranch to where no one can find us. We'll live off the land. Off grid all the way to where they can never find us.*

Justin must have felt her attention because he turned and offered her an encouraging smile.

Some help that was.

She huffed out her impatience and wondered if Fort Belvoir had a special *paranoia pheromone* that was released into the air to make everyone who came near— okay, she had to laugh—paranoid.

The guards apparently dubbed her electric toothbrush nonlethal and released them into the wilds of the fort.

Michael led them out of the shack and across a patch of neatly trimmed lawn and the parking lot.

Kara guessed that no explanations were forthcoming while they were still out in "public." She searched for a neutral topic to break the silence and to distract her own nerves.

"So, where did you and the wife go for your leave? Did you get any leave?" Best she had at the moment.

"We managed to go fishing for two days in Montana with some friends, Mark and Emily." Michael continued moving smartly along. He was so smooth that she found herself staring. If she blinked, he just might disappear into the shadows never to be seen again.

Michael and Claudia were with their friends Mark and Emily...? The founders of the 5D, Mark Henderson and Emily Beale! Two of the most celebrated names in SOAR. And Michael and his wife had gone fishing with them?

Kara had rarely felt so young and out of place.

She didn't actually fly…like they did.

She didn't risk anything…like they did. Like Justin did.

She'd been part of the 5D only a few months. And she, of all people, was the one they'd called to Fort Belvoir? Were they frickin' nuts?

Kara wasn't used to this desire to run away. It didn't sound like her. Usually she was the one champing at the bit—another goddamn cowboy metaphor to plague her ass. She'd always wanted the next level, but this time she was fairly sure that she wouldn't like it when she found it.

That she wanted to run away with a cowboy sounded even less like her. However, that she wanted to do it with Justin…that was…truth. *Crap!*

"You better be worth it, Cowboy."

Justin grinned at her. "Yes, ma'am."

Well, she certainly hadn't meant to say that aloud.

The low brick building had a nondescript entrance of glass and aluminum doors that reminded Justin of an insurance office. Inside, they slammed into a much more serious security wall than at the Pence Gate.

"Empty your pockets into your duffel. You will be given a chit. Any items other than standard clothing will not be allowed."

Justin emptied his pockets, though Kara had to grumble about it first. When they pointed to his hat, Kara was the one who reacted.

"It *is* part of his standard clothing." She spoke up

fast. "You take that from him, and it's like pulling the bung on a keg; all his Texas starts leaking out. I know you don't want to have a bunch of Texas dripping all over you."

Justin was amused. He glanced at a wall clock, still a few minutes to midnight. Hadn't they just spent most of this afternoon getting all over each other? Made him smile to think how much they'd both enjoyed that.

"It's all right," he managed and reached for it.

"Nope, Cowboy. You take that off and I'm not going in with you."

He tried to puzzle out why Kara was suddenly making such a big deal about his hat or was she just sassing him? He couldn't tell. But if she wanted him to keep it, he'd keep it.

He tugged it back into place and turned to the two men operating the inspection station. It was now their problem.

Rather than cutting up stiff, they looked to Colonel Gibson who had been waiting patiently beside them. As far as Justin could tell, Michael didn't shift his stance or so much as blink, which was apparently enough to spook the two guards. It certainly was enough to unnerve Justin.

Michael's studied non-reaction left it entirely up to you to imprint what he might be thinking on that dead-pan visage. And with a Delta Force colonel, the imagination of consequences was never a good place to go.

The guards waved Justin through an enclosed metal detector booth. When he stopped inside, it hit him with a blast of air that he knew would be swept up and sniffed by an explosives detector.

Apparently none of the three of them were in any way

objectionable. They were allowed to proceed through another set of doors that had a heavy bolt released by an armed guard inside.

Justin remembered his first trip into the 160th SOAR's compound on the back lot of Fort Campbell. He'd been as impressed as any greenhorn by the layers of security, a huge step up from the 10th Mountain. Now he wondered at how lax they'd been. He'd arrived there with a full draw of gear, lacking only a rifle and sidearm which he'd turned in to the armorer when he left the 10th Mountain. The Night Stalkers hadn't checked anything beyond his orders matching their orders, and that his ID and thumbprint really were him. Here he was grateful not to be left strolling down the hall in his briefs.

Michael led them down a corridor.

"Hey, no security cameras." Kara's voice echoed down the wide concrete passage.

Justin looked along the ceiling and then back behind them. Nothing.

Michael simply waited for his question.

"Oh"—Justin figured it out first—"if there was ever a group that would know—"

"—that a security feed could be hijacked," Kara cut him off, "it would be—"

"—these folks." He finally managed to get in the last word before she could say *The Activity*. He couldn't let Kara go through life without a dose of her own interruption medicine.

They stopped at a door that had no keypad, doorknob, or other means of entry. Michael didn't knock; he simply stood and waited.

The door slid aside.

Justin had expected a small office. A couple of guys hunched over a conference table or an electronic map. The standard bastion of military mission planning.

Instead, it was a large room, noisy with conversations. There must have been twenty people tucked into cubicles, all open toward a central table.

It felt more like Justin had always imagined those software places to be. Instead of drab gray, there were bright colors. The prints on the walls were mostly of jets launching off carriers, tanks splashing through rivers and the like, but they weren't military slogans and protocols of the day.

The air smelled of coffee, sugar, and popcorn. There was an energy here that buzzed and hummed and made him feel more awake despite the long and busy hours since taking his mother to the airport that morning.

"This room is fully secure." Michael finally spoke for the first time since taking their car keys, his voice raised to be heard above the overlapping conversations going on around them.

He indicated the circle of desks.

"The Ring, as they call themselves, are specialists from two dozen security agencies, including the British SAS. This room is about sharing, not compartmentalizing information. There isn't a person in here without top secret clearance. There are no sensitive compartmented information structures in this room."

"Whoa there." Justin stopped and grabbed Kara's arm to keep her in place.

Again Michael stopped and waited for him to ask the question, though Justin could see he already knew what it was.

"Are we even cleared to be in this room? To fly where we do, we both have top secret clearance, but what if someone starts talking about a special access program we aren't authorized to—" He didn't bother finishing.

"That is why your arrival was so precisely timed. This room goes through a full security scrub every night at midnight. For the next two hours, the only files that will be opened or mentioned are those you are cleared for."

Kara was damned glad that Justin was there close beside her. She'd thought this would be a grand adventure: their entry into the inner sanctum.

Now she felt as if she were on the teetering edge of some rediscovered old subway excavation that had mystically opened in the middle of a New York sidewalk, and if she fell into the hole, no one would ever see her again. She'd just disappear beneath the city streets with no one the wiser.

She'd thought to shake off Justin's tightening grip on her arm; now she hoped he never let go.

Michael led them, stumbling like automatons, into the center of The Ring—it definitely deserved the capitals. Twenty sets of eyes turned to look at them, blue ones with glasses, browns in soft faces, greens in hard faces. She felt as if she were riding a Coney Island Tilt-A-Whirl until she spotted a familiar face coming from beyond the circle of curiosity about what alien slime mold had just landed in their midst. Were they about to call the Ghostbusters?

The recognizable face gave her a focus. At first a

relief and then, once she identified its owner, a place to aim a chunk of the craziness that had built up inside her.

"Major Willy Wilson." She almost said, *Did you lose another team?* but recalled Justin standing beside her and managed to clamp down on her tongue before the thought slipped out that way. Instead she singled to right field with, "What does Willy need the 160th SOAR to fetch for him this time?"

Tact. Kara Moretti practicing tact!

Justin was a very bad influence.

"From you, Brooklyn, I—" Wilson stopped with fists on hips as if ready to go to battle. Then he glanced aside as Michael loomed beside her, somehow growing taller and fiercer without moving an inch. "Ah…we can discuss that later."

At least his recovery was far lamer than hers. In comparison she hadn't hit a home run, but it was at least a double.

A man who had an entirely different manner stepped forward from close beside Wilson. There was a calmness about him that was a lot like…Justin's.

He and Justin were shaking hands like they'd known each other forever. The dude practically broke out in song.

"Didn't see your face behind your visor and mask last time, Captain Roberts. Just wanted to say thanks again for getting me and mine out. Hell of a piece of flying, brother." Oh, The Activity guy Justin had rescued.

"I want to thank you for being as good a driver as you are," Justin tossed back as if they were playing backyard catch. "We're most of the way to making that pickup a repeatable event without coming quite so close to bucking us all to the ground. Name is Justin."

"Blind luck, I assure you. Next time I'll crash you for sure."

"Looking forward to it, Tom."

"If it gets any more macho in here," Kara observed sotto voce to Michael, "I'm gonna have to scythe these dudes back down to size. What do you think? They past harvest time already—gone from male to stale?"

Michael didn't answer of course, but it did cut through all the glad-handing that was going on.

"So, anyone care to tell us why the hell I'm here when I'm supposed to be on leave?"

The big guy that Justin had addressed as Tom nodded approval. "Lady gets down to it. Good call, Michael." He waved them to chairs around the central table.

Kara took her time turning the chair, sitting in it, and turning back. It allowed her to scan the whole room.

Most of The Ring returned to their work, but a couple kept their attention on the conversation. Kara guessed that they were the most likely elements to be involved, though no sign or signal identified one from another.

It also allowed her time to assess the fact that she was Michael's selection to be here. There were a lot of obvious reasons, such as being the AMC and RPA pilot on the mission. She wondered what the less obvious ones were.

Once she turned to the table, *Tom*—not a chance that was his real name—nodded to her. "We extracted evidence that there is a Hamas terrorist cell embedded inside Ramon Airbase—four members, all on the inside. We can't tell the Israeli Defense Force or the U.S. Air Force, as they'd want to know how we know. Telling Mossad would have the same issue."

"Tell them anyway. We'd be doing them a favor."

Tom nodded again. "We considered that. But the fact that Hamas managed to place a cell inside the air base itself implies that there is a mole higher up—so four on the base and one outside who managed to get them in place. That's why we were inside. The U.S. isn't the only one with sleeper agents embedded throughout its country. The evidence we gathered uncovered a route to the mole that is being pursued by separate forces."

A look went around the table. There wasn't time to read all of their expressions, but Michael, Justin, and Tom obviously agreed on the proper fate of such individuals. Wilson's brief look was harder to interpret. Maybe he wanted the terrorists for questioning and *then* dismemberment.

"So, you have terrorist Palestinian extremists camped out on a remote and key Israeli air base and we're going in to extract them?"

The silence around the table was deafening.

She watched as Justin swallowed hard.

"What?"

"I just realized…" Justin wasn't speaking to her. He was talking to Michael. "I've never seen handcuffs on a Delta's combat gear. I'm thinking that Delta wasn't exactly formed to make arrests."

Kara felt her own throat go dry. Deltas were said to be the best shooters in the world. Shooters, not policemen.

"Sometimes we carry cuffs. Not often," Michael said softly. "Not this time."

Justin was glad he'd retained his hat after all. By slouching and tipping his head down, he could stare at the table and hide that all the blood had drained out of his face a quarter of an hour ago, and that none of it had decided to come back yet.

A month ago he hadn't believed in The Activity any more than he'd believed in the Wizard of Oz. Or that he'd already met the only woman for him.

Now he was supposed to believe that they'd mapped out a complete mission to insert a strike team, eradicate the terrorist cell, and disappear with no one the wiser.

He was hoping that Kara was one of the ones who was "no wiser" about the nature of the mission.

The Activity had two specialties, SIGINT and HUMINT.

Signal Intelligence was handled by the knob-turners of The Activity. The ones who could track cell phones by 1990. The ones who now ran the unblinking eye over war zones that allowed them to see a car bombing and then run combined RPA and satellite video *backwards* through a day or more to identify the bomber's point of origin.

Justin had flown some of those missions, being instructed second by second as the intelligence rolled backward in time and the attack he delivered from his cargo bay rolled forward.

Human Intelligence was guys like Tom going in on the ground and interacting with people. None of Justin's crew had been allowed near the Humvee that they'd extracted from Ramon Airbase. What, or maybe who, had been in the shadowed interior of that vehicle?

There was the question he didn't want Kara even thinking about, let alone asking.

Fooling yourself, boy, if you think she doesn't see it also. Nothing slips past Kara's guard.

Well, nothing except for himself. Somehow he'd slid past her defenses. He still didn't know how to make sense of the last few days. It was as if he'd been a different person, lost in a city, practically drunk on his joy of being around Kara.

Had he gone home for leave, he'd have ridden, maybe done some teaching with the kids, and not given a thought to any of his actions. Instead he was wrapped up in New York City and the Morettis, and totally lost out on the wide prairie that was Kara.

Kara.

To her the last days had probably made perfect sense. To her this meeting—

Justin jerked upright.

"Wait a sec," he cut in on the ongoing logistics discussion. Three or four of The Activity analysts had now rolled their chairs up to the table. They were in a heated discussion on best methods to circumvent perimeter security, which would certainly have been heightened due to last month's raid.

Michael looked at him though the others kept talking. "Hey!"

"Is for horses," Kara responded, finally coming out of whatever tactical haze she'd descended into.

"Does it make sense?"

Tom started to speak but Justin waved him to silence.

"Think, Kara. Something's wrong here. The Activity not willing to communicate with Mossad about a possible mole. How much you want to bet that one of these desks normally has an Israeli intelligence agent sitting at it? Maybe it does even now." He looked around The Ring. "Any of you Mossad?"

A half-dozen analysts popped their heads up to look at him through narrowed eyes.

"Never mind, you wouldn't tell me if you were."

But he'd seen where Wilson's gaze had drifted, to one man who studiously kept his head behind his monitor. One of the analysts who had been paying close attention throughout the meeting without coming forward.

"You." Justin pointed. "If you wouldn't mind joining us, we'd like to know quite what's happening that we aren't being told."

The man shrugged and rolled his chair over. His attempts to make it look casual were wholly ineffective. He was really wound up about this for some reason.

"Hi. I'm Yussel." But it didn't come out as casually as the words intended.

"For today," Kara muttered.

"Actually, that is my real name. I do use it on occasion."

Justin would feel better if there was even on lick of a smile on the man's face. There wasn't.

"They've been giving it to you straight up," Yussel insisted. Which told Justin something else about what was happening. There was some "next-level bullshit going on," as Kara would say.

"These guys are all taking themselves too seriously." Justin kept his conversation aimed at Kara. "The horse and rider that win the rodeo are the ones who ride easy in the saddle, but these guys are acting like high-strung East Coast jockeys. No offense, guys."

Major Wilson looked pissed; Tom looked thoughtful. Several of the analysts were about to tell Justin he was completely wrong, which would only prove him right. The Yussel guy looked ready to come across the table at him to defend how serious he was about his country's security.

Michael had frozen in stillness as if scenting a change in the wind and not yet knowing what to make of it. So he wasn't in on it either, but he obviously agreed with Justin now that he'd pointed out the problem.

Kara was nodding. "They're more on edge than a Mafia capo with heartburn and an FBI tail. Giving me another reason to like you, Cowboy."

———————

Kara kicked Justin in a friendly fashion under the table. Usually his smile or his body dazzled her, but this time it was his brain. He'd picked up on exactly what was wrong with this whole meeting and then had the guts to lay it straight out on the table.

Now that he'd pointed it out, she'd felt the tension building throughout the briefing.

Now she and Justin had shifted into a perfect sync of their own. Like when he flew and she felt she was right inside his head. Like when they made love in such perfect synchronicity.

"They made a mistake, didn't they?" she asked him, wanting to rub their noses in it.

"I reckon they did." Justin laid on the Texas drawl as thick as barbecue sauce.

"What?" Willy Wilson snapped out. She loved that Justin could just crawl under that creep's skin.

"Y'all"—she gave it a deliberate Brooklyn nasal twang—"focused on distracting little ol' me because I'm the 5D's Air Mission Commander. You forgot there's a reason the cowboy is in the room and it's not only because he's pretty. He's also one of the best helo pilots there is, anywhere. That means he ain't some down-home cracker; instead he's sharp as hell."

"But he is so very pretty." A tall blond walked into The Ring from somewhere out of their range of sight. She had one of those figures that was impossible to ignore and her tight T-shirt and form-hugging slacks did everything to display it. Her English was accented and as lush as her curves. There was an obvious strength to her, a soldier's strength. Her straight hair swung along her jaw as she sashayed over to the table.

The Yussel guy clearly was as puzzled as Kara was by the woman's identity.

Justin's stare had been riveted in place before she'd even crossed half the distance to the table.

Kara kicked him again, not so friendly this time.

He jolted—she'd forgotten she was still wearing her new boots—glanced at Kara, and then shook his head as if trying to shake off a case of hypnosis.

Kara wasn't prepared for the deep surge of jealousy that shot through her. Did she really care that much about where Justin's attention drifted? So he was looking at another woman who was astonishing and deserved a second look. That she was blond, beautiful, and much closer to Justin's height didn't help; they would look amazing together. But that didn't make the taste in Kara's mouth one bit less bitter. *Since when did Kara Moretti get all possessive over a man? Never…until now.*

The woman settled into a vacant chair as if she were the queen ruling the room—a queen wholly aware of the raw sexual impact she wielded with every gesture.

Out of the corner of her eye, Kara could see Michael

exchanging nods with the woman. It was a nod of deep respect in both directions. Major message there. The only person who would impress the top operator in all of Delta Force would be...

Kara glanced at Justin who had also noticed the silent exchange.

He nodded his agreement with Kara's assessment.

She wasn't sure if it was okay to say the word aloud, then she considered that they were sitting inside a planning room for The Activity, perhaps *the* main planning room. Not many more secure places anywhere.

"James Logan," Justin said, making Kara snort with laughter. He grinned at her and she felt the warmth there. It made her less ticked off by how he'd stared at the blond.

"Oh God, that's perfect, Cowboy."

Everyone else around the table looked mystified. She'd learned that Michael was a very linear thinker without much of a sense of humor that she'd ever seen. The woman, Kara could see, was almost there. Was it a cultural gap that kept her from seeing the joke, or wasn't she sharp enough? Easy to find out.

Because Kara still felt so out of her depth and wound up, she decided to compensate by tipping her chair back and propping the heels of her pretty new boots on the table before speaking.

"James Logan? A particularly lethal and contrary comic book hero."

Still the blank looks all around. Wasn't a soul at the table other than Justin who was up on their comic lore.

"James Logan," Kara repeated once more, then sighed. "Also known as the Wolverine from the X-Men."

The woman burst out laughing. It was a bright merry sound and left Kara feeling far more kindly disposed toward her.

Tom grunted and Michael's brow finally cleared as he caught up with the analogy.

"Wolverine," Justin explained for those around the table who were still lost. "In the last few months I've met the women of SOAR's 5th Battalion, D Company"—he tipped his hat to Kara—"Delta Force operators, and The Activity. I figure that the Wolverine must be showing up next, now that I've met a Kidon operator."

Yussel flinched and his eyes shot wide. Tom began nodding as if now things were making sense. Major Wilson simply looked confused, as if he had no idea what they were talking about.

The woman's smile was radiant as she addressed Michael but kept her focus on Kara. "You were right, Colonel Gibson. They both managed that with so few clues. It is very good."

"Anyone care to give me a goddamn clue?" Wilson snarled.

"Willy Nilly"—several people around the table chuckled at Kara's nickname for him—"I'm shocked that you haven't heard rumors of Mossad's elite counterterrorism squad. They put the CIA's Special Activities Division to shame for both effectiveness and secrecy. Of course, I never believed the rumors of their existence; they were even sparser than The Activity's. But it was the only piece that fits the puzzle this woman presents."

"Tanya," the woman acknowledged without confirming or denying her membership in Israel's Kidon kill squad.

Kara nodded her head. They were in a world of

first names only. She felt exposed that she, Justin, and Michael were clearly so well known. Since there wasn't squat she could do about that now, she shrugged it off.

"Okay, Tanya. Spill it." Then Kara remained tipped back in her chair to listen.

"How completely do you trust your people?"

Kara considered Tanya's question. "Varies according to their abilities and my experience with them in general. The personnel of the 5D, immensely. The cowboy"—she hooked a thumb at Justin—"I'd trust him with my life."

Which startled both of them.

Kara's boots slipped off the edge of the table and thunked to the floor, making everyone jump. *That couldn't have just come out of her mouth!*

Kara only trusted family. Cops' kids learned that one early.

Don't trust outsiders, ever.

Growing up she'd seen too much trouble between even cops and their partners. And though in her neighborhood her parents were typical in still being married, in her military life any marriage that lasted five years beneath the grinding wheel of military deployments was considered a major success. Ten was almost as mythical as Wolverine himself. Outside of the 5D, she didn't know of all that many military marriages that survived even two years.

Trust was for the person who had your back during the firefight...except she'd never been in a firefight.

She'd heard military teams trusted each other with their lives. Kara supposed they had to. Yet another way she didn't fit in. She'd always been safe, outside the action team. She trusted their actions, but it was never her life on the line.

So how was it that the 5D trusted *her?* How did she become their AMC? It made no sense. The arrogance that she displayed in thinking she could—

"Easy there, Brooklyn." Justin's voice was a soft whisper and stopped her crazy spiral.

What if—

"Let me get this straight." Justin leaned into the conversation to give her a moment.

He really did have her back, even against her own internal craziness. It was a heady feeling. The possibility of a touchstone in her life. Justin was as rock solid as they came, and somehow it was her that he was there for. She listened to his voice, trusted it to guide her, and let it lead her back into the conversation.

"How many missions fail due to leaked information?" Justin looked at Michael.

His grim expression spoke volumes. "Fewer than fail due to poor intelligence. Which is the purpose behind this group." Michael addressed the last remark to Tanya.

"We do suffer a higher percentage of security failures because Israel is so young and so much less secure," Tanya acknowledged. "On occasion we need assistance with…security issues to remove them."

"But in this case…" Justin prompted.

"But in this case"—Tanya sighed—"the problem may be on our air base, however, it is not actually 'ours.'"

"The American Camp." Kara knew she was right as soon as she said it. She'd just found the next-level problem.

Tanya tipped her head toward Tom who nodded.

"Shit!" Justin's curse sounded in the suddenly silent room.

"The *mole*"—Tanya's tone bore anger as deep as any Kara had ever heard—"the Americans insist, will be Washington's problem. Not because we cannot find him, but because they don't want anyone else knowing about their dirty laundry. So he must be your FBI's to resolve. Our job is to clean up the mess in Israel with no one the smarter—not your people, not my people."

"Captain Moretti." Michael Gibson's voice was soft, pacifying. "I promised Tanya our very best assets to resolve this matter with absolute discretion."

Kara couldn't react. All she could do was stare at the Delta Force Colonel. What the hell was he whistling out his ass? She'd been SOAR mission-qualified for only a handful of months. She'd been the AMC for a handful of weeks.

Granted she was in the 5D, but she was supposed to... Shit! She was...

"We're going for a walk." A deep voice cut through the ringing in her ears. "Come along, Kara. Walk and talk." Justin coaxed her to her feet and she stumbled after him, letting him lead wherever he wanted.

—∿∿—

As they stepped back out of the building and into the darkness, Justin was thankful for the fresh air, but Kara was still in shock. Justin had thought she was good, but he hadn't known she was that damn good. Apparently neither had she, which he rather liked about her.

Feet planted on the ground, that was Kara Moretti.

He led her across the mostly empty parking lot and

into the trees, maple and oak. They smelled so different from home.

Home.

He suddenly ached for it. It was May. The plains would be carpeted in a hundred varieties of yellow wildflowers. Amarillo was called the "Yellow Rose of Texas" for a reason. Butterfly bush and Russian sage would be scenting the night air. The strong southerly winds carrying the warmth of the Gulf Coast northward and the wettest season of the year coaxing the land to bloom with soft rains or rolling thunderheads. Back home the winters were dry and cold, the summers warm and wet. Give him a nightjar call or a screech owl hoot and he'd feel right at home even at one in the morning.

He wanted to show Kara the grasslands and the canyon country. He wanted…so much.

But now was not a time for dreaming. Not of home, not of the woman beside him.

He found a white oak with a heavy, low branch reaching sideways only a few feet above the ground.

Justin lifted Kara up until she was seated on the rough bark and then scooted up beside her. He took her hand. She returned the handclasp as if it was the most natural gesture in the world, not the constant miracle he felt it to be.

"She's pretty," were the first words Kara managed.

"Who?" Not what he'd been expecting at all. "Oh." Why was Kara thinking about Tanya the Kidon agent?

"Good thing I'm not the jealous sort."

"Good thing." Justin could feel himself smiling. "Sweetheart, if you think there's another woman on this planet that I want to be seeing naked more than you, you're even more addle-headed than your average Yankee."

She leaned in and kissed his shoulder. "You're all right for a Texan."

"I take it that's Yankee for you're madly in love with me. I can work with that."

He'd been ready for the punch on the arm that Kara delivered with an impressive force despite the fact that she was laughing.

"Damn, but you're tenacious, Cowboy."

"Inherited it from Ma." Which made him feel homesick all over again even though he was farther south than Annie was at the moment, what with her still being up in Syracuse, New York.

"Stubborn." Her laugh still died off too fast for Kara Moretti.

"Guilty," he admitted, wondering how to help her. "Of course, if there was a second woman that I wanted to see naked…"

"She's all show." But there wasn't any heat behind it.

And he'd wager that the one thing that the Israeli agent wasn't was all show.

"Too bad she isn't what's bothering you."

"Yeah, too bad." Kara sighed. "Shit, Justin. I've taken out plenty of bad guys before, but American bad guys? I never had to think about the possibility. What's a girl supposed to do with that?"

Justin hadn't come at it quite that way. Bad guys. *Take 'em down* was as far as his thinking ever carried him.

It hadn't been Hamas that had killed his crew, but it might as well have been. If he could, with a single stroke, stamp down on every single extremist group and grind them out of existence with his boot heel, he wouldn't be asking if it was right.

The ones who flocked to al-Qaeda, Hamas, or a Ku Klux Klan lynch mob were all the same to him. Not the most compassionate view.

Kara's heart was bigger than that.

"You're a hard woman to live up to, Kara Moretti."

"I… What? Why on earth would you say that?"

Justin looked up at the canopy of oak leaves. So dense, only the occasional star shone through. If not for the thin crescent of the waning moon, it would be as dark as a cave here in the Virginia woods. Then the rage came from so deep and at such a full gallop that it just snapped out of him.

"I don't get how you extend your heart to people you've never met despite what they've done. I care about *you*, Kara. I care about my family and my crew. I like your family and what folks I've come to know on the *Peleliu*. But someone who's out there killing folk because they can? Or because they believe different than other folks do? Any pity I had for them went south the day my crew's lives were burned into my back. Don't ever give me the codes on the Bomb; I'll launch it right up their asses."

Justin clamped his teeth down on his tongue to try to stop his anger from spilling out even more. *Breathe slow*, the post-action counselor had told him…after he'd finally woken up in Walter Reed Hospital, ten thousand miles from his dead crew.

If the counselor guy were here now, Justin would use his fist to let him know just what Justin thought of that particular advice. He took a deep breath and did try to let it out slowly. Maybe it even helped…maybe.

Kara kept her silence, used her free hand to start playing with his fingers where they were interlaced with hers. It helped him calm down and focus more than any goddamn breathing routine.

"I remember saying once that you should have just gone and gotten mad at me, Justin." She tugged at his index finger, then his thumb. "Must say, I'm rethinking that idea."

Justin tried a dutiful laugh, but not much came out.

"You keep that down deep. World doesn't get to see you mad much."

"That's 'cause I'm a deep guy."

"Deep as shit, Cowboy; I've stepped in it and can't seem to climb back out."

Before he could take that wrong, she lifted their joined hands and rubbed the back of his hand against her cheek.

"You're most of the way to convincing me I don't want to climb out either. Next thing I know, you'll have me all snugged down in that pig wallow of happiness of yours. Because no matter what it feels like on the inside, you're pretty incredible from the outside, Cowboy."

Justin was half tempted to say exactly what it felt like on the inside but then decided he'd be far better off keeping his trap shut.

"I'm not deep. I just want to be damn clear about what I'm doing before I go and do it." Kara kept his hand between hers and her cheek. "I'm just a girl from Brooklyn, Justin. They want an AMC who can go the distance and not get the team killed along the way. That so ain't me."

Justin laughed. He couldn't help himself.

"What?"

"That is *so* you, Kara. You have no idea, sweetheart, but that is so you."

"How—"

"You're the goddamnedest mama bear I've ever met, maybe even more than the queen mama bear that gave birth to this boy. You'd kill yourself to protect your family. And you've got fences a mile high as you choose who you'll let in."

"I don't have fences." Kara's protest was emphatic as she tried to drop his hand, but he didn't let go.

"Damn, sweetheart. That's bad news."

"Why?"

Justin wished he could see her face, but the night's shadows were too dense. "Because, Kara, my only hope of winning your love is that I simply haven't climbed over those high barriers of yours. If you don't have fences, then it means that I'm simply not good enough. Don't particularly like the sound of that."

Kara jumped back down to the forest floor and tugged at their joined hands to make him drop off the branch and stand in front of her. Then she slid in against his chest so that he could nuzzle the top of her hair.

"Oh, you're plenty good enough, Cowboy. You cleared those heights long ago. Which is what's scaring the crap out of me."

For lack of any better answer, Justin kissed her, kissed her with his whole heart.

She kissed him back just the same, with her heart wide open.

"Ready to go get 'em, Mama Bear?"

"Ready, sweetheart," she answered with her terrible Texas accent that came out sounding more like a female Humphrey Bogart.

It was good enough for him.

Chapter 23

JUSTIN DIDN'T ENVY THE RIDE THEY WERE HAVING IN the back of his Chinook or the Little Bird gunship that Claudia was flying close behind him. They had discussed a dozen scenarios to insert the action team, and the one they'd chosen wasn't a smooth ride.

A jump from a high-altitude aircraft was out of the question. Israel had one of the most advanced radar missile-detection systems ever built. It was used to spot incoming Scuds from Jordan or Egypt, or mortars from the West Bank. A plane entering Israeli airspace at any jump-capable altitude would certainly be spotted and fired upon.

Ramon Airbase was eighty kilometers from the nearest international waters so a HAHO jump was also out. By jumping from a high altitude and opening a flying chute right away, a team could travel forty kilometers and be very difficult to detect. But eighty was out of the question.

With water out of the picture, the only other HAHO jump option was to come in over the Sinai Peninsula, deliberately pop up until they showed on everyone's radar, and release the jumpers to fly the twenty kilometers across one of the most carefully watched borders in the Middle East to Ramon Airbase. Egypt was not what Justin would call a friendly country for launching a U.S. mission against America's closest ally in the region.

Fast and low was the answer. Fast and low in a hundred feet of helicopter meant a very rough ride for those in back.

That wasn't Justin's problem. His problem was getting them there in one piece. For reasons he couldn't explain, this flight was far more nerve-racking than his first foray in and out of the Negev Desert. Of course last time he hadn't had a chance to think about the flight beforehand. It had been an emergency exfiltration.

This was a preplanned mission, and it was white knuckle the whole way in from the coast. This time he'd had almost forty-eight hours to worry as assets were selected and recalled from leave, then traveled to the *Peleliu* for the detailed planning sessions.

"Danny, we need a flying song."

"*I'm leavin' on a hee-lo.*" His copilot started them off rather than complaining. It meant he was as tightly wound as Justin was, not a good sign. Not a bad voice either.

"*Didn't know that we'd be back here again.*" Carmen picked up the tune.

A surprise bass came over the intercom from Raymond at the rear ramp. "*Oh man, I really got to go.*" Like he was looking for the bathroom.

"Piss off the ramp," Carmen said quickly to not interrupt the song and got some laughs.

"*All our guns are packed, they gave us the go.*" Justin kicked off the verse.

"*I'm seeing hard rock right outside our door,*" Talbot observed from his position at portside minigun.

"*I really hate to think we're all gonna die…*" Danny's morose tone drew laughter, and the song continued pinging around the *Calamity Jane*.

As it did, Justin could feel his nerves and those of his crew easing down and finding the groove. His crew's state of mind really shouldn't matter to him. He'd sworn it wouldn't.

Good luck with that, Justin.

When he'd first come back to flying from the hospital, he'd sworn he'd never get so close to a crew again. Never again risk having so much to lose. But this crew had grown on him until once again it was impossible to imagine flying with anyone else. If anything, he was in even deeper than he'd been with Mariko, Rom, and the other members of his first crew.

Like Kara Moretti. He was in so deep—they both were—that it was past imagining. Right at this moment, as he slewed around the edge of another wind-carved tower of stone, he finally understood her fear. How had he been supposed to see that the problem was she cared too much about him, rather than not enough?

He waited until the *Jane* was low in a canyon and their signals could only be intercepted by something directly overhead, like Kara's Gray Eagle *Tosca*.

Justin flipped his mic out of the helicopter's intercom circuit for a moment as he twisted through a hard ninety-degree turn in the dry streambed.

———

"Hey, sweetheart."

Kara jolted in her chair inside her coffin. She'd been so absorbed in monitoring the flight and the ongoing silence of the Israeli defense perimeter that Justin's voice was a visceral shock.

She had both *Tosca* and the small ScanEagle

replacement bird aloft as well as two helos in flight, all of which kept her plenty busy.

The tactical display showed that Justin was down in a canyon, so it would be safe for him to transmit. But she was pushing the high ceiling of *Tosca* and any signal she sent from that big Gray Eagle would have a broad spread. She could listen, but outside of an emergency, she wouldn't transmit—and the bastard would know that.

"Just figured out some things," he continued.

Always thinking, aren't you? And he was; the man was always puzzling at his world until it felt all neat and orderly. Kara was more likely to beat it into submission until it fit her plan. She could hear the grunt that the g-force slammed out of his diaphragm as she watched him slalom through another hard turn on her display.

"Reckon I think too much." As if he'd heard her unspoken comment. "Finally understand I'm not the only one crazy in love. Wanted to let you know. I'm not the sharpest one in the herd, but I get there. Looking forward to it, sweetheart." He released his mic.

He'd called in the middle of a mission flight to tell her that? To tell her that she was *crazy in love* with him? He was *such* an idiot.

Of course she was—

She tried desperately to make that into a *wasn't* but it didn't come out that way.

Of course she *was*? Crazy in love with a cowboy currently deep inside a country that would blow his ass out of the sky if they spotted him and ask questions later?

Kara really needed her head examined. Or her

heart, because it was being pretty stupid about this whole situation.

"Two minutes to target." Tago drew her focus back in. He glanced over from his own armchair and offered a smile that was encouraging rather than angry. She liked Tago's protectiveness of her, but she—Oh crap, she was going to say it or at least think it!—loved Cowboy Roberts.

Damn him! And he'd left her with no reasonable way to respond.

She double-checked Ramon Airbase's alert status. It had remained quiet during last night's overflight to inspect the base for security changes. It was equally quiet and normal for the three hours she'd already had *Tosca* on station tonight.

Well, time for that to end.

What did you boys and girls learn in the month since we were last here?

Both SOAR helos were in position.

Claudia Jean Gibson was hovering the stealth attack Little Bird *Maven II* to the north of the air base, masked by a single convolution of the land.

And roaring up the wadis from the southwest were Justin and his crew in the *Calamity Jane*. Two birds was a minimum flight for mission safety reasons. They also needed both birds for this to work, as well as for the extraction plan to stand a chance.

No need to send a signal. One of the trademarks of the 160th was they could place themselves anywhere within plus or minus thirty seconds of plan. It didn't matter if it was a thousand kilometers into bad-boy land or meeting an aerial tanker during a Red Flag aerial combat exercise over the Nevada desert—at plus or minus thirty seconds they'd be there.

The 5D's goal was plus or minus ten seconds. *We'll damn well beat that tonight!*

We! Kara surprised herself. It was "We." That much had become clear during the planning aboard the *Peleliu* as she worked scenarios and built the mission team. She might be sitting back in her safe and secure GCS coffin, but the only one who thought less of her for it was her own self.

Dumb, chick! Real dumb. Get with the effing program.

Captain Kara Moretti was in the 5D. And the 5D rocked.

Sure enough, at exactly thirty seconds to the witching hour, on schedule to the second, Michael's wife, Claudia Jean, kicked an illumination flare up and over the ridge that masked her from the base. Then she laid down the hammer and was scooting west, deeper into the hills.

The base took fifteen seconds to wake up instead of the nearly sixty it had taken them during *Calamity Jane*'s first visit. Also, instead of coming alive in sections, the whole base snapped to at once.

Perimeter and runway lights flashed on together, dimmed a moment at the unexpectedly heavy load, and then brightened once more as the electrical grid stabilized.

Moments later, lights kicked on in two of the hardened hangars where they'd be warming up a pair of fighter jets as fast as they could. If they were on warm alert, the planes could be airborne in as little as three minutes, more likely six.

Humvees tumbled into action at various points around the base, but they were all inside the perimeter fence and Claudia's flare had been high up on the hill, well away from any perimeter gate. Ground forces weren't a threat, and hopefully *Maven*'s stealth setup and rapidly changed position would mask Claudia from the jet fighters.

All attention shifted to the airfield itself along the northern edge of the compound.

———∿∿∿———

Justin rolled down out of the southern hills close beside the Israeli residential area of Ramon Airbase.

"Ten seconds," he announced over the intercom.

A small area of salt pan and sand lay inside the perimeter fence but had been left rough. It was either for training exercises or the Israelis were serious fans of motocross.

It had several advantages for clandestine entry.

A small fold of land hid the exercise ground from the closer structures if Justin stayed low enough. He was nineteen feet from wheel to top of rear rotor. The fold of land would mask him as long as his wheels stayed within three feet of the barbed wire topping the perimeter fence.

Advantage two: the sandpit was at the far corner of the base from the airfield, meaning very little attention would be on this area at the moment.

And finally, the training ground was rough enough for their inserted team to disappear in moments even if his helo was spotted.

At five seconds, Raymond had the rear ramp open.

At three, Justin hopped the *Calamity Jane* over the perimeter fence with his wheels a foot above the wire.

At one, he was moving at fifty kilometers per hour and his rear ramp was inches off the sand.

"Rolling," Carmen called.

At zero, he could feel the weight shift as the Humvee they'd stolen last month rolled out the back of the helo, off the ramp, and hit the dirt.

At contact plus five seconds, the Humvee was on the sand going one way, and after less than a hundred meters inside the fence line, Justin had the *Calamity Jane* back over the razor wire and racing once more into the southern hills.

If the Humvee was spotted, it would look exactly as if it belonged—after all, it actually did. There wouldn't be any problems as long as no one looked too closely at the soldiers inside.

It was driven by Tom from The Activity exactly as it had been when it left the air base. He knew the airfield like no other and was there to positively identify the targets. Colonel Michael Gibson and Lieutenant Bill Bruce, Michael's right hand, rode as shooters, as did Tanya of Mossad's Kidon. The four of them were now out of Justin's hands until their mission was complete.

The *Calamity Jane* was at least two minutes ahead of the Israeli alert fighters—that's if they kept engines idling and cockpits manned. Hopefully it would take them a full five minutes with cold engines and pilots in a ready room.

Justin needed the five minutes.

He cut south and then, against what they'd expect, he turned east away from the protecting hills.

"You better be right, girlie," he muttered to himself. Kara had insisted the fighters would be scouring the hills, never expecting an invading force to move deeper into the Israeli desert and expose itself on the flats of the Central Negev.

He kept as low as he dared, might have even spun his wheels a time or two on a bush. Eight kilometers east across the central basin lay the ruins of an ancient city, Avdat. It was a leftover from the old Incense Route that had moved valuable spices across the barren desert for over five hundred years in the times of the Greeks and Romans. Kara had told him all about it during the briefing. Woman's brain was a steel trap for details.

The Avdat ruins climbed the face of a hill above a parking lot. A complex jumble of buildings fronted the slope. Atop the crest was a large rectangular building, rather than the remaining outer walls of one. The rectangle was cut in two by a midline wall, making two temple squares.

Kara had gotten all excited about kings and spice routes.

All he cared about was the deep-walled courtyard that would hide his helicopter. The squared-off area to the rear was big enough for the *Calamity Jane* to hide through a few hours of the night.

Even if the IDF's jet patrols spotted the heat source generated by his hot engines, they wouldn't think to investigate in the middle of a World Heritage Site. At least he hoped not.

Four minutes after invading Ramon Airbase and delivering a kill squad of Delta and Kidon, he was parked within the ancient limestone rock walls. Inside of thirty seconds, the only sounds aboard the *Calamity Jane* were the bright pinging of cooling metal and the final thuds of the slowing rotors. Soon there was only the desert and his crew sighing with relief.

He couldn't agree more.

Chapter 24

KARA TRIED TO KEEP AN EYE ON EVERYTHING AT ONCE. She had the ScanEagle in an automated slow circle at its max altitude of twenty thousand feet, its cameras offering a wide-area tactical view. Tago had the controls of *Tosca* and was keeping his focus on the air base from twenty-nine thousand.

Willard Wilson was perched on a stool behind her. He'd been so busy hovering over her shoulder that she'd finally laid down a strip of red tape four feet behind her and Tago's seats.

"You cross this, and I'm gonna kneecap you. You talk to me while I'm running this op, same thing." To emphasize her point, she dialed open her small gun safe, then loaded and holstered an M9 Beretta. So far he'd believed her and kept both his distance and his silence. She didn't wear her sidearm often, but SOAR had made sure she was damned proficient with it. Yet another piece of training she'd never appreciated before.

At four minutes after contact, midnight dark and four minutes, Justin was tucked away in his World Heritage hidey-hole.

Claudia's Little Bird helo was a dozen miles west parked close beside the Egyptian border at the bottom of a canyon so narrow that only a Little Bird and an exceptional pilot could be parked there. That she did it at night just meant she was a member of SOAR's 5D, because no one else could. A patrol would have to stumble on the position by pure chance to find her.

Now all they could do was wait.

Kara hated waiting.

They would either be signaled to come extract the action team—she found that phrase more comfortable than *kill squad*—or they'd depart two hours before first light and return tomorrow to wait once again in the depths of the dark desert.

It took nine full minutes for the first pair of alert fighters to make it off the Ramon runway. Fourteen minutes for the second pair.

Didn't learn enough, boys and girls. Americans took fifteen minutes—from full stand-down. If they had massive civil unrest in countries both to the east and west and then add on the Gaza Strip to make matters worse, U.S. Air Force would definitely be under the five-minute mark.

"Condition four," she transmitted, *the IDF is in the air with four birds*. She received back nothing but silence from the two helos and one ground team. Now it was their turn to be silent under all circumstances as the Israelis searched downward for any sign of an intruder. Of course what they should be watching for were two tiny vehicles shrouded in a stealth casing and flying high above where the jets were looking. But they didn't know that and she wasn't telling.

The Humvee that they'd delivered to the air base had progressed out of the exercise grounds and was moving quickly along the roads as if it was also responding to the alert status. They had thought about painting a large X on the roof in infrared paint to make it easy to spot from above, but the Israelis had top-quality American night-vision gear and would see the marking. They'd finally opted for a narrowband, highly directional radio ping. A fifty millisecond burst every three minutes on a preprogrammed rotating frequency pinned down the vehicle's location on *Tosca*'s tactical display.

All Kara's players were where they should be. Now they had to get through the long, slow second lap of this horse race.

Horse race? Damn, Justin was ruining her.

"Okay, smoke 'em if you got 'em." Not much of a joke; none of Justin's team smoked, not with working around Jet A fuel as often as they did. Plus the peak physical fitness their jobs required. The least hint of impaired breathing would earn you a scratch from active flight duty; few SOAR and no one from the 5D was willing to put that at risk for a cigarette.

"Two on roving patrol. Danny and Raymond, you're short straw."

"Thanks, bro. Needed to stretch my damn legs," Danny groused as he grabbed a radio and clambered down from the cockpit.

The man would grouse about winning the lottery, but he was an exceptional tactician. Justin was trying to teach him the bigger picture, but since Justin's brain was also tactical, it was hard. However, it meant they flew together fantastically well. He clapped the man on the shoulder before he climbed down.

Kara, on the other hand, saw big picture strategy so fast and so completely that a mission must look like a single gestalt to her. She made him feel like a cow looking at a new gate. He just wished she didn't do it quite so often.

Justin made sure the radio mounted in his vest was active, pulled off his piloting helmet, and almost stepped out into the night air.

Then he thought about Kara and how upset she'd be if all his "Texas leaked out" in the heart of the Negev Desert. He reached back for his cowboy hat before popping open his door and stepping down. The shortest projection was that they'd be three hours on the ground. He grabbed a battery-powered night-vision rig just in case and tucked it into his vest above where the folding FN-SCAR MK17 combat assault rifle hung across his chest.

Outside, the desert night was cool, moonless, and alight with stars. The desert air was even clearer than Amarillo. It was also so achingly dry that he'd need a water bottle before long. He wanted to ask Kara how much rain fell in the Central Negev just to hear her voice. She'd probably know too—would certainly be on top of tonight's forecasts, though shining stars and a sharp desert chill answered that one clearly enough. But he couldn't risk the transmission, and not talking to her about anything other than the mission had grown plenty annoying.

"So…" Sergeant Carmen Parker's silhouette materialized beside him in the darkness, a shadow among shadows. "Should I be singing the 'Wedding March'?"

"Should you what?" He kept his voice down because it was so quiet that it felt like the whole desert was listening. And because the shock had knocked the wind right out of him.

"Oh, c'mon, Captain, we all want to know. You and Moretti are so cute together that it makes our friggin' teeth ache. I bet you hold hands when you walk around in your civvies. We've got a pool going on when you'll pop the question. You haven't already done it yet, have you? If you have, Talbot will take the pool."

Justin was fraternizing with a fellow officer, and she was asking about wedding plans?

Wedding plans?

Shit! He needed to sit down. Being in love with Kara was one thing; stepping into marriage was serious business that was going to take some thinking. He really wished his dad was around so Justin could ask how he'd proposed.

Justin almost laughed aloud. He'd bet Kara's new boots that Annie Landau Evans had done the proposing.

"We haven't talked about such things yet."

"Well, you better, Cap. You don't get a move on, she's likely to ask you first. You at least got an answer for when she does?"

Justin snaked out an arm and snagged it around his starboard-side crew chief gunner's throat and hauled her into a loose choke hold. He rapped his knuckles atop her head, then kissed her on the crown of her head.

Her elbow shot out and bounced off his vest armor.

So he kept her in a friendly headlock a few moments longer.

"Tell you what, Carmen. You can fight with my sister and Danny for which of you gets to be best man. But if you lose, you're gonna have to sing at the ceremony. Solo."

"Deal, Cap." Then her voice softened. "It would be a privilege."

"Right back at ya." How could he not be weak in the head for this crew? He let her loose.

Marriage? He really hadn't gone there.

Marriage with Kara Moretti? Easy to picture that woman in a form-hugging gown and cowboy boots.

Kids with Kara Moretti? Now that was an image he could really see.

Took his damned breath away like a quarter horse in a full-mile race.

—*m*—

On Kara's tactical display in the coffin, she could track the Israeli jets. The first pair of them were running along the Egyptian border scanning for any sign of breach or aggression—probably close enough to the border to be freaking out their neighboring country. Though it was probably safe enough because the Egyptians were embroiled in their own problems; they were on their fifth or sixth government in half as many years.

The second pair of jets were drawing and quartering the Negev Desert. Twice they came close to Claudia's Little Bird hidden deep in the canyon by the Egyptian border. They never went anywhere near the Avdat World Heritage Site. Why would they? It was too nearby, just eight klicks away from the air base. You could probably see the ruins from the air base control tower.

Thankfully no one thought to look straight up, not that there'd be much to see. The ScanEagle was full stealth and the Gray Eagle was rated as "very low" for radar signature. Even if they thought to look straight up, she was probably secure, as long as the jets didn't climb up to her altitude and start nosing around.

Kara's main concern for now was the Humvee roaming across the active compound. The Gray Eagle's powerful camera made it easy to zoom in tight and keep a close eye on it.

The vehicle made it over to the special project buildings where she'd discovered Tom's men hiding the first time. The four people of this action team wore standard U.S. gear to blend in. Such gear included small IR reflecting patches on their shoulders that made them stand out in one of her views despite the five-mile-high altitude she was cruising at. In minutes they were inside one of the buildings. Two minutes later they were back, except there were five of them; four with shoulder patches, one being escorted none too gently.

The five figures piled into the Humvee, but it didn't go anywhere. For six long minutes, through two blinks of the every three-minute locator strobe, they remained immobile.

Kara tried not to imagine what was going on in the back of the Humvee. Maybe it just had to do with some kind of secret truth serum that took time to work.

She shared a look with Tago. All color had long since drained from his face and he was swallowing hard. Yeah, about what she figured as well.

Chapter 25

IT HAD BEEN OVER AN HOUR SINCE THE HUMVEE HAD pulled into the American Camp at the northeast corner of the base and Kara's team of four had exited the vehicle. No sign of Mr. Passenger Number Five.

She fought down a wave of nausea. Maybe it was better not to know. For once she truly appreciated not being on the forward action team.

Kara checked the other two teams. Claudia had been overflown several more times by the Israeli jets but remained undetected.

Two of them were now on a long approach back to the air base, swinging wide over the Central Negev before turning onto the final leg of the runway's landing pattern.

She watched the jets sliding side by side across the night sky, clear of Avdat and Justin's position by a bare kilometer.

Even as she watched, one of the jets dissolved in a massive fireball.

"What the fuck?"

The other jinked to the side, but not before a bright streak intersected its wing. The wing blew off.

At over three hundred miles per hour, it tumbled the last five hundred feet to the ground in just over a second.

No parachutes.

"Shit! Tago, wind it back."

He scrolled the flight recording backward in time.

The jet hauled itself back off the desert floor and regained a wing.

The other one imploded from fireball back into a jet streaking on short final back toward home.

Now she could see the two lines of light that had taken out the jets faster than their pilots could react. They came from just out of frame on the Gray Eagle's close-up camera.

"The ScanEagle!" She toggled over to the ScanEagle's controls.

With a few practiced flicks, she had its wide-area video feed on her central screen. She found the two flame-filled craters in the desert that moments before had been IDF F-16Is. Zooming in, she centered on the two fireballs and then hit rewind.

Once again the jets rematerialized and the bright streaks of attack moved away from them. She tracked the streaks back along their path.

Minigun tracer fire, very different from a missile's track. She'd seen it enough times to recognize it instantly. On the infrared vision the tracer fire looked like dual streaks of green flame, making it easy for the gunner to steer his weapon using night-vision gear, but otherwise close to invisible.

Green tracer fire, like the kind shot by the U.S. military.

It had arced up from below and sliced apart the jets' underbellies. At four thousand rounds a minute, it might as well have been a buzz saw, hitting a bomb or fuel tank on one jet and cutting off the wing on another.

She continued back along the path until she found a helicopter, a model she recognized instantly. It was an MH-47G Chinook twin-rotor, just like…

"Justin?"

She fast-forwarded the recording, staying centered on the helicopter this time.

The helo flew down low over the burning jets, raking them with additional fire.

"He's gone renegade!" Wilson shouted from behind her. "He just killed two Israeli jets."

"No way." Kara words felt dreamy as the helicopter she was watching took another run at the downed jets, apparently finding a fuel tank or unexploded bomb as a fresh explosion erupted from the wreckage.

"He has! Just look, goddamn it. Where's he going now? Is he going in to kill my team?"

The helo was on the move, lumbering through a turn.

"*Jane*." She finally remembered that she had a radio. "This is *Tosca*. Break off. I repeat, break off."

She was answered by static.

"He's going to kill my team! You gotta stop him, Moretti. That's a goddamn order. Shoot him! Shoot him now!"

Kara couldn't make sense of it.

She tried again, still no radio response.

She zoomed back. The helo dipped and swerved, but finally centered on Ramon Airbase and began moving forward.

Someone was screaming at her.

Ordering Tago to launch missiles.

The demands.

The noise.

Time moved so slowly that the words ringing off the steel walls of the coffin made no sense.

She could practically see each beat of the *Calamity Jane*'s rotors.

A glance at the wide area feeds. The other two Israeli jets were too far away. They'd flown nearly to the Gaza Strip in case that's where the original attack was centered. They were turning back even now; the bright flares of afterburners creating sky-sized rooster tails of heat across her infrared vision.

She called the *Jane* again, knowing she'd have no response, but she had to keep trying.

"Goddamn it, Moretti!" A hand clamped down on her shoulder and shook her hard. Wilson. "Goddamn Roberts is one of the sleeper agents. Launch your fucking missiles!"

She pulled out her M9 Beretta, cocked it, flipped up the safety, and aimed it at Major Wilson's forehead using his reflection in her main monitor. Kara didn't aim for his knee, she pointed it right at the center of his forehead.

"What did I say about crossing the tape line and keeping your mouth shut?"

He stumbled backward, cursing as he stumbled over his seat and crashed to the floor.

She reset the safety and holstered the weapon.

And wished to God that Wilson wasn't right.

Justin had gone renegade. He had killed two Israeli pilots and downed forty million dollars' worth of jets.

Kara had four Hellfire missiles at twenty-nine thousand feet. Eighty pounds of high explosive. Running at Mach 1.3, a thousand miles per hour, she had a lead time of eighteen seconds. At cruise speed, the *Calamity Jane* would reach the air base in ninety seconds, just over a minute at never-exceed speed.

She allowed herself twenty seconds; all she dared spare.

Radio response was nil.

The two Israeli jets still returning from the Egyptian border were fully six minutes away despite having reached supersonic flight.

Based on their earlier response time, Ramon Airbase was still five minutes from launching any more alert fighters.

Who could she call for advice in the next fourteen seconds?

Michael Gibson was on the ground, probably unaware of what had just transpired deep in the Negev unless he'd been looking in the right direction to interpret the massive boom of destruction.

Captain Claudia Gibson was parked in a deep and distant canyon and would know nothing. No flash of light. No shock wave.

Lieutenant Commander Boyd Ramis would only know about his ship, the *Peleliu*, not about this highly classified mission being run from a steel box on his hangar deck.

Chief Warrant Lola LaRue was in transit from her leave in the U.S. She wasn't due back aboard until midday and it was only midnight now.

And Justin.

Nine seconds.

She couldn't ask Justin because he wasn't answering his radio.

Six seconds.

Her only guidance was the Air Mission Commander, one Captain Kara Moretti.

Four.

She wanted to have faith that there was a reason

Justin had broken cover to down two Israeli jets and was now turning to attack Ramon Airbase.

Three.

Kara wanted to trust him.

Two.

The *Calamity Jane* shifted direction. Not toward the Israeli housing, nor the main operations base of the air base. Instead, it veered toward the American Camp's housing. Base personnel lived there. Families. Maybe children.

One second.

Kara centered the Gray Eagle's targeting crosshairs on the Chinook helicopter.

She selected all four Hellfire missiles and hit the fire button.

Wilson gasped in shock or relief behind her; she didn't care.

She held the laser guidance on the center of the helo and counted seconds until impact.

These weren't some flares that would light up a hillside to spook the Turkish OKK during an exercise.

Her heartbeat stroking slow and steady, counting seconds in perfect sync with the timer.

A single Hellfire was a tank killer, able to punch through the heaviest armor.

She kept a thumb near the abort-destruct switch that would destroy the missiles prior to impact and called one last time on the radio, knowing it was in vain.

At fifteen seconds she removed her hand from the switch.

Four Hellfires...

At sixteen, she whispered into the mic that she loved him.

…striking a thin-skinned helicopter…

At seventeen, she still held the laser guidance steady.

…were annihilation.

At eighteen seconds, the Chinook disappeared from the sky in a massive ball of flame.

Chapter 26

Some part of Kara continued functioning. She didn't know how.

She fielded messages from the inserted team.

Rousted Claudia from her hidey-hole two hours before sunrise.

All focus from Ramon Airbase had turned to the destruction of three aircraft in the desert: two jets in the heart of the desert and a million tiny bits of an American helicopter close outside the air base's perimeter fence.

The eighty pounds of explosive and the eight hundred gallons of Jet A that the Chinook helo had carried— Kara could no longer stand to think of it as the *Calamity Jane*—burned long and hot.

Four Hellfire missiles.

Hopefully nothing identifiable would remain.

She shied away from the thought.

Kara guided the *Maven II* in across the desert, and Claudia extracted the four-person team more quietly than they'd arrived. Their job was done.

Fifteen minutes after their departure, there was one more nasty surprise for the Israeli air base. The Humvee that had gone missing three weeks earlier had reappeared in a far corner of the base, on fire. The unusually intense vehicle fire killed four American soldiers who would probably get honorable burials back in the States no matter how little they deserved them.

She let Sergeant Santiago Marquez solo the *Tosca* to provide a watchful eye over the *Maven*'s departure from the Negev and her return to the *Peleliu*. There was no need.

Nobody was watching for the tiny stealth helicopter's passage or the four shooters she carried back to safety.

All the Israelis cared about was the graveyard in the desert.

Time disjointed on Kara.

Wilson was gone, pissed as hell about something. At her. At the dead pilot she'd just killed in a foreign land. It didn't matter.

The *Maven* was over the Negev. The West Bank. The Mediterranean.

Santiago handed off the *Tosca* Gray Eagle to the Incirlik ground crew.

And Kara watched the replay on the screen.

Two Israeli jets descending back toward base after a fruitless search exactly as expected.

Tracer fire from two miniguns arcing into their bellies as the Chinook climbed out of its hiding place among the ancient ruins of Avdat.

The jets flaming, exploding, augering into the desert floor.

The Chinook turning for Ramon Airbase. The long, long silence. Thirty-eight seconds from the final turn until it exploded. Until Kara killed...it.

Gone.

That simple.

Gone.

The helicopter.

Her crew.

Her pilot.

Captain Justin Roberts dead in the desert.

No body to deliver back to his mother. His mother who had begged her to protect her son.

Instead she had killed him.

Kara rewound the tape and watched it again, etching the images on her heart.

At some point, Claudia arrived with Michael close beside her.

She fought when they lifted her from the chair, but they overpowered her easily.

They carried her to her cabin where Justin and she had—

That's when she broke and the tears finally came.

Chapter 27

KARA HAD NO RECOLLECTION OF SLEEPING, BUT WHEN she awoke, Claudia was still there. So were Lola, Connie, and Trisha.

"What are you all doing here? Why—" And then she spotted the fifth woman crowded into the small room that was Kara's berth.

A tall, stunning blond.

For half a moment, her mind still foggy, Kara was afraid that Annie Roberts was impossibly here and Kara was supposed to tell her something.

Something bad.

Then she recognized Tanya of Mossad's Kidon counterterrorism unit and it all flooded back.

Worse than bad.

Kara had killed the only man she was ever going to love. Shot him right out of the sky.

"Go away." She wished they'd all go away so that she could curl up and die…

Like Justin.

What could have gone wrong?

Someone took her hand.

Kara would have shaken her off if it had been anyone other than Connie.

The sympathy was worse than the pain. The pain was hers, but the sympathy made no sense. They didn't know. They couldn't know. Their husbands were all safe, all secure—probably down in the officers' mess razzing each other.

"Tell me." Connie's voice was barely a whisper, but it carried in the otherwise silent room.

Kara was past decision making, didn't know what was right, wrong, allowed… A glance at Claudia, then the woman from Kidon. Each nodded in turn.

So Kara forced her body upright until she sat up on the edge of the bunk, still holding on to Connie for strength, and told them.

Recounting each moment. Second by second.

Clear.

Cold.

She'd been teased enough times by Carlo the opera singer about her heart being frozen against him.

It was frozen now as she offered a chill retelling of the facts. If there were any emotions, she was past feeling them. Maybe later the pain would return, but for now it was banished into some steel vault deep within her. Lost behind the high fences that she had denied to Jus—

Shove the thought aside.

Continue the debrief!

So she did.

When she was done, she hung her head. Then she saw that she still wore the beautiful boots that Justin had given her.

Kara tested for feelings, like poking cautiously at a sore tooth, but nothing happened. No regrets, no shock—they were simply pretty boots that someone had given her.

Shock.

She was in shock.

Great. She absolutely needed another problem for her brain to work on at the moment.

"I can show you the tapes. I have every second of it on tactical display down in the"—she couldn't manage *coffin*—"ground control station."

"We'll need to look at those," Lola commented. "As soon as we can. I need to understand how we lost a fifty-million-dollar helo and her five-person crew."

Kara wanted to find offense. Wanted to find Lola more concerned about the money and equipment than the people, but even in her current condition, she knew better. Which told her something about her own mental state.

"Let's do it now while I'm still too numb to care."

Connie squeezed her hand, but it made little difference. Connie's husband was still alive and waiting for her when this was over.

Kara had finally learned exactly what it meant to forward deploy into a battle zone. The man closest to you could die between one moment and the next.

But how many soldiers had pulled the trigger on their teammate themselves?

—⁓—

It was early evening as they all trooped down to the coffin on the *Peleliu*'s hangar deck. Somehow Kara slept through the day, her body shutting down to protect her.

Well, for now her brain was still shut down and she was glad of it.

Major Wilson was waiting for her. He went to pull her aside. "Kara, honey. I need to get into the ground control station and Sergeant Marquez wouldn't let me in without your clearance. C'mon, let's go."

Kara looked down at where his hand was clamped possessively around her upper arm.

He turned to face the women who'd accompanied Kara from her berth. "Thanks for getting her here, but this is a secure area and secure information." Wilson began dragging her over to the keypad of the door lock as if he was trying to hustle her out of the way before the women could react.

Well, Kara still had her sidearm.

Once again she had it out and the safety off before she knew what she was doing. She tucked it up under his chin and pressed hard enough that all he managed was a startled "Gurk!" as he tipped his head back.

"Way over the line, Wilson. Now go away, *honey*, before I kill an officer. I've already done it once today."

He tried a protest that might have started with *court martial*, but he couldn't speak past the additional upward pressure she applied.

Major Wilson finally backed off, spewing imprecations about classified information and getting Lieutenant Commander Boyd Ramis down here to arrest her and confiscate all her data.

As if Kara had anything left to lose.

Once he was gone, she put away her sidearm and unlocked the door.

"Shit, girlfriend." Trisha clapped her on the back just the way a guy would. "Knew there was a reason I liked you."

The others laughed.

Kara didn't.

They watched the tape in silence.

Then they went back and watched it again, discussing flight paths and angles of attack.

Kara felt an itch.

Halfway through the third replay, there was a pounding on the coffin's door. She delegated the unwelcome intrusion to Lola as the leader of the 5D to go deal with Ramis and whoever else Wilson was dragging into this mess.

Words she couldn't quite make out. Ramis's thoughtful ones, cut off by a spate of diatribe from Wilson.

It started to sound ugly and then everything went quiet.

Then Michael's voice. Soft. Two words, but perfectly clear. "Back. Off."

There was no argument.

Claudia sighed happily. "I do love that man."

The door clanged shut once more.

Kara ignored the brief spurt of pain as Lola returned with Colonel Gibson in tow. Claudia kissed her husband, and Kara turned away to restart the tape.

Trisha started back in making some point about the angle of attack.

Kara cut Trisha off mid-sentence by rewinding the tape and letting it roll again from the moment of the attack.

The shoot down.

The helo's passage over the crash sites as the miniguns continued to pound the downed aircraft.

The slow, lumbering turn toward the air base.

"What are you doing, Justin?"

The others watched in silence.

The helo didn't twist like some goddamn light-footed rodeo pony.

It—what was the word she'd just thought? Her brain was moving like mud. Just like the helo.

"It's lumbering. Justin never flew like that a day of his life."

The slow course change toward the American side of the camp. An overcorrection before landing back on course.

She brought up the vector analysis routine and watched his speed increase. The acceleration was agonizingly slow for a SOAR pilot.

"That isn't Justin flying," Lola said before Kara could. "I've flown beside him too many times."

"Nor Danny," Trisha put in. "I took him up in my Little Bird for some cross-training and he's pretty hot shit at the helm. Look, there. No dip down to follow the ground contour."

"Was he dazed?"

"No."

"Path is too straight, no wobble. It's just not a SOAR-level skilled pilot."

The voices were pinging around her.

"One of the crew chiefs?"

"Why would they fly to attack the base?"

"It wasn't Justin or his crew at all." Kara's declaration silenced the room. She wasn't expressing hope; it was fact. They might have already been dead, bleeding out on the cargo deck of the Chinook, but no one from SOAR had been at those controls.

None of the actions made sense. The flight style characteristics weren't Justin's. The murders of the IDF jets and their pilots weren't the actions of a SOAR crew. Even if one of them was a sleeper agent, that wouldn't explain the coordinated effort necessary to capture a Chinook, fly it, and kill the two jets.

"How far back in time does your video go?" Connie asked close beside her, hand still on Kara's shoulder.

"All the way."

——✴——

Kara wound it back once again, jumping quickly to the moment of the attack and then slowing the rewind speed.

She zoomed out to a wide view as the helo and the two jets retreated backwards across the sky. When the jets disappeared, reversing up the Central Negev, she followed the helo instead.

Even in rewind, she could see that it wasn't flown by a SOAR pilot. Whoever it was knew the craft and how to guide her, but while maneuvering they didn't hug terrain or ease into deep wadis. They were keeping a ridge between the helo and the approaching jets, but they weren't doing a very good job of it.

Good enough, she supposed the two dead pilots would protest.

A road. Some low buildings. The geometric shapes of limestone walls that she recognized as the Avdat World Heritage Site ruins.

The helo reversed back into the courtyard, an awkward, uneven motion.

The bright sparks of the rotor blade tips striking airborne dust painted two circles of light. As the rotors slowed, the circles dimmed, then disappeared.

She let it run backward for a long time at ten times speed.

"Can you zoom in any tighter?"

Kara shook her head. They were looking at a tiny segment of the ScanEagle's wide-angle video from four miles high. The whole helicopter was little bigger than her palm in the center of the image, one pixel per meter more or less. The walls of the courtyard made a visible square. Beyond that, nothing but dark, cold desert—black under infrared light.

Everyone watched the unchanging image in silence until the rotor disks spun back to life and the helo was once again airborne backwards. The motion of the flight was wholly different.

"That's Justin," she managed without her voice cracking. "He was still alive at zero-zero-eight hours last night when he landed there."

"So what happened between eight minutes after midnight and one-ten hours?" Connie asked. Her voice was so calm, it was the only thing that kept Kara from flying apart.

She reached out to brush her fingers over the cold glass of the screen, but felt closer to Justin for the gesture. Past hope, it was perhaps as close as she'd ever be to him again.

Kara ran the hour and two minutes of video that the helicopter had spent parked on the ground at four times normal speed. For fifteen and a half minutes, the only sound in the coffin was the shuffling of feet.

Nothing.

She wound it back to Justin's landing and let it play forward in real-time speed.

"At this distance, it is unlikely that the camera can pick up an individual's heat signature unless they are all gathered together." Kara switched off the coffin's lights so that she could see the main screen that little bit more clearly.

She could feel the others gather more closely behind her. She tried to draw comfort from that but—

"What's that?" The silhouette of Trisha's pointing hand was outlined against the screen, but Kara had already hit the pause and was rolling the pixelated image back frame by frame.

"Pilot side," Lola noted.

Sure enough, the vague bright spot, sometimes two pixels across, sometimes one, shifted back toward the pilot's side door as she rolled backward.

His last steps?

She flipped from infrared to normal light view, which should have shown nothing in the dead of night.

The black helicopter disappeared into the darkness.

But the bright spot grew brighter.

Her heart beat for the first time in what felt like forever.

Only one thing she knew of on the helicopter that would reflect starlight more brightly than it radiated heat.

She began scrolling forward frame by frame, synchronizing the two views.

Once again, Justin stepped away from the *Calamity Jane*.

On one screen Kara placed the infrared view of the site. Heat signatures showed the cooling helicopter, the dark line of the ruin's walls that had cooled faster than surrounding soil, and that elusive hint of motion by the pilot's door.

On the other screen, in visible light, she followed the

one bright spot on a field of pitch-black as it moved away from the helicopter.

A white cowboy hat.

Chapter 28

JUSTIN FELT A GROAN TRY TO ESCAPE AS HE RETURNED to consciousness and did his best to suppress the sound.

He cracked open one eye cautiously and wished he hadn't; a headache slammed to life and blurred what little vision he had.

The darkness was near complete. Light that might have been sunrise or sunset was either barely begun or spent for the day.

A lamp flared, a small oil lamp; the sudden brightness made his head hurt even more. He closed his eye and tried to assess. Gagged. Bound feet. Hands as well, thankfully in front. Lying on his side. No obvious point of outside pain. Intense inside pain.

His last memory? Holding Carmen in a loose choke hold because she'd completely deserved it for teasing him about setting a wedding date.

Justin had let her loose, then looked up into the barrel of a rifle centered on his face.

Behind him, someone stuck a needle in his neck and the world went away.

Drugged equals headache. He'd have to remember to request a different sedative next time.

He'd been within a dozen steps of the helicopter. How in the world had they gotten past the outer patrol?

Because Raymond and Danny had been down before Justin had even exited the *Jane*.

Please God, don't let him have lost another crew. He'd rather be dead himself.

He risked the one eye again.

The man who'd lit the lamp was staring right at him. So much for subterfuge.

Justin shrugged his chagrin and the man nodded in what seemed to be a friendly way, or at least an understanding one.

Black face mask and a green headband with foreign writing. Justin didn't need his handy-dandy terrorist guidebook to recognize a Hamas militant. The man also was wearing a SOAR vest and had several weapons dangling about his neck, probably including Justin's own.

Justin tried to rock himself upright.

The guard didn't threaten to shoot him.

Once Justin was up, the headache redoubled, but he could see more of his surroundings.

They were in a chamber made of stone. Old stone, dry laid without mortar. Above them were four curved arches of stone spanning twenty or more feet and equally high. Pretty impressive engineering actually, each block angle cut, each a meter square and probably weighing a ton or more. Over the arches lay a tarp that would block any searches from above.

The Baptistery at the head of the colonnade. He recognized it from Kara's briefing. He was still at the Avdat World Heritage Site.

There was only one entrance to the chamber, beyond the guard. Through the open stone arch, Justin could see that the tarp had been folded aside and now the last of the daylight was fading in the quick desert twilight.

If they were still here, then the *Calamity Jane* was

parked nearby. If there was some way they could get back to it… He filed that idea for later.

They!

The thought finally pounded its way through his headache.

His crew!

On the rough stone floor around him lay four bodies. Bodies… *Please God no*.

A pained groan had to be the sweetest sound he'd ever heard. Danny sported a livid black eye, but he was alive.

The others… He could see Talbot wincing and Raymond breathing.

His crew was alive.

For how long was a different question that he'd worry about later. They were all alive for now.

Weren't they?

He kicked Carmen's boot.

She kicked him back.

Justin tried to remember the last time he'd been so happy.

—◦◦◦—

Kara nursed the two-pixel white dot across the black terrain of last night's video. It disappeared for long moments. Maybe he kept tipping his head. Then she'd find it again a dozen feet on and moving away from the helicopter.

"There, upper left," Tanya called out.

Kara didn't know whether to chase them all out so that she could concentrate or bless them every time someone spotted Justin's hat a moment sooner than she did.

She re-centered the screen before shifting to the next frame. The problem was complicated by the circling view of the ScanEagle on its automated orbit high above. She prayed that they didn't drift off the edge of the image. Direction had become meaningless.

For the moment, only the hat mattered. Bless the man for such a ridiculous habit.

It took an impossibly painstaking hour to trace the hat across the site. They'd gone through archways, down passages between courtyards that were impossible to see into, but the hat always emerged from the other side eventually.

The mission clock on the video showed that less than five minutes had passed for their hour of tracing him, but now he was on the far side of the temple from where he'd landed in the heart of the Byzantine fortress. They'd passed through the second-century Roman temple and the Nabataean temple to King Obodas. Justin had walked through eight centuries before being lost in the colonnade that had long ago greeted the spice caravans as they crossed from Petra in Jordan over to Gaza.

"Did he walk under his own power or was he force-walked? Or was he carried?" she asked herself and hated the final image.

"Hard to tell." Michael spoke for the first time. "Can you play the whole sequence in real time without the image rotating?"

Kara made a note to stop talking aloud to herself when the ground control station was packed, but she had the playback set up in a few moments, overlaying the map of the temple she'd found while researching the site.

She started the video, tried to imagine Justin going for an amble among the ruins, his long legs stretching out in front of him with each step.

Kara couldn't make it work.

He moved in fits and starts. The white dot reached an archway and stopped. Then moved through a passageway, but with a stop on the other side. A few of the halts were a full minute in duration.

Finally they lost all trace of him in the colonnade.

She stopped the run.

"Lights," Michael said.

She found the switch and flicked it on.

Many in the room shaded their eyes and groaned.

"He was carried."

Kara's worst-case scenario.

Michael appeared unaffected by the sudden change in illumination. Did they teach Delta Force tricks to instantly adapt their eyes to changing light conditions? The more she knew him, the more mysterious Colonel Gibson became, rather than the other way around.

"My best estimate," he continued, "is that he and his crew were moved at the same time by an insufficient number of attackers to move them all at once as a unit. The timing would work for three groups of two individuals moving the five crew members. Initially slow to collect them from various points where they were taken or shot—"

Kara gasped at the idea. She didn't know why. An hour ago she'd firmly believed that she'd murdered Justin and his crew. But the idea of him being alive and now dead again left her emotions in chaos.

"I'm inclined to assume the former. If they were

shot, there would be little point in taking the time to move them. If alive and captive, then the scenario makes more sense."

Kara had pulled up her legs without realizing it until her knees were against her chest, her heels on the edge of the seat, and her arms wrapped around the soft leather of her new boots.

"Alive eighteen hours ago. I'm going to hold you to that."

Michael offered a grim smile in acknowledgment.

"Now we must find out whether he remains on the site."

"How are we supposed to do that?"

Connie pointed at a side screen. "Isn't that the ScanEagle's engine readout? You're still aloft."

Kara spun back to face the ground control station, her booted feet hitting the floor as she did so.

There it was.

She'd been too fried last night to remember to bring the ScanEagle home. It was still aloft, circling on autopilot over the Central Negev with its engines and its cameras running. It still had seven hours of fuel.

Kara zoomed the image back enough to be able to see the parking lot and fast-forwarded to sunrise.

"No vehicles arrived during the night. Now let's just hope that if they moved them, they didn't move them far. I'm only scanning about ten square kilometers."

—᠕᠕᠕—

Justin didn't want to reveal that he spoke some Arabic, just in case there was anything to overhear. But with sign language he managed to get permission to pull his gag, though he made no effort to unbind his hands.

The man kicked a canteen in his direction.

Justin sipped only the smallest amount, in case it was all they were getting. He moved slowly to each of his crew, pulled their gags, and gave each of them a sip of water.

Danny looked as if he'd been hit upside the head with a rock. There were scrapes and scratches all around his black eye. He'd lost some blood, but not much. He nodded that he was okay, then winced revealing he was sorry for having done so.

"Don't try singing," Justin whispered to him.

The guard hissed, but Danny's wry smile was worth the risk.

Raymond had had a much rougher time of it and was still out. He looked as if he'd been taken down by a band of jackals.

"*A good fighter, that one*," the guard said in Arabic.

"Eh?" Justin asked him.

The guard shrugged and was silent again.

The others were okay.

Was there one man or a dozen guarding them? If one, they had a chance. If a dozen…

The chamber they were in was twenty feet square. The walls reached up nearly eight feet before the four arches soared overhead. There were gaps between them, the ancient roof no more than a memory. The walls were rough enough to climb easily, if he and his crew weren't bound and guarded. And Raymond wasn't going to be doing any climbing soon; he was still out cold.

The guard sat twenty feet away with a FN-SCAR rifle

held casually across his lap. It had a magazine in and Justin could see the safety was off.

Mr. Guard didn't have all of their gear either. Two vests and three rifles were unaccounted for. Which probably meant at least two more guards.

"Y'all don't need even three guards when one could stop us'n just fine," he spoke his conclusion aloud to warn his crew.

The guard mimicked his own earlier "Eh?"

None of them were likely to survive a charge into a fusillade of 7.62 mm rounds.

For now, it was time to sit and wait.

He moved back to his original spot and leaned against the wall. Nearby he spotted where his hat had been knocked off. He dusted it off as well as he could with his hands bound and tugged it back on, felt much better for doing so.

He wouldn't mind a song just to cheer up his crew, but what he really wanted to do was let Kara know he was alive.

She must be worried sick.

———

"What we know…" Kara turned away from the console and faced her team. "One, no vehicle transported them off-site last night."

Her team. She liked the sound of that, because she really needed them right now.

"Two, no obvious transport during daylight hours. Three, our last estimated location for Justin's hat…"

That earned her a few chuckles.

"…is in the Baptistery at the head of the colonnade. This

area is masked by a tarp, but the tarp is showing higher-than-ambient temperatures right now, suggesting that there may be multiple people under it. Recommendations?"

"You're the boss man, lady." Trisha spoke up. "You tell us."

Yeah, right! Kara almost said, appreciating the irony. But it wasn't ironic. These were some of the most skilled fliers and, between Michael and Tanya, operators in any military. And they were looking to her for a mission plan.

Her.

She was about to send a combined Delta-SOAR-Kidon team into the fray to recover Justin and his crew, combined as she saw fit.

Every minute that passed increased the danger to the captives and the chance they were about to be moved.

What was needed was clear, at least to her. And she was the Air Mission Commander, so her plan was going to be it—even if she still wasn't used to the idea.

"Fine. Here's what we're going to do."

But this time she wasn't going to be sitting in some quiet little corner.

Chapter 29

KARA SAT IN THE BACK OF THE DAP HAWK CARGO BAY with a ScanEagle portable command station set up in front of her.

Lola piloted the heavily weaponized Black Hawk with her husband, Tim, as copilot and weapons specialist. The DAP was unique to SOAR and about the deadliest damn machine imaginable…deadly to the enemy.

Connie and Big John sat at the two side-mounted miniguns at the front of the cargo bay.

Kara liked having all of that wrapped around her.

Michael was aboard Claudia's Little Bird *Maven II* along with Tanya.

Trisha and Bill, the other SOAR and Delta couple, were in the *May*.

All three craft were stealth modified and moving at top speed mere feet off the dirt of the Negev.

Kara had watched hundreds of flights from on high. In SOAR training, she'd ridden along on a number of familiarization missions aboard each of the 160th's crafts.

Never before had she flown into a battle zone where everyone was putting their lives on the line. And this time they were doing it based on the belief that her intelligence analysis was accurate and her action plan sound.

It wasn't just her desire to finally participate in the fight that had sent her aloft. Her nerves hadn't let her stay aboard the *Peleliu*. She didn't know why, but they were jangling there.

Of course the team hadn't told LCDR Ramis that they were flying a mission; what the Navy didn't know wasn't going to get them court-martialed. In fact, no one aboard the ship knew that Kara was even aboard this "training flight." Not Tago and definitely not Wilson. As a precaution, she'd even changed the coffin's security code so that Wilson couldn't browbeat Tago into providing him access. If she died on this mission, well, it wouldn't be her problem to figure out how to break back in without triggering an automatic all-systems erasure.

There hadn't been time to prep and fly the *Tosca* the three hours down from Incirlik. The ScanEagle was a much simpler craft. It had no payload other than its cameras and comm gear. No Hellfire missiles, no signal jammers, complex navigation systems, or other heavy-duty systems. It didn't even have landing gear; recovery required snagging a rope line with a wingtip.

It was designed to fly and peek without being spotted; and the stealth modification made it very good at that.

She circled it down from twenty thousand to ten thousand feet, doubling her image resolution.

The arched room of the Baptistery still registered warmer than the rest of the structure. At this altitude, she should be able to see an individual person in motion out in the open.

The flight of helos was still twenty-five miles out when she spotted trouble. She clicked on the intercom.

"I have a truck arriving at Avdat parking lot. It's big enough to move the whole crew and a number of guards."

"Any chance that it's normal traffic?" Lola asked.

"Four hours after the park closes and it's too dark to see your own nose? Get a grip."

"You *are* from Brooklyn, aren't you?"

Kara reviewed her words. They didn't sound that rude to her, but maybe they were. How was she supposed to know?

"Brooklyn, New Yawk!" She did her best to channel Justin. "Best dang city in them there union of states."

"Your accent sucks, Kara," Big John rumbled from his minigun. Right, the big man was from Oklahoma.

"So, I've been told." And she was just going to keep believing that she'd be seeing the man who'd told her so real soon. "We're twenty miles out. If we jump to never-exceed velocity, we'll cut nine minutes down to six."

"We can't outstrip the Little Birds," Lola informed her, but Kara could feel the helicopter nosing down to gain speed. "They're carrying our snipers. I'm accelerating to their V-max. As a result, we're all going to be flying several feet higher. Hope the Israeli radar is watching the other horizon."

Kara knew the Little Birds would assess the DAP Hawk's changed flight and adapt rapidly without the need to risk a radio transmission.

She watched the truck's leisurely approach. Reinforcements would not be a good thing right now. But neither would firing a long-range missile and risking blowing up a World Heritage Site if they missed the truck.

The truck eased up to the gate.

"Come on, guys," Kara encouraged them softly. "Get into an argument over who has to climb down and open the gate."

Which appeared to be exactly what they did.

They repeated the act at the second gate and began driving up the winding road toward the temple. The road switchbacked sharply, which the driver had difficulty following in the dark.

She wanted to scream for Lola to hurry up, but the SOAR pilots were the very best people at doing their job, so rather than watching over their shoulders, what should she be doing?

Watching the air base!

She spun her cameras to look east.

No jet patrols.

Except for the two jerks roaring down the runway and up into the air.

She held her breath and clicked her boot heels together three times.

It appeared to work; as soon as they were aloft, the two jets turned away toward the Egyptian border, moving away from them and the Avdat site as if on a routine patrol.

SOAR continued its invasion of Israel without any notice.

She spun her view back to the truck. Old enough that even the low grade at the front of the temple appeared to be slowing it down.

—⁓—

Justin listened to the truck grinding up the hill toward them. Full dark, you didn't need to tell him they were in trouble. As long as they were at Avdat there was a chance of getting back to the helo. Or of someone finding them.

It had been a full day; someone must have noticed they were missing.

But there'd been no rescue at full dark. Two hours later, there still hadn't been a rescue after the amount of time necessary to cross the Israeli border and the Negev after dark.

Once their captors moved them, there wasn't a chance in hell of them being found. He really didn't want to end up as a shaky videotape on Al Jazeera. He didn't want his mother to see that, and he definitely didn't want Kara to see that.

His military life was a risk. He knew that every time he flew to battle. A combination of realism seasoned with a touch of denial let him keep flying. He knew that he protected his country in some way or other with every flight. This time taking out a terrorist cell, hopefully. He hoped the ground team had made this whole mess worthwhile at least.

And he was good at his job. He knew what he did counted.

The denial was there though, the need to believe that he was untouchable. The explosion that had killed his first crew had disproved that, but something like that didn't happen twice to the same guy.

Except this time it had.

Justin knew that if he had the chance to do it again, he would. If he could make Kara and her family one minute safer by doing this duty, he would.

But that truck really worried him.

It stalled, backfired, started, and ground forward once more.

No question it was bad news.

Then there was a loud bang followed by a high hiss and the truck halted again.

Their guard had sat calmly and hawk-eyed through-out the entire approach.

At the latest noise, he sighed.

It sounded like the truck had just gotten a flat tire.

———∧∧∧———

"Nice shot, Michael."

Kara could see the truck sagging down at the front left. Nice shot, hell. He'd punched out a truck tire from a hovering helicopter a half mile from its target with no one the wiser. The shot was out near the theoretical limit of his PSG1 sniper rifle.

With the truck momentarily disabled, the two Little Birds split wide and went to ground.

Kara took one last look at the air base—still quiet—and concentrated on the World Heritage Site.

Michael, Bill, and Tanya hit the dirt moving before the helos were fully down. No need for Tom from The Activity on this mission. This wasn't gathering intelligence; this was pure action.

This time, Kara felt no compunctions about what was going to happen. "Take 'em down hard," she'd told the team during planning.

The Little Birds pulled up and back; the 5D was *not* going to lose another helicopter on the ground tonight. They started a slow orbit of the site, far enough out that there wasn't a chance of them being heard. Close enough they could respond in seconds.

Kara offered a play-by-play over the DAP Hawk's intercom as the two Delta operators and one Kidon agent worked their way forward:

"Inside the perimeter.

"Michael is coming in from the very back of the temple.

"Bill and Tanya are in position on opposite sides of the truck.

"Michael through the temple, closing on Alpha One."

Before they engaged, they wanted to make sure that the people they were looking for were present and alive. A body recovery operation would be…something she wasn't going to think about.

"Michael outside the Baptistery."

———

Justin wished that the guard would at least blink. Not that he was going to start a rush on him, but it was unnatural for a man to be so watchful.

Maybe he slept with his eyes open.

Justin shifted slightly to one side and the guard's gaze snapped to him, his rifle rising a few millimeters before settling back across his lap.

The boredom must be really setting in for Justin to even try something that dumb. The headache had worn off, but now he was getting plain old stupid. *Don't antagonize the man with the gun.* Good rule. He must remember to tell it to Kara when he saw her. If he ever saw her again.

At least she knew how he felt about her. She had to.

He wished he'd proposed. Wasn't that something a girl would want to know? That someone loved her that much. Seemed an important thing a man ought to say once it was true, whether or not she had high fences to deal with.

Kara would come around. She'd—

The guard jolted slightly and then looked at Justin

strangely for a long moment before sagging forward over his weapon.

Justin was on the move in that instant. He'd mostly freed his leg bonds where he'd hidden his ankles behind the still-prone Raymond. He'd been wiggling his toes every few minutes to get circulation back into his feet.

As the guard flopped forward, Justin shoved off the wall in a diving roll over Raymond. He came up with his feet free and moving. It was more of a stagger, but it would get him there.

A man rose from behind the guard, extracting a long blade from the back of the guard's neck.

He held up a finger to his lips, signaling silence, and Justin stumbled to a halt.

Then Colonel Michael Gibson keyed his mic and whispered, "Five secure. Proceed."

Justin could hear the whispered spits of silenced rifle fire sounding nearby.

Then everything was silent.

Kara circled the ScanEagle at a thousand feet and watched the infrared signatures carefully. This low she could see the three shooters clearly. And she could see that there were multiple heat signatures beneath the tarp.

The truck driver and his assistant were down. A roving guard was also down.

"Checking back of truck." She circled down low so that she could see inside the open back. "Boxes blocking view, but unclear if there are heat signatures."

Tanya moved forward. She eased up onto the truck bed with a handgun out and leading the way.

There was one heat flash and then another.

Then she jumped down off the bed. "No longer is it a problem."

"Clear," Kara announced over the radio, but she continued to circle the area.

Moments later the DAP Hawk drove ahead fast and dove down to the dirt close beside the Baptistery. A group came hobbling out of the covered area.

Kara tried looking out the helo's door, but she wasn't wearing night-vision gear. She actually had a better view of what was happening close around her on the console across her lap.

Five mobile, one being carried.

Please no! She felt awful for thinking that, *but please don't let it be Justin.*

Then she spotted the bright signature of the hat, but it was on the shortest figure in the group.

Had she been following the wrong—

They slid in the injured man. He cursed in a slurred voice, so he wasn't dead. And he wasn't Justin. Three more came aboard, including a woman wearing Justin's hat.

Then, looking disheveled and so powerful she almost wondered if they'd picked up a Greek god of old along the way, Justin climbed aboard carrying a rifle in one hand and a pistol in the other.

A double slap on the hull and they were aloft.

She watched on her screen as the two Little Birds came in close. The shooters clambered aboard and the helos pulled back aloft.

In seconds all three of them were moving low and fast toward the Mediterranean coast. She set the ScanEagle to follow as well as it could.

The disabled truck and the dead Hamas agents would be left as a puzzle for the Israelis. It might suffice for them to explain the loss of the two F-16s the prior night.

"You gotta pay more attention, Cap," Carmen shouted over the roar of the DAP Hawk's rotors. "You dropped your hat when you tried to tackle Michael." She pulled it off her head and slapped it down onto his.

Justin wrapped his arms around his crewmate and kissed her on the nose.

Kara was so glad to see him alive that it was hard to begrudge him anything. But this was asking a hell of a lot.

Then he hugged each of his crew in turn. Holding Raymond's hand for a moment as the others found some blankets to tuck around the injured man.

Then he looked up and caught sight of Kara.

—∿∿—

Justin had to blink twice to be sure he wasn't imagining things. He considered slapping himself, but that was too much out of the funny papers.

"Kara?" He barely mouthed it, but she heard all of the questions in it clear as day.

"Hey, Cowboy. You know you caused people a whole lot of trouble yesterday, what with getting yourself kidnapped and all."

He tried to stand up and banged his head on the low ceiling of the DAP Hawk. Thankfully his hat gave him enough warning before he brained himself and was just shoved down low over his eyes. He worked it back loose and scooted across the deck to her.

His hand reached out tentatively and touched her on the arm. "You're here!"

"No, this is just an illusion of me. Of course I'm here. Had to see how the other half lived."

He'd never been so happy to—

He leaned around her control console and crushed her to his chest. To hold her for even a moment was the best—

"Hold on there." He sat back on his heels and kept his hands on her shoulders. "What in the wide world are you doing here?"

"I wanted to make sure you were okay."

"Okay? Okay! Goddamn it, Kara! All this time, I kept telling myself it didn't matter what happened to me as long as you were safe back aboard the *Peleliu*. How dare you risk yourself out here! What if I'd already been dead? You're not supposed to face shit like that."

Kara brushed a hand over his cheek. "You have the most beautiful face, Cowboy. I plan to spend a lifetime looking at it. But sometimes you are as dumb as one of your horses. I already killed you once; I wasn't going to let it happen again."

And she told him the story of the night he'd missed.

"You shot down *Calamity Jane* thinking I was aboard?" She nodded.

And then she'd found him and flown to his rescue.

"I don't deserve you." It was the only conclusion he could reach.

"You're stuck with me anyway, Cowboy. You did hear what I said?"

"Uh." Justin tried to think of what she could be referring to. Her impossible bravery at taking the right action even when thinking he was aboard? That was even harder than merely losing your crew.

Or that he was dumb as one of his horses—

"Wait a sec."

"Ah! The light dawns."

"Now just hold on there."

Kara folded her hands neatly in her lap and did her best to look sweet, innocent, and endlessly patient. He knew full well that she was sweet only when it pleased her, not one ounce innocent, and about as patient as a golden retriever waiting for a tennis ball.

"You said something about my face."

"Did I?" Kara played innocent all of a sudden.

Well, two could play that game. "Huh, guess not. My mistake." He rose to a low squat and turned to fall back into the seat beside her.

The punch on his arm felt like he'd just come home.

"You know, there's one thing I can't figure out."

"Like how to ask a girl to marry you?" Kara teased.

"No, no. Wasn't that." He gave it right back.

She actually growled at him.

"Like how they knew exactly where my helicopter would be and to have a crew waiting that was capable of flying it. An MH-47G isn't exactly a Toyota pickup. A man needs training to fly it."

"That's been bothering me too." She leaned her shoulder against his as the DAP Hawk took a hard banking turn. "I didn't know what it was until you said something, but it was like an itch."

"One your future husband could scratch for you?"

"Asshole."

"Love you, Kara."

"Jerk!" But she leaned into his kiss plenty hard.

He could never tire of the taste of her or the way they responded to each other.

Even Raymond joined the round of applause from his crew by thumping his uninjured hand against the deck.

"Thank you. Thank you. Thank you one and all for staying alive and sticking with me. You're the best flight crew alive."

They cheered and laughed; it was a good moment.

But Kara wasn't the only one with an itch, and he'd had a few thoughts about it during his long hours as a hostage.

Chapter 30

KARA FOUND THAT IT WASN'T HARD TO LOOK AS exhausted as she felt. She wanted a joyous reunion, a celebration of everyone surviving a difficult and challenging mission. She wanted a goddamn day off after what she'd just been through. The last time she'd slept just might have been on the car ride from Brooklyn to Maryland; she didn't count the comatose hours during which she'd thought she had murdered Justin.

Instead she was standing beside the coffin and waiting for Michael to return with Major Willard Wilson.

They finally appeared down the far end of the hangar deck and began the long walk. It was still dark night, though dawn was coming soon. The deck was dimly lit by work lights, and the two figures moved in and out of shadow until they stopped before her.

"Thanks, Michael. Hey, Willy Nilly." She did her best to sound genuinely disgusted. Not hard.

"Hey, honey. You doing any better? Hard thing you did yesterday, shooting down one of your own. Real tough."

"You call me 'honey' one more time and you might be wearing a cowboy boot in your balls."

"Sure thing, honey." He grinned down at her and she barely resisted the urge to do as she'd threatened; would have under any other circumstances.

"I…haven't been feeling well. But you wanted to get the records of the Ramon Airbase mission?"

"Yeah, I really do. I want to secure those before someone sees them who shouldn't."

"Uh-huh." Kara kept her thoughts to herself as to who that might be. She turned to the coffin, keyed in the new code, and leaned down for the retinal scan. The bolts thudded aside. She swung the door wide and Major Wilson hurried forward.

On the threshold to the door he stumbled to a halt. "What the hell? You aren't supposed to be here."

"Don't you mean I'm supposed to be dead as a beaten horse?" Justin stood just inside the coffin's door.

"No. Yes. No. You're supposed to be—" Wilson clamped down on his tongue.

"I'm supposed to be in the hands of the bomb makers."

"What bomb?" Wilson asked. "The Hamas cell was making nerve agent."

Tom stepped out from behind the still-closed half of the door. "Funny thing, Wilson. I never mentioned what my team recovered at Ramon. Never said it was nerve agent."

"Sure you did." Wilson backed up and bumped against Michael.

"Neither I nor my team." Tom stood shoulder to shoulder with Justin. "Then we analyzed who knew where the *Calamity Jane* would be landed during the operation. That's a pretty small circle."

"I'm guessing," Kara joined in, "that based on their last course change, the Hamas flight crew were supposed to use the *Jane* to eradicate our ground team before they could be recovered and expose you with the information they forced from the Hamas cell buried in the American Camp."

"Thing was"—Michael's voice was so cold that it

sent a chill up her spine—"none of them knew who you were. Just a voice on the phone. You were just a faceless moneyman to them."

"If you hadn't figured on using the *Jane* to make a suicide run against our team inside Ramon Airbase—" Justin began.

"—we never would have suspected you, Willy Nilly," Kara finished.

Wilson spun to face her, his face contorted with rage. "That's the last time you call me that, bitch! I can't believe you were so goddamn heartless that you'd shoot down your own lover. Guess spreading your legs for him didn't mean shit! Should have fucked you myself— just a common whore!"

And he struck out at her.

Before Kara could even think to react, a massive hand clamped down on Wilson's wrist, stopping his fist inches from her face. Justin twisted Wilson's arm up and back, then used it to steer the man's face into the steel side of the coffin. Hard.

Keeping him pinned there, Justin moved up close behind Wilson. "We thought about what you were planning—to dump a nerve agent in the American Camp food supply inside the security perimeter of Ramon Airbase."

"Hundreds of dead Americans in a place where only the Israelis could be blamed." Tom continued the analysis, because that was the part he had figured out. "You'd break up a beautiful friendship. By causing a major international incident between Israel and the U.S., we might even have pulled all support from Israel, destabilizing the whole country. Exactly what the Palestinian Al-Qassam Brigades of Hamas would want."

"At first, we couldn't figure out what motivated you. Murdering American servicemen and women. Betraying your country." Justin's voice was thick with anger at that.

"But then I had this little idea," Kara said lightly, as if she were shopping for a scarf.

"We'd already done complete and deep background checks on you," Tom put in. "We knew it wasn't family or ideology."

"Money, you fucking creep." Justin hadn't eased up on Wilson's arm, and he cried out as Justin wrenched it further.

Kara was right, seeing Justin mad was not a safe place to be unless you were on his side. The easygoing cowboy wasn't a facade; it's who he was. But down inside he was the baddest papa bear imaginable.

"Of course." Tom leaned casually against the door frame of the GCS. "The Activity does have some capabilities, ones you have drastically underestimated. Your millions are gone despite the offshore account shuffle you did. Your Hamas contact is already in Kidon custody, and we expect to have your moneyman soon."

"Even I don't know who he is," Wilson grunted out.

"Oh, but we do." Tom's smile was not a friendly one. "A renegade Saudi Prince's Lamborghini Huracán is about to have a regrettable accident."

"You know, Willy Nilly"—Kara got right up in his face and drawled out his nickname thickly—"we talked about what to do with you. But then someone else had an excellent suggestion."

Tanya came around from behind the coffin. "Hello, Major Wilson. Israel, particularly Mossad, we would very much enjoy showing you our country, a very small piece of it, and talking with you there…for as long as you last."

Kara could see Wilson's eyes shoot wide, then Michael injected the knockout drug he'd held ready. Justin leaned in moments before Wilson lost consciousness.

His voice wasn't a low snarl. It wasn't a shout. It was one of the quietest and most dangerous sounds Kara had ever heard, little more than a whisper.

"You never strike a lady."

Chapter 31

THE DAWN LIGHT WAS WASHING ACROSS THE SKY where Kara and Justin were standing on the fantail of the *Peleliu*'s hangar deck and looking down at the ocean gently rolling out behind the big ship.

"I guess your mother was right, Justin." Kara wished she had laughter or joy in her at this moment. It had been a lot of long hard days since the moment they'd left Brooklyn. But she didn't dare miss the chance. She had to get this done before he flew again. It was too important to put off.

"She usually is." Justin shifted to stand behind her. Wrapped his arms around her and pulled her back against his chest.

Safe. Safest place she'd ever been on the whole crazy planet.

"What did she say this time?"

"Your mother…" Kara tried to focus on speaking, but being in Justin's arms made it difficult. "She said I was going to have to be the one to propose to you."

"Did she? Don't that beat all."

"So Justin—"

"Nope. I'm gonna stop you right there, sweetheart." He planted a kiss atop her head.

"But—"

"Said nope, and mean nope."

"Justin—" He was about the most irritating man ever.

"I'm going to propose to you. But this isn't the proper place or the proper time."

"Oh, what is?" She tried for "arch with disdain" and feared that she landed closer to "goofy with delight."

"I'm going to propose to you"—he nuzzled her ear—"in this place I know where there won't be another soul for ten miles about. We'll ride out there among the yellow and blue flowers of Texas. I will make love to you all night."

"Outdoors?"

"Of course outdoors."

Kara had never done that. Wasn't really the thing in Brooklyn, but she liked the way it sounded.

"And in the morning—"

"In the morning?" she managed to prompt him dreamily. She was completely gone on this man for a reason.

"A time like now, right about dawn, when the sun glows as bright as you do, I will get down on bended knee and beg you properly to marry me and stay with me until the end of our days."

"I'll wear my pretty boots."

"I'm counting on that. And I'll offer you my granny's ring; it will look beautiful on your hand."

"Father's side or—"

"Direct lineage of Annie Landau Evans Roberts. I already asked permission."

"Oh." Kara tried to catch her breath without very much luck. "I'd like that. I'd like that a lot."

"I was thinking you might."

Kara lay back against him as they watched the sun rise off the stern of the warship. They'd fly together.

And when they were done, they'd ride together. Them, and their children.

"Justin?"

"Yes, sweetheart?"

"My answer will be yes. Just so you know."

"Pleased to hear that." He rested his chin atop her head so that she was fully against that wonderful broad chest of his. "There is one other thing I should mention as it is nonnegotiable."

"And what's that, Cowboy?" Of course he'd wait until she was total putty in his arms.

"Gotta get you a cowboy hat."

She turned in his arms and pulled him down so that she could kiss him at the first break of day. Before their lips did more than brush, she whispered one more thing.

"You mean a cowgirl hat."

"Yes, ma'am."

Read on for a sneak peek at the
next book in the Firehawks series:

Flash of Fire

AN ALARM SHATTERED THE PRE-DAWN SILENCE. NOT SOME
squeaky little beeper. Not Macho Man in the Morning on
the radio. And, thank all the gods there ever were, not the
bloodcurdling "Incoming enemy fire" siren that Robin
Harrow had heard a lifetime's worth of during her six years
of Army National Guard service—both in practice and
during a pair of six-month deployments in Afghanistan.

But it was just as strident.

Wildfire!

Robin lay in her bunk a moment longer, as grunts
rolled out of their own racks up and down the barracks
hall, heels thudding to the floor, moans and groans
sounding through the thin plywood walls.

She'd been awake and glaring at the blank darkness
of the bunkhouse's low plywood ceiling for hours, only
now coming visible in the first light through the thin curtains. Awake and ready to go. Day One on the job, also
Day One of the fire season. She'd lain there wondering
just what she'd signed up for and how long it would take
for the action to start. Part two had just been answered;
not very long.

Bring it, people.

In the interview for Mount Hood Aviation, they'd

promised her that when it hit she'd be scrambling. She was absolutely down with that no matter how little she actually believed them.

After the worst of the clatter in the neighboring dormitory rooms had settled, Robin dropped out of her bunk. She'd used her dad's firefighter trick—at least her mom was pretty sure her dad had been a firefighter, so she'd watched a lot of fire movies and learned what she could. Her flight suit was pre-slipped with fire-retardant cotton long johns and the legs of her flight suit in turn were already in her unlaced boots. In thirty seconds flat she went from sleeping bare on top of the covers to lacing her boots.

She'd spotted the job opening for a temp one-season piloting job and, needing to get out of her post-service life in the worst way, answered the ad. Her time in the Guard had included certifying for heli-bucket brigade on out-of-control wildfires. It was a damn sight better than her gig in her mother's truck stop restaurant playing the "Hi! I'm Robin!" perky waitress. She'd had way more than enough of that as a kid and teen.

Phoebe's Tucson Truck Stop—founded by and named for Grandma Phoebe Harrow—was one of the last big independents on the routes. A massive complex that sat on the I-10 just south of Tucson. They could fuel over a dozen rigs at a time and park hundreds. Truck wash and basic service, certified CAT scales, motel if you wanted a night out of your rig, barbershop, and—the bane of her existence—Mom's Grill.

Peddling herself as a waitress was part of the gig, or at least pretending to: tight—and too goddamn short—outfit to reveal her soldier-fit body, her light-blond hair kept short with that chopped look that men thought was so cute—and she liked for its low maintenance. She really did do it herself with a pair of scissors.

Robin double checked her Nomex pants and her leather Army boots, now that's what a girl should wear, not some damned hot pink mini-skort. She pulled on a white cotton tee—screw the bra, she'd never liked the damn things anyway and on a Harrow woman they weren't mandatory. Nomex jacket in one hand, personal gear bag over her shoulder, and she was good to go. Nobody was going to mess with Robin the firefighter pilot.

She headed out into the hall of the now silent dormitory. Not a soul in sight. She put on some hustle down the dark and narrow hallway. But she'd gone the wrong way and hit a dead end. Turning back she went looking for a way out of this place. The corridors weren't long, but it was a maze worse than dodging the trucker's with straying hands.

Despite Robin's constant battles at the truck stop, the tips had been really good; Grandma Phoebe's pointers on how to work money out of the late-night guys' soused brains—and their deeply overinflated illusions of what was *never* going to happen—paid well, but…GAG!

Much to her surprise, when she told Mama and Grandma about the ad for a seasonal firefighting job, they'd shuffled her ass out the door and over to the airport so fast it had left her head spinning. Robin had always assumed she'd eventually settle into the traces to become the third Harrow woman to run Phoebe's Tucson Truck Stop, but maybe not. At least not this season.

Robin zagged the other direction through the MHA camp's labyrinthine barracks after hitting a second dead-end corridor. She spotted a few guys coming out of a door, holding their toothbrushes. But when she arrived, she didn't see any women's bathroom close beside it.

Robin gave up on finding the women's bathroom and walked into the men's. While she leaned over the cracked porcelain and brushed her teeth, the guys who were rushing by half-dressed gave her odd looks reflected in the sheet of scratched steel screwed to the battered wood wall as a mirror. In moments she was the only one there, staring idly at the "Jimmy + Theresa" inside a heart and a thousand more inscriptions carved into the fir-plank wall with a penknife over the years.

Robin pocketed the toothbrush and rinsed her face. If this were the AANG, grunts would all be formed up on the line by now, but the civilian world…the men would still be moving slow and the women were probably back in their rooms doing their hair. She stroked a damp hand through her short hair and she was done with that. Robin headed for the field.

Robin headed down the hall and banged out the doors ready to leap at the fire…and was staring at the gravel parking lot. Not a soul here. The lot was crowded with dusty pickups that had seen a better life a long, long time ago, an impressive array of muscle cars—enough to make a good drag race, and several motorbikes—some hot and some not. But no people.

Damn it! She'd come out the wrong side of the building.

—◊◊◊—

"How was the wedding?"

Mickey Hamilton was moving too slow to avoid

Gordon's cheery punch on the arm. He'd pulled in late last night and he'd been more stumbling than functioning since the fire alarm had rousted him. He'd had enough hours of sleep, but he really needed some coffee.

"Morning, Gordon." Mickey rubbed at his eyes, but it didn't help. The first day of MHA's fire season he should have been allowed to sleep in. But no-o. Sunrise hadn't even hit the horizon yet, though it was only minutes away, and the first call had come in. Most of the team were already at the base of the airfield's two-story control tower even though it was less than five minutes since the alarm. MHA tried to hit fifteen minutes from alarm to airborne and no one wanted to screw it up on the first day.

The rising sun was dazzling off the glaciered peak of Mt. Hood that loomed to the west. The air smelled ice fresh and pine sharp on the June breeze—especially after spending four days back home in the Eastern Oregon where the grass was already going dry and dusty. It was going to be a hell of a fire season.

He breathed in deep. Here the Doug fir and spruce that surrounded the camp rolled for dozens of miles in every direction, except up the face of the mountain which spilled glacier-cooled air down through the warm morning.

The grass strip runway split the ramshackle camp buildings behind them from the line of beautiful firefighting craft parked down the far side. Straight across stood Firehawk One. He could almost see a frown on its blunt nose because Emily wouldn't be aboard. But his own Bell 212 was three down the row and was just as eager to get going as he was.

"Smells like a good morning to go fight a fire."

"Avoiding the question, Mickey. Tell me, was the bride hot?"

"My sister, Gordon. Get a grip."

"Right, sorry."

Vern, one of the Firehawk pilots moseyed up looking about as awake as Mickey felt.

"Hey Mickey. So, was the bride hot?"

Mickey sighed. "Yeah, she was…" and he left the guys hanging for several very long seconds. "But not as hot as the Number Two bridesmaid."

"Yes!" Gordon pumped a fist. "Details, Mickey. We want details."

Mickey scanned the crowd gathering. MHA's pilots, smokejumpers, and support personal were all hustling up. The team's leaders, Mark and a spectacularly pregnant Emily, and Carly, their genius fire behavior analyst were all conferring on the platform landing one story up the control tower stairs. But they didn't look ready to announce anything, so he turned back to his audience, which now included Steve the drone pilot and Cal the photographer.

"Suzanna Rose. Went to high school together, but we never hooked up. Saw her at rehearsal dinner and let's just say I saw a whole lot of her after that."

"It's those blue eyes of yours."

"Nah, it's because he looks like an ex-Marine."

"Which I'm not." Mickey had started flying helicopters before he started driving cars. Actually, he'd flown his first helicopter on his tenth birthday and never looked back. It had been a ten-inch-long, radio-controlled wonder with red-white-and-blue racing stripes that he'd crashed and rebuilt a hundred times. He'd been fifteen before his first real bird. Had been with MHA for eight years since graduation, all of it flying to fight wildfires.

"Women don't care."

"It's because you're so pretty." Gordon tried to pat his cheeks until Mickey fisted him lightly in the gut.

"Let's just say it was an awesome wedding."

"Seeing her again?" Vern, the cowboy tall pilot from Washington State.

"Nah." Mickey tried to sound casual about it. A part of him—a past part—should have been pleased by how neatly it all worked out, but another part of him—one he didn't know well—was disappointed. "She's leaving for a job in Europe next week. Be gone at least a year."

"Perfect!" was Gordon's response, but Vern looked a little sad for him only reinforcing the feeling of disappointment that Mickey didn't understand.

Of course Vern was biased. He'd gone and fallen in love with the gorgeous and diminutive MHA chief mechanic over the winter. Oddest looking couple, but it was working for them which was…good? There'd been a whole lot of weddings lately among the MHA top staff and it was…odd. He sighed, but kept it to himself.

"Oh, hey. You gotta see the new pilot. Emily's replacement. She's amazing!"

So she'd finally found a replacement? Flying without Emily Beale in the lead this season was going to be like having one of your arms amputated and no one telling you. You just kept reaching out and getting nothing but air. Of course one look at her huge belly as she stood there next to Mark up on the first-story landing of the tower and he wondered how she'd even fit between in the pilot's seat for the candidate-interview flights.

They'd gone on for weeks. Hopefuls—all guys— showing up, sometimes several a day, trooping into the Oregon wilderness and driving up to the high Mount Hood Aviation base camp. To substitute for Emily, someone was going to have to be seriously good. She was the best heli-pilot Mickey had seen in a decade of flying and eight years on fires.

After nearly a decade of fighting fire, Mickey could see the failures almost as fast as Beale had them back out of the sky. Military-quality control, but no feel for a fire—not even the flaming steel drums set up mid-field. Weekend aviation jocks who thought that flying fire was just about taking the certification course—MHA wasn't a place heli-aviation firefighters started, it was where they strove to end up.

And then she'd hired a female pilot. If it was anyone else than Emily Beale, you could claim gender bias, but not her. Emily only cared about finding the very best. She set an amazing standard.

"So…" Mickey turned back to the other guys as Betsy the cook worked her way through the crowd with a stack of Styrofoam and a pitcher of coffee. Everything stopped while they all loaded up, then reconvened gripping cups of Betsy's best brew. "So, what's the new recruit like other than hot?"

About the Author

M. L. Buchman has over thirty-five novels and an ever-expanding flock of short stories in print. His military romantic suspense books have been named in Barnes & Noble and NPR "Top 5 of the Year," *Booklist* "Top 10 of the Year," and *RT Book Review* "Top 10 Romantic Suspense of the Year." In addition to romantic suspense, he also writes contemporaries, thrillers, and fantasy and science fiction.

In among his career as a corporate project manager he has: rebuilt and single-handed a fifty-foot sailboat, both flown and jumped out of airplanes, designed and built two houses, and bicycled solo around the world.

He is now a full-time writer, living on the Oregon Coast with his beloved wife. He is constantly amazed at what you can do with a degree in geophysics. You may keep up with his writing at www.mlbuchman.com.